ANGLES ᴏʀ ANGELS?

David Stokes studied history at Oriel College, Oxford and is an emeritus professor at Kingston University. His wife Sue managed to prevent him naming any of their children with names beginning with Æ.

Other publications by the author include:

The Happy Ending
Small Business and Entrepreneurship

Testimonies from beta readers:

'A tour de force! Very convincing flavour of Anglo Saxon Britain.'

'A dramatic tale of actual people in 7th century Britain, supremely well-researched and skilfully told.'

'If you want a highly entertaining read whilst learning more about the Anglo-Saxons, then don't miss this exciting historical novel.'

'Once I began reading, I just could not stop. A particular bonus for me was the extensive historical notes at the end of the book. These give you further insights into the period so that you know what is in the historical and archaeological records and what the author has made up.'

For more information about the author and the Anglo Saxon period, including free downloads, go to:

davidstokesauthor.com

ANGLES OR ANGELS?

David Stokes

Matador
9 Priory Business Park,
Wistow Road, Kibworth Beauchamp,
Leicestershire. LE8 0RX
Tel: 0116 279 2299
Email: books@troubador.co.uk
Web: www.troubador.co.uk/matador
Twitter: @matadorbooks

ISBN 978 1789018 400

British Library Cataloguing in Publication Data.
A catalogue record for this book is available from the British Library.

Printed and bound by CPI Group (UK) Ltd, Croydon, CR0 4YY
Typeset in 10.5pt Adobe Garamond Pro by Troubador Publishing Ltd, Leicester, UK

Matador is an imprint of Troubador Publishing Ltd

Angles or Angels?
is for
Jasmine, Jamie, Dylan, Bryher, Jack and Otto

Late sixth century Britain: regional kingdoms are engaged in a ruthless struggle for supremacy. To the south, Saxon kings predominate, but in the north, British leaders are combining in a final effort to overthrow their Angle rivals in Deira and Bernicia. Amidst the tumult, the word of Christ begins to be heard again.

Contents

Map: Northern Britain
viii

Place Names
ix

Characters
in order of appearance
xi

Acknowledgements
xiii

Prologue
ANGLES OR ANGELS?
Bede's Ecclesiastical History of the English People
xv

Part One
Catræth
– AD 600 –
1

Part Two
Degsa's Stone
– AD 603 –
143

Historical Notes
282

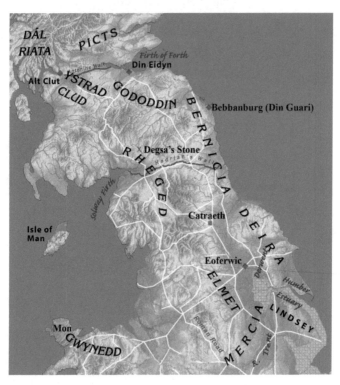

NORTHERN BRITAIN c. AD 600
(Adapted from Wikimedia Commons)

Place Names

Alt Clut – Dumbarton Castle, Strathclyde, capital of Strad Clud

Bebbanburg (Din Guari) – Bamburgh Castle, Northumberland

Bernicia – Angle kingdom approximating to modern Northumberland

Catræth – Catterick

Dál Riata – Irish kingdom in the Scottish Highlands

Deira – Angle kingdom approximating to modern Yorkshire

Deere Stræt – old Roman road that ran north from York and past Hadrian's Wall into Scotland. It runs through Catterick and close to Ripon. The modern A1 follows its route in part.

Degsa's Stone – the site of the Battle of Degsastan, now unknown. Possibly near Dawstone in Liddesdale on the Scottish Borders.

Din Eidyn – Edinburgh

Din Guari (Bebbanburg) – Bamburgh Castle, Northumberland

Dunadd – capital of Dál Riata, a hillfort near Kilmartin Glen in Argyll, Scotland.

Elmet – British kingdom around modern Leeds

Eoferwic – York (Roman Eboracum)

Frankia – France

Frisia – small islands off Holland

Gododdin – British kingdom based around Din Eidyn (Edinburgh)

Gwynned – British kingdom in North Wales

Humbris – Humber Estuary

Hyripis – Ripon in North Yorkshire

Isle of Mon – Anglesey, Wales

Manaw – Isle of Man

Mercia – Angle kingdom in the West Midlands of England

Pictland – north east Scotland, home of the pre-Roman Picts

River Swæle – River Swale, tributary of the River Ure that flows into the Ouse, though York and into the Humber estuary

Rheged – British kingdom approximating to modern Cumbria

Strad Clud – British kingdom in Strath Clyde, Scotland

The Wall – Hadrian's Wall, Northern England

Characters

in order of appearance

Bold indicates that they appear in contemporary written history, and so almost certainly existed.

St GREGORY – Pope Gregory 1st, 590–604, sent a mission to Kent in 597

ACHA – daughter of King Ælle of Deira. Born c. 585

EDWIN – son of King Ælle of Deira. Born c. 588

LILLAN – thegn in the service of the Deiran royal family (originally Lilla in Bede)

FORTHHERE – thegn in the service of the Deiran royal family

ÆLLE – King of Deira c. 570–600

ÆLFRIC – brother of King Ælle

GUTHLAF – merchant trader from Frisia (islands off the coast of Holland)

ÆTHELFRITH – King of Bernicia from c. 593, grandson of Ida, founder of Bernicia

THEOBALD – Æthelfrith's brother

HERIN – son of Hussa, one of many grandsons of Ida, founder of Bernicia

ANEIRIN – British poet of the period credited with the early Welsh poem *Y Gododdin*

CYNON – hostage to Æthelfrith, son of Lord Clydno, survivor of the Battle of Catræth

BEBBA – consort/wife to Æthelfrith

MYNYDDOG – King of the Gododdin, a British kingdom based at Edinburgh

GORTHYN the Great – warrior in service to Mynyddog

OWAIN – King of Rheged (modern Cumbria), son of Urien

RHYDDERCH – King of Strad Clud (Strathclyde) c. 580–614

ÁEDÁN – King of Dál Riata (western Scotland), son of Gabráin

RHUN – monk, brother of Owain, son of Urien of Rheged

CEREDIG – King of Elmet, British territory around modern-day Leeds

TYDFYCH the Tall – British warrior at the Battle of Catræth

HILDA – healer at the Deiran court

LEAX – head of King Ælle's guards or 'hearth-companions'

MAELUMAI mac Baeton – king's champion warrior from Ulster

CONAING – son of Áedán of Dál Riata

CADFAN ap Iago – British king of Gwynedd, north-west Wales

CADWALLON – son of King Cadfan of Gwynedd

CEARL – Saxon king of Mercia

CWENBURG – daughter of King Cearl of Mercia

Pagan gods are also mentioned:

WODEN, THUNOR AND TIW – Anglo-Saxon gods of war

FRIGG – goddess of love

LOKI – the Norse trickster god

Acknowledgements

I am indebted to all those who have contributed to the creation of this book. In particular, I would like to thank those who read through draft chapters and gave me honest feedback during the formative stages: Isabelle Thurley, Josh Greenaway, June Collis, Kit Stokes, Martin Geech, Richard Humble and Sue Gross.

Thanks to Bryony Stokes who kindly and expertly edited an existing map to conform to the requirements of this book.

Various book clubs and writers' groups, including Jericho Writers and Hampshire Writers' Society, have given me encouragement and support. The editorial and production staff at Matador and Troubador all demonstrated great patience and skill during the production phases. Any errors that persist are my own.

Perhaps the greatest debt of gratitude is due to an eighth century monk without whom we might not have known of the existence of many of the personalities in this book: the Venerable Bede.

Prologue

Angles or Angels?

It is said that some merchants arrived in Rome one day and set out their goods in the market place. Some young boys with fair complexions, handsome faces and striking hair were amongst the merchandise for sale. St. Gregory came along with the crowds and he inspected the boys with interest and asked where they had come from.

'They are from the island of Britain where all the people look like this,' the merchant said.

'Are they Christians or heathens?' Gregory asked.

'They are pagan,' came the reply.

Gregory gave a heart-felt sigh. 'How sad that the lord of darkness should have people so bright of face in his grip, that their graceful, outward form should conceal minds that are ignorant of God's grace. What is the name of this people?'

'They are called Angles.'

'Good, for they have the face of angels and such people should be fellow-heirs of the angels in heaven. What is the name of the kingdom from which they have been brought?' he asked.

'They are from the kingdom of Deira,' was the reply.

'Deira? De ira! The wrath of god! They've been snatched from the wrath of god and called to his mercy. And what is the name of the king of this land?' Gregory asked.

'He is called Ælle.'

Playing on the name, Gregory replied, 'Alleluia! The praise of God the Creator must be sung in those parts.'

From Bede's
Ecclesiastical History of the English People,
Book II, Chapter 1.

PART ONE

Catræth

– AD 600 –

One

The Angle boy raced quietly across the hut, taking the girl by surprise as he flung himself, naked, onto her back. She shrieked and jumped to her feet, twisting to shake him off.

'Edwin, you wretch! Look, you've made me all wet.'

He fell onto the mattress, gurgling with glee. She took a towel from the maid who should have been washing him in the bathtub.

'And now you're soaking my bed, you horrid little brother. Enough of your horseplay.'

Edwin squirmed and wriggled. 'Acha, Acha is a horse's arse!' he spluttered in a singsong voice.

Acha lifted the towel and slapped him hard on his bare buttocks.

'Didn't hurt, didn't hurt,' he sang.

Acha slapped him again, even harder.

'Didn't hurt,' he continued, although she could see from the red weald on his fair skin that it probably did.

'Who taught you that disgusting song?' she asked, holding his feet together so that he couldn't move. 'It was the thegnsons, wasn't it?'

'Shan't tell, shan't tell.'

She knew that she was right. She would have words with them later. They wouldn't get away with that.

Edwin squirmed into a sitting position, and the maid tried to rub at the curls that dripped water onto the bed.

'I was going to tell you a riddle, but I don't think I will now.' Acha half turned away.

Edwin shook his head free of the maid's towelling. 'Yesss! Riddle time. Riddle time. I've got one too.'

Acha nodded to the maid, who hurried to a box of blankets.

'Only when you're tucked up under a warm cover, ready for the night.'

Edwin pattered to the next bench along the wall, threw himself onto the straw mattress and laid flat on his back, eyes tightly shut. As the maid drew a blanket over him, Acha couldn't help smiling at his chubby nakedness. When he put his thumb into his mouth, she scowled and reached over to pull his hair with one hand, yanking the thumb from his lips with the other.

'Æthelings don't suckle their thumbs. How many times do I have to tell you?'

Edwin sat up, frowning. 'What *do* æthelings do?'

Acha loosened the top of her tunic but stopped, remembering she no longer liked to undress in front of him, now that she was becoming a woman.

'Æthelings become kings if they are strong. And to be strong, you need lots of sleep.'

Edwin thought for a moment. 'When I'm king,' he said slowly before continuing in a rush: 'I can have you whipped because you're a horse's arse.' He disappeared under the blanket, giggling and wriggling.

Acha sighed. 'Pity, I had a good riddle for you. Now you've spoiled it. I'm going.'

His head shot up from under the bedding. 'I'll be good, I promise. And strong.'

Acha turned, trying not to smile. 'On your oath?'

'On my oath.' He wiped his eyes with his bare arm and sniffed. 'Your riddle first.'

With a wave, Acha dismissed the maid and tried to recall the words of the bard who had recently visited the royal encampment to recite in the feasting hall. It was one of the few occasions when she had been allowed to remain there after sunset but only for the riddles and the opening poem. Once the mead had begun to flow, her father, King Ælle, had told her to be gone. It was a start. It wouldn't be long before she could join the other hall-women who watched from the side while the men ate, drank and insulted each other around the mead benches.

'I am a creature with many teeth,' she began as Edwin gazed at the tapestry on the wall with a faraway look. 'My mouth is lined with useful beaks that point down while I gently scratch the slopes, searching for plants. I uproot those that have no use and leave living the ones of value. Who am I?' She brushed a bead of water from Edwin's brow and pulled the blanket higher.

'A cow,' he blurted.

'No, cows don't have beaks. '

'A duck then.'

She shook her head. 'No, they only have one beak, not many.'

Edwin frowned. 'Give me another clue.'

Acha thought for a moment. 'I am a friend to man but if you should mistakenly put a foot on my teeth, I will hit you on the head with my tail.' She chuckled, pleased with her invention.

'Are you a dragon?' Edwin snuggled lower down the bed.

'No, they don't live in fields around here, do they? Do you remember how you hurt your head during the feast of Eostre when you ran into the barn full of field tools?'

Edwin fingered the mark that still showed on his forehead. 'Yes, I trod on a… ' His eyes widened with understanding. 'A rake! It has teeth that pull up weeds and when I stood on them, it wacked me in the head, made me feel dizzy. You're a rake.'

Acha clapped her hands and leaned forward to kiss the spot where he had been injured. 'Well done. What's your riddle?' she asked.

Edwin fidgeted with the curls that hung over his ears. 'What was it? Oh yes. I grow very tall, erect in my bed. Like this.' He struggled to his feet, letting the cover fall so he stood, naked on the mattress and giggled nervously. 'And I'm hairy underneath.' He put a hand on his bottom.

Acha bit her lip, fearing what might be next.

He sniggered, barely containing his excitement. 'A girl grabs me, peels back my skin and puts me in her pantry. What am I?'

Acha glowered, not amused in the slightest. 'Who told you that?' she snapped. 'That's a rude riddle that foolish men tell in the feast hall over their drink, not one for you. It was those stupid thegn-sons, wasn't it? They told you.'

Edwin's eyebrows knitted together in confusion. 'It's not r… rude. It's an onion. The answer's an onion. Lillan said it would make you laugh.' He was almost in tears.

Acha's cheeks reddened as she thought of the thegn-son who had set him up for this prank. She may have let Lillan kiss her, but that did not mean he could take liberties with her brother. She swept Edwin into her arms and squeezed him hard.

'Yes, it is an onion. But it can also mean the pisser that you boys carry between your legs. That's what makes it rude, so you keep it to yourself until you carry your spear and sit with the warrior-men.'

She laid him down onto the bed, running her fingers through his hair.

'Now, it's time for sleep.'

Edwin shook his head to rid himself of her hands that were untwisting the knots in his curls.

'But I'm not tired. Another riddle. I bet I'll get the next one.'

She pinned him down by the shoulders. 'Alright, but if you get it wrong you go to the dream-maker straightaway. Agreed?'

He nodded and she thought again of the poet in her father's feasting hall who had entertained them with riddles so difficult that even the wise-ones could not answer. She smiled as one came to mind that should be hard enough to baffle Edwin. Dusk was falling and she wanted to slip outside while he was asleep and be a grown-up for a while before it was too dark.

'My mother and father forsook me for dead when I was first born but another woman kindly took me under her care.'

Edwin interrupted, frowning, 'What does "forsook for dead" mean?' he asked.

'It means they left him, believing he was not alive.'

His frown deepened. 'Like my mother. She forsook me, didn't she?'

Acha twisted a piece of straw sticking through the weave of the mattress in annoyance, realising she had made a bad choice of riddle.

'No, our mother did not forsake you. She died after your birthing but she knew you were alive and well.'

Acha was about to continue but Edwin still frowned.

'Did I make her die?' he asked.

7

She shut her eyes tightly for a moment to stop the tears.

'No, of course not. Many women die during the birthing time. Shall I carry on?'

'I've forgotten the beginning. Can you start again?'

She tucked him more securely into the blanket, trying not to show her frustration.

'Who am I? A woman, who was not my mother, brought me up. She took care of me and she was as kind to me as she was to her own children. She fed me so that I grew big and strong, but she had less of her own sons and daughters because of what she did for me.'

She hoped his puzzled expression meant he was thinking of the riddle and not their mother.

'Me. It could be me, couldn't it? You are bringing me up and you're not my mother.'

'No, it's not you because I don't have any children of my own, do I?'

'You might have some soon though. Your breasts have got bigger. I've seen them.'

Acha sighed. 'It's rude to peep at girls' bodies, you know that. There will be plenty of time for me to have my own children once you can stand with the spears.'

She hoped that would be true. With her dying breath, her mother had asked her to watch over her new-born brother and she was still doing just that, ten summers later.

'Is it someone else?' Edwin asked quietly.

'No, it's not a person,' she said, gently brushing his cheek with the back of her hand. 'You can have one more question, then I will tell you the answer. And you will go to sleep.'

He did not speak for several moments and she glanced anxiously under the door to judge how much the light had faded.

'It's an animal, isn't it?'

'No, it's not an animal. It's a feathered-flyer that you will hear calling in the distance if you are quiet when you wake in the morning.'

He was still looking puzzled but his eyelids were drooping.

'Cuck-oo, cuck-oo,' she sang softly.

His eyes shot open. 'A cuckoo! But why… oh yes I get it. I've got another one for you.'

'We made a bargain, remember? The dream-maker is waiting.'

'But what if he gives me a bad dream?' He pulled at her arm as she tried to stand.

'You tell him that your big sister ordered a lovely dream for you. It's about… about rabbits. Yes, fluffy rabbits that are hopping out of their sandy homes to play with you.'

When she saw his eyes finally flicker shut, she crept to her corner of the hut. She undid the two brass buckles at her shoulders so that the plain tunic fell to the floor. Ignoring the night shift the maid had laid out for her, she found her most colourful gown, pulled it over her head and ran a cow-bone comb through her hair. Blowing Edwin a kiss, she gently lifted the latch of the door, hoping the hinge would not squeak, and slipped out into the night. She paused under the thatch to breathe the evening air whilst she listened for any sign of wakefulness from her brother. Good, he wasn't stirring. She would become a mother again in the morning.

Now it was time to be a maiden and choose herself a man.

Two

S he hurried along the trail towards the eerie stone structures that were casting long shadows in her direction. Some said they were the work of giants who had once governed the world from strongholds like the one that lay crumbling around her village. Her father, King Ælle now ruled here at Eoferwic and he and his followers preferred to live under warm thatch supported by posts of oak. But the ruins left by the giants still had an important use: the toppled walls provided the king's elite warriors – the thegns and their sons – with an ideal location for battle practice.

That was why Acha wanted to reach the ruins before dark. She could sense the gleam of semi-naked bodies as young men wrestled in the overgrown courtyards or climbed the disused towers. She was in her thirteenth summer and such thoughts were new to her, but with no mother to guide her, she could only follow her instincts.

And they told her that her childhood was over and she needed to become a woman.

The cloud of the day had given way to a clear evening sky, so Acha knew the thegn-sons would still be busy with their mock fighting. She picked her way over the rubble and rotten timbers towards the ruins of the old citadel. It was said that the ghosts of men in war gear could still be seen in the roofless houses where they had once lived and prepared themselves for war. What she saw now were not spirits but real warriors flexing their muscles in mock battles. The thegn-sons were lifting fallen remnants of stone, struggling to outdo each other in the size of slabs they could carry. They did not grow strong from ploughing fields or scything wheat, like farmers' sons. They were born for battle, following their king into whatever fight he happened to pick, sworn to protect him from his enemies, or to avenge him should he fall.

She stopped herself from calling to Lillan so that she could admire his body as he strained to move a boulder. He was taller and leaner than the other youths. When she'd first teased him about his size, he'd retorted that he had the supple strength of the willow rather than the unbending might of oak. Secretly, she always preferred taller men and particularly liked his slim, clean-cut look. He waved and scrambled to retrieve his tunic amidst the masonry as soon as he caught sight of her.

'Acha, I thought you were never coming.'

'I had problems calming my little brother. Some oaf had taught him a vulgar riddle.'

Lillan's sudden look of guilt was unmistakable. 'Oh did he… what was… ?'

'It concerned a young girl who put an onion in her pantry. He said the halfwit who told him was called Lillan. But that couldn't be you, could it?'

He pulled the tunic over his head, hiding the blush in his cheeks. She tugged the shirt down to see his face, enjoying seeing him squirm.

'No, I knew it couldn't be you, because the same thickhead had taught him a rude ditty about me. And you told me that my

11

face reminded you of a golden sunflower. Not the hindquarters of a horse.'

A tall youth with the beginnings of a beard ran over to join them.

'Help me, Forthhere,' Lillan said, putting an arm on his shoulder. 'I am being slain by a sharp tongue.'

Acha glowered at the newcomer to stay out of their conversation, but Forthhere just laughed.

'I'm oath-bound to protect this princess,' he said, bowing towards Acha. 'So I cannot help you. But I would remind her that a trader arrived on the quayside today promising to show a sample of his wares in the hall.'

He immediately had Acha's full attention.

'A trader? From where?' she asked. Visiting merchants were rare and much depended on their origin. Most brought only weaponry and ironmongery that had no interest for her.

'From Frisia. I'm told he has the latest ornaments and weavings from Frankia,' he replied.

Acha could not hide her excitement. Merchandise from overseas was always more exotic than the drab offerings of local pedlars.

Lillan took her hand. 'Shall we go and see what he has to show? It's nearly sundown so we'd best hurry.'

She disentangled her fingers from his.

'Yes, but I haven't finished with you yet.'

*

The feast hall was brim full, bustling with the followers of the King of Deira. Table-women elbowed their way past slaves and thegns alike to cover the tables with brightly patterned cloth whilst others brought out wooden goblets and silver spoons. Acha squeezed in through the door, inhaling the smell of the cooking that sizzled over the fire as she strained on tiptoe to see across the hall.

'Good, we are in time. I can always rely on my father to be late,' she said to Lillan, brushing past a tapestry to make her way along the wall. 'Although I'm not sure I will be able to see much. Everyone seems to be here. Even my toad of an uncle.'

'Ælfric? Oh yes, I see him. He's brought his thegns. Maybe he's expecting trouble.'

At that moment, Acha caught sight of the grizzled face that she knew so well. Her father was making his entrance. She tutted as she saw the plaits in his white beard; no doubt the whim of some new slave-woman he had found to his liking. At least he had chosen to don the old boar-skin cloak that reminded her of his former glory. One of the earliest memories from her childhood was watching her father wrap that hairy garment around his wide shoulders. His warriors had just taken Eoferwic – the town of the wild boar – from its British king and they had cheered wildly the first time that he had donned the boar-skin cloak, a symbol of their supremacy over the ancient capital of the north. Now, it hung loosely on shoulders stooped by a lifetime's burden leading the kin. She just hoped he could stay awake tonight; she had heard that his head sometimes joined the platters and bowls on the table before the end of the feasting.

The buzz of conversation died as he took his place at the high seat and banged three times on the trestle.

'Let the mead flow!' he called.

'Thanks to the feast giver,' the hall-folk replied as one, followed by the scraping of benches as they scrambled to sit whilst the table-maidens filled their goblets from jugs brimming with golden mead. Acha and Lillan remained standing with the thegn-sons and daughters who lined the wall hoping for a nod from the king that they could stay longer.

Ælle waved to a newcomer with a weather-beaten face to sit beside him.

'Before you feast on Eoferwic's fine food, I would welcome an old friend from over the seas. Guthlaf of Frisia has berthed here and trades with us with my blessing,' the king announced in a booming voice that defied his withered frame.

The audience tapped on the benches to acknowledge the trader whilst their king paused, weighing his words. 'His next port of call is to the north, in the land of the Gododdin, where Mynyddog the Wealthy is anxious to receive him. Mynyddog, it appears, has summoned warriors from the old kingdoms to join him for feasting in Din Eidyn. And he sent word to Frisian traders, like my friend here, to bring him new war blades, shields and battle gear. I wonder what his purpose might be?'

The king scratched his greying hair and feigned a puzzled expression, to the mirth of the hall-folk. 'Maybe he is doing all this to amuse himself before his ancient bones finally fall apart. He is hosting a festival of the Old North, we hear tell.' Ælle slowly shook his head. 'Mynyddog the Mean some call him. He would not waste his wealth on mere feasting. No, his hosting is for a hostile end; he is gathering a great warband that he will turn on his neighbours. The question is which one?' The king paused to sip from a silver chalice, and the hall erupted in a hubbub of chatter as opinions were shared on the news.

'How far away is Din Eidyn?' Acha asked Lillan anxiously.

'North of the Wall, almost in Pictland,' he replied as the king continued in his thunderous voice.

'We will find out soon enough. If he turns his miserable band on us, our spears are ready, are they not?'

The benches erupted in a roar as thegns leapt to their feet, waving their fists, banging on the tables. When the tumult had died down, everyone returned to their seats except for a well-groomed figure with a portly stomach who remained standing.

It was Ælfric, the king's brother who dared to question him.

'I hear that Mynyddog would be our friend. His real enemy is Æthelfrith, the upstart who is threatening the Gododdin's borders as well as our own. With Mynyddog's warband to the north and our warriors to the south, we could crush Æthelfrith's Bernicia like a nut between us.'

Ælle rounded on the speaker, glowering and waving his hand for him to be seated. 'Not now, Ælfric, we have visitors in our midst,' he hissed.

Ælfric did not budge. 'When then? You have not called for the Witan's wisdom for many moons.'

The king glanced around the audience, who had stayed very quiet during this altercation. Acha could see he was shaken by his brother's defiance. Many times before, he had railed about him in her presence, cursing his stupidity and vanity. To openly question the king in his own hall before his sworn thegns was tantamount to rebellion. Ælle held up his hand to stop the serving-women from advancing further with their bowls and jugs.

'It is I, brother, who will decide if Æthelfrith and the men of Bernicia are to be our friends or our foes. Sit with us quietly. Or leave us to our feasting.'

The hall-dwellers shifted uncomfortably on their benches while the two brothers glared at each other. Acha gripped Lillan's hand tightly, hardly daring to breathe.

Ælfric did not budge. 'Before you make your decision, lord king, I would give you certain information I have come by. And I would give it to you now. My wife is at her birthing-time and I must return to her to see if I have an heir.'

Ælle looked hard at him for a few more moments, before banging three deliberate blows on the table.

'Let the feasting hall be cleared of all except lords and thegns. No more guests tonight,' he said, glancing meaningfully at the wall where the younglings stood.

Acha kicked at the stones along the walkway towards her hut.

'So much for seeing the trader's wares. How I hate that stupid uncle. He's a horse's arse, no mistake.'

Lillan took her arm. 'Not so stupid. He knows that his life can go one of two ways. Languishing in luxury on his estates or winning glory as the next king.'

His words stopped her in her tracks. If only her elder brother, Edwulf, was still alive. He would have put an end to Ælfric's posturing. All the thegns had loved Edwulf and would have willingly accepted him as the next ring-giver. But the tusks of a wild boar had ended those hopes when Edwulf was out hunting. Her brother, Edwin, had become his father's heir in only his eighth summer.

'You really think Ælfric will try to make himself king before Edwin grows up?' She tried to see into Lillan's eyes but it was too dark.

'Not many kings die in their beds. But your father has ruled longer than anyone who can be remembered and he still has the loyalty of the thegns. Don't worry, no one is strong enough to challenge him, not even a sly fox like Ælfric. Not yet.'

Yes, father will just have to keep living until Edwin can take his place, Acha thought. And it was up to her to make her little brother strong and wise enough to become a great king.

As they approached her hut, she tugged at Lillan's tunic. 'I must go in. But first, you must go on your knees to beg my forgiveness.'

'Me?' Lillan put on an innocent look. 'Edwin didn't learn the chant from me. He's always hanging around the older boys. He would have learned it from them.'

His eyes told her that he was speaking the truth, and she knew the problem. Edwin had worshiped his elder brother and had followed him everywhere like a puppy-dog. He had replaced him with other youths since his death. And some were taking advantage of him.

'You must protect him more. You're oath-bound to him.' The wind whipped a wisp of hair into Acha's face but she left it to fly. 'And you must stop asking him to tell me rude riddles.'

Lillan looked at his feet. 'I do admit to that one. It won't happen again.'

Good, she was enjoying his grovelling but she wasn't sure if he had done enough to merit the goodnight kiss that had become their custom. No, she enjoyed it too much herself to punish him that way.

'I best go to my bed. Edwin always wakes me early,' she said.

He put his hand on the beam by her head to stop her passing. 'Why doesn't his maid take him?'

She gently took his hand from the beam and ran a finger over his knuckles.

'He's not that easy. You only see him when he is boisterous, charging and cavorting like a wild dog. I see him when he is quiet, not saying a word, staring into the distance. A seer told me that a mother who dies in childbirth can give their baby strange spirits. Sometimes he tries not to sleep for fear of his dreams. I'm not sure what worries him, but the straw in his sleep bench is often wet in the morning.'

He gingerly put his hand onto her shoulder and pulled her closer. 'And what about you? Do you worry?'

She pushed him away. 'Are you suggesting I moisten my bed too?' She laughed then put a hand to her mouth to stifle the noise. 'Ssh,' she said, trying not to giggle.

'This will keep us quiet,' he said, brushing his lips on hers. *Alright, just one.*

Three

A cha awoke to find that she was alone. Good, she thought, Edwin must have gone out and left her to sleep.

I have the hut all to myself! I can wash before I dress in case I bump into the thegn-sons.

Pouring water from a jug into a wooden bowl, she caught sight of her reflection.

Is that a spot on my chin? No just a mark from Edwin's grubby hands.

She studied her face more closely as the ripples on the surface of the water calmed. Was she really as beautiful as Lillan liked to tell her, or did he say kind things merely to please her? He seemed to like her eyes best of all. They were as blue as the sky on a summer's day, he'd said. Today they looked tired, more like the grey of autumn. What of her nose? To her, it looked straight and rather delicate but Lillan had never commented on it. Maybe he preferred the snub nose of Forthhere's sister. She had caught him gazing at her more than once. Her breath rippled the water, distorting her image as she turned to admire her hair. She was happy with her generous head of hair, even if her father did joke that it would be good to spin and weave into blankets. Some men might prefer the red mops of the British, but she liked her hair that shone like gold when she brushed it hard. If only she could find more bear-fat to rub in, but all she had was pig-render that smelled so vile she had to mix it with lavender.

Thank the gods, I don't have Edwin's girlish ringlets.

As if in rebuke, her brother rushed in through the door.

'Acha, Acha, you have to come. Lillan says. The trader is displaying his wares in the hall but he is leaving on the tide,' Edwin panted.

'Close the door! Do you want every passer-by to see a princess as she dresses?' Acha shouted as the curtain around her billowed in the breeze. 'Why is he sailing so soon?'

Edwin thrust his head between the curtains as Acha quickly wrapped a gown around her shoulders. 'Don't know. Everyone's in a hurry this morning.'

Knowing that Lillan was waiting for her, Acha took one more glance into her washbowl as she finished dressing. Her hair was knotted in places but it would have to do. New merchandise seldom arrived at their court and she did not want to miss it.

*

Edwin tugged at her hand, pulling her along the walkway so quickly that she had to catch her breath when they arrived at the hall. Straightening her clothes and hair, she peered inside, half-expecting to see the usual muddle of menfolk sprawled around the long room. Today it bustled with women, not just wives but younglings like her, even children. She eagerly pushed her way into the throng, gasping at the vibrant hues of the linens and silks laid out on the trestles.

A table of body-ornaments caught her eye. Their shapes and sizes seemed very strange to her. The brooches were made up of several round metal discs like small shields, piled one upon the other, each decorated with tiny garnets lined with gold foil. Could such fine jewellery support the weight of a garment, she wondered, fingering one of the heavy brooches that pinned her own robe to each shoulder, or were they just for display?

Edwin reappeared and tugged at her gown. 'Come on. Guthlaf's over there with Lillan.'

He dragged her through the crowd to the high table where the Frisian trader was surrounded by a gaggle of thegn-sons, all talking animatedly about the wares on display. Forthhere held aloft a pair of soft leather boots with eyelets threaded with long thongs.

'These would take forever to lace up. Pity the sheep if you were called out in the middle of the night to ward off wolves and first had to put these on,' he laughed.

Guthlaf tugged at his grey beard. 'No, they wouldn't be of much use on my ship neither. But the Frankish-folk all wear them at court.' He paused to incline his head to acknowledge Acha's approach. 'Perhaps this young lady has more appreciation of the modern fashion.'

'Guthlaf, this is Acha, daughter of King Ælle,' Lillan said moving aside with a smile to welcome her into their circle. 'Have you seen anything you like?' he asked her.

She lightly squeezed his hand. 'Oh yes. I've never seen such rich colourings. The red cloth is quite stunning. I'm not so sure about the jewellery though. Have you no amber beads, Guthlaf?'

The trader nodded knowingly. 'Funny you should mention that; I don't know why but amber is suddenly less popular. Beads too. Pendants set with amethyst or garnets is what I have brought from the Kentish kingdom. Maybe it's the influence of the Roman god that has spread there from over the Straits.'

Acha raised an eyebrow. 'Which Roman god?'

'Why, the Christ-god. Haven't you heard? Gregory, the bishop in Rome, sent over converters to Kent at the invitation of the king's wife, who is of the Frankish folk. All of a sudden, everyone is a Christ-man and wants to dress like they do in Frankia.'

'Well, we don't here.' Lillan disdainfully held up a pair of fancy legging-garters. 'You can ship these straight back to the Kentish court.'

Guthlaf quickly swept up a roll of mauve material from the table.

'I'm sure your father would like you to wear something in this latest colour,' he said, holding a fold of the fabric to Acha's chin. 'Perfect for your complexion. I can just add it to the king's reckoning. He as good as said he expected to buy you a new robe.'

Acha doubted that her father had said any such thing but it might be worth the risk to gain a new garment, something not too grand that might pass unnoticed on her father's account. She could hardly be blamed for believing the trader.

'Perhaps you could show me the hood trimmed with fur on the table over there?' She grabbed Lillan by the arm. 'And you can come too and tell me what colours you like to see on me.' She turned to Forthhere. 'Could you watch over Edwin? He'll be bored with us.'

*

The sun was descending towards the horizon when she finally made her way back to her hut, weary but delighted with her day. Behind her trailed Guthlaf's boy, his arms piled high with the fine linens and silks that Acha had chosen. She rubbed admiringly at the ornamental central-boss of her circular brooch. It would make a fine fastening for the new cape that she would sew from the purple cloth. She could use the scarlet silk to edge the cloak. No, better keep that to trim the sleeves of the ruby-red robe. Lillan had said she would look stunning in that. Fingering the garnet-headed pin in her hair, she felt glamorous for the first time in her life.

Edwin had arrived before her and was slurping broth at the fire. She looked aghast at the leather hat crossed with metal ridges that swamped her brother's head.

'What's that on your skull?'

'It's a combat cap. You can hit me and it won't hurt.' Edwin grabbed a poker and tapped his helmet with it. 'See?'

'I do see but I do not understand why someone who has not yet seen his tenth summer would be dressing in battlegear.'

'Guthlaf's tiller-man said every ætheling should have such a cap. I have to be ready.'

'Ready for what?' Acha squatted next to him and ladled some soup from the cauldron.

'Ready for when the war-dragon flies.' Edwin thrust the poker in the air, cutting it left and right.

'Ouch, this soup is hot.' Acha wiped her lips, dropping her spoon back into the bowl. 'And when is this dragon meant to fly?' she asked, breaking a piece of barley bread and soaking it in her broth.

Edwin lowered the poker and turned wide eyes towards her. 'It already has.'

'I haven't seen it,' Acha said, testing the temperature of the broth-soaked bread on her lips.

'It has flown from the mountains of the painted-people to the lands of the Gogoggin.'

'Gododdin,' Acha corrected. 'The tiller-man told you this, did he?' she asked, concerned that the boatman might have fed her brother with just the right ingredients for a bad dream.

Edwin nodded. 'He saw it himself, curling its scaly tail around the black rock of Din Adin.'

'Din Eidyn,' corrected Acha. 'Did he see it actually fly?'

Edwin looked surprised. 'Of course he did. That's why I need the war-helmet. It's coming this way.'

'I see. And did he gift you this... this cap?'

'Father came by and said his barter-bill was becoming so big, one more small item wouldn't matter.' Edwin glanced mischievously towards the cloth pile by Acha's bed. 'Oh yes,' he continued. 'He said to tell you that he would like to see you before sundown.'

'Why didn't you tell me before?' Acha snapped, snatching the pin from her hair and brushing the bread from her tunic. 'It's nearly dark now.'

She ran out of the door along the short path to the king's quarters. One of the guards at the door bowed and went inside while she waited, impatient to know how many of her purchases she would have to return. Perhaps she had been rash to take so much. It was just that...

'The king will see you now, my lady.' The guard held the door as she paused on the threshold to allow her eyes to become accustomed to the shadows of the room.

Ælle sat in his high-backed chair in the centre of the hut dressed only in a simple tunic. His once-golden hair hung loose and grey down to his shoulders. Acha was pleased to see he had lost the plaits to his beard. Quickly scanning the depths of his living space, she saw no sign of the young slave-women he normally liked to have around him, whom she blamed for such affectations.

'It's so dark in here, father. I don't know how you can see anything.' She moved in slowly, careful to avoid a stack of shields scattered around the king.

'Just like your mother. You chide me for a welcome. You'll tell me next to tidy the war tackle I leave about,' the king rumbled in a gruff voice as he replaced the shield he was polishing onto the pile. 'Come closer so I can see you. By nightfall, my eyes grow weary of the brightness of day.'

'Sorry father, I did not mean to reproach you.' She inwardly cursed her thoughtlessness in forgetting her father's sight problems. 'I should be thanking you for your generosity in offering me a small selection from the trader's merchandise.'

He slapped his knee and threw back his head. 'Ha, not so small by all account. No matter. I have few enough chances to dress you like a true princess. Would you like some honey drink? It's in that jug.' He indicated a table, set with ornate drinking cups for two.

As she poured, Acha tried to remember the last time he had prepared refreshments for her visit, or been so generous with his gifts. Something was different.

'Besides,' the king continued, 'you serve our kin well with your devotion to Edwin. He is even more precious since…' Ælle paused to sip from his goblet and Acha saw his eyes moisten. '…since he became my only son. That is why I asked you here.'

Acha studied his face with surprise. Had she done something to Edwin that displeased her father?

'I am fearful for his future,' he said slowly, stroking the moustache that drooped past his mouth to his chin. 'I have to make arrangements to protect him, if…' He took another sip from his cup. '…if I am not here to protect him myself.'

Acha's eyes widened in alarm. 'Are you ill, father?' She moved closer, tucking a fur cloak around his shoulders.

He gratefully put a hand on hers. 'No, I'm not ill. But I grow old and weary.'

'Not so old, father.' She put an arm around his neck and ran her hand through his hair. 'See how thick your head-hair remains.'

He patted her arm. 'Yes there's life in this old dog yet, but the pups around me are yapping louder and it will be some time before Edwin can stand with the spears and relieve me of some of my kingly burdens.'

Acha pulled over a stool and sat at her father's feet. 'I am really trying with Edwin, father. He is becoming stronger but since… since he lost his brother, he seems to… I'm not sure how to put it.'

'Lack conviction?' the king suggested.

'Yes, that's it. He's too easily led. He believes too much of what others tell him only for their own purpose.' Acha paused, surprised at her own openness. She had never spoken of her brother like this to the king before. 'He needs to find his own mind.'

'And he will,' Ælle said. 'But he needs time. Time that he might not have if anything should happen to me. Which is why I need your help once more.' He stretched forward and took Acha's delicate hand in his gnarled paw.

'Once, I had to ask you to become a mother to Edwin. Now I have another role for you.'

Acha involuntary gripped his hand tighter in anticipation. Maybe she was to become trained in some special skill at the loom or spindle.

'I need you to become a wife.'

She did not believe she had heard correctly. 'A wife? Did you say wife?' She moved closer to his chair, her mind whirring.

'I would have waited until you had grown into full womanhood before choosing your husband,' the king continued, patting her hand. 'But I cannot delay.'

Her brow furrowed in incomprehension. 'You want me to marry now? Why? Have I wronged you in some way?'

'No, no, on the contrary, I need you to become a peace-weaver to protect the kin.'

Acha stood, knocking over the stool. It could not be Lillan if she was to be offered as a political ploy to another clan. Her dreams were crumbling like the ruins nearby.

'Peace-weaver? I am to marry into a rival kin?'

Ælle reached over and righted the stool. 'Sit down and let me explain.'

'Just tell me who it is. If I am to be sent to some foreign court, at least say which one.' She turned her back to hide her tears.

Ælle stood with a groan and put heavy hands on her shoulders. 'There, there, don't fret so. He is of our race.'

She span round. 'Who then? Just tell me who you have in mind.'

'Æthelfrith, King of Bernicia.'

His words echoed around the hut, ringing in her ears like an alarm bell. She had heard mothers threaten their children with Æthelfrith's fury if they didn't behave. Æthelfrith the Ferocious, they called him, wild as a wolf in battle.

She swallowed hard. 'Why him?' was all she could say.

'Sit down,' the King said as gently as his gruff voice would allow, steering her back to the stool. 'This is how it is. The kings of Rheged, Strad Clud and Gododdin, have formed a great battle-host ready to march. They are desperate to take back the lands they say we have usurped, even though they vilely misused them when they ruled here. I learned from Ælfric yesterday that they are to be joined by warriors from Elmet and Gwynedd who are on the move from the south.

Edwin's words came back to her. 'So the war-dragon is flying here,' she said.

'That is unclear. The last time the Britons put aside their ancient quarrels, they struck, not at us, but at Æthelfrith's forefathers in Bernicia and drove them into the sea. But once Æthelfrith became their king, he took back the land they had lost. They will be wary of attacking him again.'

Because he is a monster, thought Acha. 'But they fear you too, father. You have fought them to a standstill over many years.'

'I have, but they see my hairs grow grey.' The king clenched one fist into another. 'And they hear whispers of dissent amongst my kin.'

Acha shivered. 'Dissent from whom?'

'Why, from those in the pack who would challenge me. Your uncle is one.'

'Ælfric? That weasel. Why don't you throw him into the bone-pit?'

The king laughed. 'If only I had more fighting men around me with your spirit. I wouldn't need a peace-weaver.'

She frowned, still numb from her father's choice. 'I don't understand. How will my marrying our vile neighbour help us?' she asked.

'If the kings that surround us march together, they can defeat Deira and Bernicia, one at a time. You must bind our two lands together. Æthelfrith and Edwin must fight side by side. After that, your sons will rule both lands so that no one can ever again threaten our combined kin.'

Acha's eyes moistened again. 'I had hoped to marry another, someone who is as fond of me as I am of him.'

For the first time, Ælle raised his voice. 'You are the daughter of a king and kings' daughters do not marry for affection. You must marry for the good of the kin, as I have explained.'

Her body sagged on the stool and she held her head in her hands. So that was it. No argument. Her fate was decided, her fine robes – her life – to be wasted on an ogre. Unless…

'What about Edwin? I still need to care for him. We've already said how unsure he is. He needs me. I cannot marry yet.' She was pleading, her words coming in sobs.

27

The king was matter-of-fact. 'There is much to discuss in this matter. I have yet to discuss details with Æthelfrith, but I have sent Forthhere as messenger to him by the trading boat that sailed on the evening tide. First, he needs to accept you as his bride. You must look your best when you meet.'

So that was why her purchases had not been questioned. Her father was preparing her like some game bird to be admired before it was plucked for the feast. No matter. It gave her hope. Æthelfrith would find that a fledgling like her was far from his taste.

Four

The warning bell jangled just as Æthelfrith was using all his youthful strength to heave earth to the top of the barricade that protected Din Guari, his fortress home. He cursed, quickly scanning the wooded lowlands to the northwest that had brought dangers in the past. His scouts had not reported any movements but they had been surprised before. He still vividly remembered the day in his youth when the British war-host had appeared out of the mist and his unprepared uncle had lost control of the fortress. Fleeing by boat to a nearby island, he had watched the flames as the barricade around his home burned brightly. Æthelfrith felt the pain of that moment as he now searched the horizon, knowing that his repairs to the new wall from recent storm damage were incomplete.

'Ship approaching from the north!'

He heard the cry and whirled around to face the ocean, his anxiety easing. Din Guari was well protected against seafaring attacks, perched high above the beach on a long ridge of solid stone. That same hard rock was almost impossible to dig into, making it a difficult base for the fortifications that Æthelfrith was now repairing. The barricade had to be made from two parallel walls of wood, in-filled with earth and rubble to anchor them to the impenetrable ground.

'Launch the guard boat,' Æthelfrith shouted to Herin, the duty captain. Seeing him nod in his languid way, he wondered if the gods had a trick to play. His uncle, who had been king when the fort had been taken on that fateful day in his youth, was Herin's father.

He grabbed the leather jerkin and sword he had hung on a post and sprinted along the turfed top of the wall towards the gate. He almost tripped in his hurry to descend the rocky steps to the small harbour at the northern end of the fortress, gratified to see that a group of warriors were already preparing to launch a boat.

'How many?' he called to his brother, Theobald, who led the men in the harbour.

Apart from their height – and the fact they had been born a year apart – Æthelfrith and Theobald could have been twins. They had the same flaxen hair, broad nose and strong chin, but Æthelfrith stood a full head higher.

'Only one boat sighted so far,' Theobald said.

'Launch a second ship,' Æthelfrith shouted to Herin who was close on their heels. 'I'll take the guard boat. You'll be in charge on land, Theobald.'

Theobald was young to wield authority but Æthelfrith had witnessed the sharpness of his little brother's mind during their childhood together. As they grew to manhood, he had found himself picking his brains more and more. He watched with a critical eye as groups of warriors, trained using Theobald's methodical drills, trooped into the harbour to carry out their appointed tasks, some straining at launching ropes, some laying long oars into rowlocks, whilst others carried shields, spears and axes and boarded the boat as it cast off.

But where was Herin with that second boat? His launching was much too casual. Æthelfrith expected to be obeyed immediately, even if Herin was older than him. Waving frantically to his cousin to speed up, he scrambled aboard the bobbing longboat and stood in the upturned prow as it was rowed steadily from the shore.

Æthelfrith noted that the visiting vessel had shipped oars and now awaited their arrival, the green flag of a peaceful trader fluttering from its sternpost. Perhaps he had been hasty to launch two armed boats to greet it. But that was no excuse for Herin's delay. You could never be too sure in these waters: pirates would use any deception to gain entry into harbour. Perhaps Herin still resented being passed over for the kingship and had deliberately ignored him. He would have to watch him more carefully. Although he appeared languid and lightweight, he was fast and nimble in combat, striking suddenly like a snake. Glowering at Herin's boat as it finally caught up, Æthelfrith signalled it to stand-by whilst he pulled alongside the visitor.

A grey-bearded figure in colourful robes waved to him from the foredeck as he approached.

'We come in peace and would convey important messages to your gracious king.'

'And who exactly would you be? I would know your origin and lineage before accepting even a message from an unbidden caller,' Æthelfrith growled.

The two boats had drifted closer so that he could now see that the messenger was no warrior and carried no sword; rather he had a merry, almost mystical look to him with a strange smile that stretched from ear to ear.

'I am Aneirin, bard and hearthside companion to the Kings of the Old North. Of my lineage I know little except that my mother was named Dwywei and she married King Dunod the Stout, although many claim I am not his son on account of my stature.' He made a flowery gesture to indicate his tall, slim figure. 'Can I board your vessel to deliver my message? Or would you have me shout it across the waves?'

Æthelfrith spat deliberately over the side of his ship. 'I have heard of an Aneirin who exaggerates the exploits of certain British kings, singing of them as heroes instead of the villains they really are. You wouldn't be related to him, would you?'

Aneirin threw back his head and laughed. 'You are mocking me, my lord, so much so that I suspect you are the very Æthelfrith I have come to see. I was told to look for a veritable giant of a man, as I see you are. I am indeed a poet who sings of the exploits of our heroic kings. One of them, Urien of Rheged, died near this very place, if I am not mistaken.'

Æthelfrith brushed at the strands of blonde hair that streamed across his face in the wind. 'Yes, I can take you to the very spot where he was cut down. But his death was hardly heroic since he was stabbed in the back by one of his fellow kings.'

He had heard the story a hundred times in the mead halls. King Urien of Rheged was an acclaimed leader and drew around him a combined army from the northern British kingdoms. He had driven the Angles of Bernicia under his uncle Hussa from their sea fortress when Æthelfrith was a young lad. But one of the British kings, named Morcant, had grown so jealous of the glory given to Urien, his commander, that he had killed him. Their war-host had drifted away in disorder, leaving the Bernicians to lick their wounds. They had been saved from their enemies, by their enemies. When Æthelfrith became king, he had sworn never to rely on such good fortune again. He had led out men to win back the land they had lost and, under Theobald's guidance, they had erected ditches and mounds to defend it.

Aneirin held up his arms in a gesture of surrender, the wide grin still splitting his face. 'Forgive me if I have misled my audiences. As a humble poet, I am armed only with words not swords, so that I rarely witness the battles of which I must speak. The message I bring today is unexaggerated and honest. It does not pretend to praise.'

'Then step alone onto my boat and speak plain. One untrue word and you will see my sword.' Æthelfrith gave the orders to ship oars and to join the two boats together with grappling irons and ropes. With the boats secured together, Aneirin was gingerly passed from one vessel to the next. He dusted himself down and flicked back his flowing grey hair, before bowing low.

'My lord-king Æthelfrith, I presume. Excuse my unkempt looks but these frail legs were made to stand on solid soil, not on wooden planks that move unexpectedly this way and that.'

'So I see,' Æthelfrith replied, frowning as his guest's cloak flapped uncontrollably in the breeze. 'I would invite you ashore but I suspect you are a spy sent by my neighbours.'

Aneirin chuckled. 'I would make a poor spy for I cannot tell a castle from a cattle-pen. No, in truth I am the bearer of an invitation – one that I would dearly wish to deliver so that I can sooner stand on ground that does not move beneath my feet.'

'The only invitation I receive from your masters is to the battlefield,' Æthelfrith snarled.

'This is different, my lord. Mynyddog the Golden invites you to attend a festival in his royal seat at Din Eidyn, a wondrous gathering that offers the finest fare of the Hen Ogledd served with a garnish of ancient sports... ' Aneirin stopped to regain his balance as the boats lurched. '... sports that test strength and skill, war games that offer combat but not killing.'

Æthelfrith turned away to conceal his disbelief and to think. He'd heard of these gatherings in the northern kingdoms that played at war, but he had never before been invited to one. The Kings of the Old North, as they called themselves, still regarded him as an unwelcome upstart even though most of his subjects were of their race. Was this a change of heart, an opening for him to be accepted as one of them? That was his ambition after all: to spread his power beyond his isolated fortress and seek glory in the hinterlands. They had failed to defeat him in battle since he had taken over as king from his uncle, so maybe they were finally ready to recognise him. Perhaps they were pandering to their special god who preferred peace and preached of love not war.

No, they were not to be trusted. This was too great a change of direction, probably a ruse to lure him into their clutches. His brother, Theobald, would advise caution, he knew that.

He turned and took a pace towards his visitor. 'What guarantee does the Mynyddog offer that this festival does not become my funeral? I cannot just accept the word of a bard whose songs I know to be untrue.'

Aneirin chuckled. 'Mynyddog said you would not trust me. Which is why he sent you hostages.' He turned to indicate two figures crouched in the stern of his boat.

Seeing them for the first time, Æthelfrith peered hard at their faces. One in particular gave him reason to stare. Wisps of fiery red hair escaped from beneath her hood and he saw immediately that she was a woman of striking appearance.

'Who are they?'

'Offspring of the rulers who would welcome you to their festival.' Aneirin waved at the pair to come forward. 'Like me, I fear they are not natural sea travellers and may not be at their best. This is Cynon, son of Lord Clydno of the Gododdin.'

Æthelfrith inspected the freckle-faced youth who glared glumly back at him, but he was keener to see the second hostage who was making slower progress along the pitching ship.

'And this is Bebba, daughter of Áedán mac Gabráin of Dál Riata,' Aneirin continued.

Æthelfrith watched her closely as she picked her way around mooring ropes. When she gave him a guarded smile, he tried not to stare knowing that Aneirin would report every glance and gesture back to his masters. But for a few heartbeats, he was held prisoner by eyes that mirrored the blue-green of the sea. She slid the hood from her head and gently shook a wave of flaming hair across a face glowing with exotic appeal. He knew he had to have her.

'Bebba's mother is of the Pictish race,' Aneirin explained, as if noticing his fascination with her features.

Bebba finally broke the spell that seemed to have turned Æthelfrith to stone.

'Good day, my lord. Perhaps you would be kind enough to escort this poor sea-sick girl to the shore?'

Æthelfrith could only smile awkwardly. 'Yes, yes of course, come aboard.' He turned to face the poet. 'I accept Mynyddog's hostages as a sign of his good faith in inviting us to his festival. We will put them ashore and follow you to Din Eidyn on the first tide.'

Five

Æthelfrith turned to Theobald, Herin and the small warband who rode behind him and pointed out Mynyddog's citadel up on the Eidyn ridge. Dragons guarded it, or so the legends said, but, seeing it perched above him on a steep outcrop of black rock, Æthelfrith did not think it needed further protection. It had been only a short sail north from their fortress home on the eastern coast, but it was the first time that they had ventured this far from their territorial boundaries. The realisation that they were now deep into what he had previously regarded as enemy territory filled Æthelfrith with excitement and anxiety in equal measure. Theobald had been against their coming in the first place. He'd argued that it was a trap baited by the beguiling Bebba, the hostage who was now awaiting their return. Æthelfrith had to admit she had almost taken away his reason on that first night in their fortress. It was all he could do to stop himself from bursting into her quarters and forcing himself on her. But she was a pleasure that would have to await his return. He believed the tournament gave him an opportunity to promote his prestige in the eyes of his northern neighbours. They still regarded him as a foreign usurper grimly holding onto his rock by the sea.

He had come to the northern capital to change their minds and win their respect as an equal.

The horse they had loaned him at the harbour was too small for his towering frame and his feet almost scraped the ground. Still, he was dressed to impress. His silver-crested helmet gleamed in the sunlight, and his wolf-skin cloak, broached ornately at the throat, fluttered in the breeze to reveal a glittering shirt of chainmail underneath. He knew it would be difficult to match someone known as Mynyddog the Wealthy in the bard-tales, but actions counted for more than gold, he told himself. As his sagging steed slowly carried him towards the stronghold perched on the dark knoll ahead, he was certain those inside would have already heard tell of the battle victories of the young warlord who was riding to meet them.

When they arrived at the palisade that fringed the black cliffs, Æthelfrith drew alongside Aneirin, who acted as their guide and signalled to Theobald and Herin to do likewise. As agreed, Æthelfrith had come with only a small group of war-trained warriors and he wanted to present a solid front as they waited impassively for the wooden gates to open. Their horses began to fidget whilst they stood in the stiff breeze that whipped around the bare stone that glowered down on them.

A head appeared above the turret by the gates. 'Who approaches?' the voice shouted.

'You seem to have dwelt too long on your mead-bench not to recognise your superiors,' Aneirin snorted. 'Your lord will kick your fat rump when I tell him you have delayed his bard Aneirin and the King of Bernicia outside your gates.'

The head disappeared and soon the great gates creaked and groaned, opening slowly. Æthelfrith looked curiously at a wide, cobbled courtyard where a lone guard-captain regarded them nervously, a small gaggle of dishevelled soldiers shuffling slowly into position behind him.

'The lord King Mynyddog would wish you welcome, I am sure. But be advised that he and his royal guests have already made their way to the festival. You can refresh yourselves here before you join them.' The captain indicated the tall hall that edged the square behind him.

'I would rest my weary bones before we join the merriment,' Aneirin answered, sliding from his horse.

Theobald leaned forward, a hand on his sword-hilt, and spoke quickly to Æthelfrith. 'I don't like the smell of this. Have you ever seen a fortress so unmanned? Even the Gododdin are not so careless.'

Æthelfrith glanced anxiously around huts and outbuildings that showed little evidence of life except for an old dog that lolled on the hall step and a couple of chickens pecking amongst the dust. It was eerily empty for the royal centre of a wealthy kingdom. Perhaps he should heed Theobald's words. If there was a trap, best to flush it out now.

'No, if the festivities are as entertaining as you suggest, we would attend them straightaway,' he said to Aneirin. 'Where are they taking place?'

'Why, in the valley behind the rock,' the guard-captain replied. 'It is but a short distance if you are sure you do not want to rest?'

'We are sure,' Æthelfrith said as Aneirin sighed and wearily pulled himself back into the saddle.

*

They heard the festivities before they could see them. As they wound their way down the rocky path, the grunts and groans of contestants and the buzz of bystanders drifted up from the valley floor. Finally, they rounded a corner cut into the blackened stone and saw the festival under way below them on a grassy field framed by craggy hills. Rows of colourful tents and pavilions encircled an arena where bare-chested men strained in turn at heavy stones and iron weights, tossing them high in the air whilst marshals ran forward to mark where they had landed.

'A strange spectacle,' said Herin in his aloof manner as they paused to watch. 'Does it have a purpose?'

'Oh yes,' Aneirin replied. 'Mynyddog does not waste his wealth on mindless competitions. He uses trials that measure muscle-might to pick and train his frontline warriors. That goliath is Gorthyn, head of his personal guard.' He pointed to a giant of a man who had just thrown an iron ball attached to a chain so far that it had scattered spectators as it skidded amongst them.

'And what of the warriors over there?' Theobald asked, indicating two small groups clutching cudgels and shields, circling one another.

'Ah, that is Mynyddog's personal invention, a war game that tests not just the strength of the combatants but their strategies too. He uses it to select the captains of his troops.'

'It looks like standard practice drill to me,' said Herin.

'Look again, my lord.' Aneirin clapped his hands together in pleasure at Herin's mystified stare. 'Each man bears only one weapon, does he not? Either a shield or a cudgel. Not both.'

'To what end?' asked Herin, covering his eyes from the sun that had emerged from the cover of cloud to illuminate the field.

'As I said, this is a game of brain as much as brawn. Each team is made up of three men who chose one weapon each, a shield or a stick. This is a true test of a warrior's wit: to attack or defend, when and how. You do not know of your opponents' choice of weapons until you have made your own,' Aneirin explained.

At that moment, the conflict below erupted as the two sides clashed with roars and the clattering of clubs on shields as one side battered at the other.

'You see!' Aneirin pointed excitedly. 'One team has selected an attacking line-up of two cudgels and one shield. They seem to be prevailing against the two shields and single cudgel of the other.'

They watched in fascination as three men crouching behind a tight wall of two shields staggered back under a fury of fierce strikes. The attackers yelled jubilantly as one hammer blow sent wooden shards flying, hurling themselves recklessly onto the defender's shield to tear it from his grasp. Æthelfrith could not help shouting his encouragement for the hard-pressed team as they turned what looked like disaster to their advantage. As an attacker held up the stolen, broken shield in triumph, a defender aimed a scything sweep cunningly low. It struck hard on the attacker's knee, turning his cry of victory into a yell of pain as he crumpled to the floor. A horn immediately sounded to signify his exit from the contest and he rolled away in agony and dismay. The combat was now three upon two and, although the smaller force fought bravely, the outcome became clear when they lost a second warrior and three surrounded the single survivor to beat him down.

'There are many variations on the tactics employed which makes it a fascinating spectacle,' Aneirin said as they made their way down into the field.

'I would rather participate than spectate, wouldn't you?' Æthelfrith said to Theobald and Herin with a twinkle in his eye. 'Good that we are three.'

Aneirin looked surprised. 'I think you will find that royal guests only attack the mead jar. They leave the fighting to their spearmen.'

Instructing a groom to take charge of their horses, Aneirin guided them around the turfed arena to a colourful array of stalls that offered food, drink and wares of all varieties. The vibrancy of the crowd that thronged the pathways reminded Æthelfrith of the harvest fairs back home and he was tempted by the traders' calls to sample all manner of tasty titbits and thirst quenchers. But he resisted and chided Herin and others amongst his men who tried to linger.

'Let's not forget where we are and who surrounds us. These people may not have heard we come under royal protection,' he warned to a nod of agreement from Theobald.

Aneirin pointed to an enclosure. 'Fear not, there will be refreshments aplenty when we reach the king's pavilion. Your host is renowned for his hospitality.'

Æthelfrith peered at the emblems on the flags that fluttered from the tented pavilion. He recognised the strange unicorn, symbol of the Gododdin, and the white stag of Rheged, but two of the flags carried simple crosses, one red on a yellow background, the other white on blue. He tugged at Aneirin's sleeve.

'I haven't seen those symbols before,' he said pointing at the flags.

Aneirin made his habitual chuckle. 'Some of our kings like to show their Christian credentials, especially as they age and want to claim a passage to heaven. The red belongs to Strad Clud, the blue to Dál Riata.'

With such illustrious kingdoms represented, this was no ordinary gathering, Æthelfrith recognised and, as he saw the royal party more clearly, he began to feel quite overdressed. They all wore colourful tunics and flowing robes, not at all like his martial attire: no weapons, no protective leather. He quietly removed his helmet and unbroached his cloak as they approached. Aneirin was right. These lords had no plan to participate in the war games but seemed more intent on quaffing the mead and scoffing the meats that adorned their tables – unless it was all part of an elaborate plot to catch him off his guard.

Aneirin bowed low before a bent, wizened figure with lank hair and wrinkled skin.

'My lord-king Mynyddog the Magnificent, may I present you Æthelfrith of the Bernice, son of Æthelfric, son of Ida.'

The king stood unsteadily. 'Ah, so you *have* come.' He turned towards his neighbour. 'I think I have won our wager, Owain. I knew he would come.' He took a swig from a golden goblet, looked Æthelfrith up and down and peered at the men who followed him. 'But you are dressed for combat and have brought a warband. Do you mean to fight with us?' He cackled, casting his bulging eyes towards the menfolk who sprawled around him in the tented enclosure. They laughed loudly in response.

Æthelfrith inclined his head to acknowledge the king, feeling his skin burn. He did not like to be the object of mirth.

Keep calm. They are full of mead and I need their favour.

'Forgive us my lord. We presumed we would partake not just of your refreshments but of your rivalries too. I am tempted to try your trial of three on three with my brother, Theobald, and cousin, Herin.' He waved his two companions forward, who in turn bowed before the king.

Mynyddog almost choked on the mouthful of mead he was about to swallow. 'Here we are watchers, not warriors. Gladiators do the fighting for us so we can be entertained, not exhausted. Come, join my companions. They are your neighbours too. You may know Owain, son of Urien, King of Rheged.'

Mynyddog indicated a tall, scar-faced figure with hair swept back into a knot behind his head who rose lithely to his feet.

'Welcome Æthelfrith. Your coming has lost me my wager but I am pleased to finally meet you, even so.' Owain's voice reverberated around the tented enclosure like an echo in a mountain pass.

So this was the son of the famous murdered king, Æthelfrith noted. He looked as cunning as his reputation.

'And this is Rhydderch, King of Strad Clud.' Mynyddog prodded a stocky companion wrapped in a green cloak who reclined in a seat next to him. He scrambled unsteadily to his feet.

'Welcome Æthelfrith of Din Guari. So we've tempted you out of your shack on the rock, have we? It was burning bright when I last saw it.' He smirked and his words were slurred.

Mynyddog flapped a hand in his direction. 'Now, now. Let us not dwell on past conflicts. We agreed to be civil to our guest.'

Æthelfrith glared back at Rhydderch. 'The fortress was in need of repair when you made your visit, so I thank you for firing the rotting timbers. I have replaced them with structures that you would find most difficult to demolish should you wish to try again.'

Mynyddog next shook the shoulders of a redheaded warrior who was oblivious to what was going on, his chin resting on his chest.

'Wake up,' he hissed before smiling up at Æthelfrith. 'He and I compete to see who falls asleep first. Seems he won today. You may not have met Áedán mac Gabráin before?'

As the wizened warrior struggled up to blink open blood-shot eyes, Æthelfrith realised he was being introduced to the famous king of the Dál Riata whose people had sailed from Ireland to claim the islands and mountains to the west of the Picts. Of more immediate interest, he was the father of his hostage Bebba. Áedán burbled at him in an accent so strong, he could not make out his meaning. Æthelfrith could hardly conceal his amazement at the crumpled clothes and unkempt red hair of one of the most feared leaders amongst the northern kingdoms.

'He asks if his daughter is safe and well cared for,' said Rhydderch.

'Do reassure him that Bebba has every comfort and security in my hall. And tell him she is welcome to stay there as long as she wishes,' Æthelfrith replied.

Rhydderch curled his upper lip into a smile. 'We thought she might be to your taste but I am sure Áedán will expect her back when you return. Intact, of course.'

Æthelfrith glanced at the Dál Riatan king who was staring wildly at him seemingly unable to speak.

'Of course – if that is his wish. But I see you like to spin the wheel of fortune here. Maybe I can win her for a while longer.' Æthelfrith sensed the anxious glance of his brother next to him as he spoke.

That seemed to excite Áedán, who let forth a torrent of words whilst gripping the table and swaying uneasily on his feet.

'He says he will gamble on fighting men and dogs but not his daughter,' Rhydderch explained.

'Wait, this young lord may have honourable intentions towards your Pictish beauty.' Mynyddog put a hand on Áedán's arm and spoke quietly. 'Let us hear his proposition.'

Áedán crumpled back into his chair. Æthelfrith had a feeling there was more understanding than it seemed behind his vacant stare.

'I am much taken with your game of three on three. I would challenge your champions to a contest. And, as I believe it is the custom to offer a trophy to the winners, I would claim Bebba as my prize,' he said.

Áedán mumbled incoherently again and Rhydderch scoffed. 'That is not a wager. You only stand to win. What if you lose?'

'I had not considered losing,' said Æthelfrith with a smile.

Owain cleared his throat to interject. 'At least you must pay a price to enter the competition, win or lose. That way we can see some return.'

'Then name your price,' said Æthelfrith, wondering where this war of words was leading.

Mynyddog waved his hand. 'This is sudden. Our guests have hardly arrived. But now you have set off along this path, I feel it could add to the festival fun. Let us discuss amongst ourselves the price for the participation that you propose and see if the father is willing to use his daughter as the stake.' He turned to Æthelfrith. 'Can we ask you to give us a few moments in private?'

As soon as they had stepped outside the pavilion, Theobald grabbed Æthelfrith's arm. 'What are you up to, brother? I fear this girl has beguiled you.'

'So you have said, Theobald. Trust me, I would not risk our fate for any woman. No, they have asked us here for a reason and I am using this wager to flush it out. In the meantime, let's eat. I'm famished.' He pulled a chair to a table laden with dishes and selected some succulent beef.

*

The sun was beginning to set when the two teams chose their weapons. Æthelfrith followed the choice suggested by Theobald, who had pointed to three shields.

'The edge of a shield is every bit as hard as a cudgel so we can use them to attack and defend,' Theobald said when he had proposed his plan.

45

They turned to see what weaponry their opposition had selected. Hitherto undefeated in the field, the burly trio facing them had gone with their favoured formation of two shields and one cudgel. They pointed in ridicule and laughed at the three shields of the Bernicians facing them.

'Isn't that Gorthyn, leader of Mynyddog's guards, who holds their cudgel, the one who threw an iron weight so far that it injured someone in the audience?' asked Herin.

'Defence is stronger than attack. If all else is equal, defence will win. That's what our grandfather, Ida, said and he never lost a battle,' said Theobald.

'I doubt he ever fought without a sword,' muttered Herin.

Æthelfrith studied their foes carefully as they settled into formation. Gorthyn was to the rear, crouching with the cudgel behind his two shield bearers, no doubt intending to strike over their heads or break out around the side to turn his opponents. He was their key man, the local hero who could win the fight for them, and Theobald had proposed a novel tactic to take him out. The three Bernicians gave their traditional shout of mutual support as they banged their shields into an overlapping defensive wall. Æthelfrith knew he could rely on his younger brother to use his powerful body and mental strength in the centre until his heart burst. Herin was quick of hand and wit but more likely to act independently, so he put him on the left, taking the right flank for himself.

He quietly unhitched his handgrip and passed his shield to Theobald, who held it as well as his own. Æthelfrith needed both hands free if their plan was to work. This was the moment he always dreaded: the waiting before the clash of metal on metal. It might be wood on wood this time but hard cudgels could still break a skull. They had watched earlier as one combatant had been carried screaming from the field after a strike to his head. He ran his tongue around dry lips as, opposite him, the

46

man-mountain named Gorthyn tapped his cudgel menacingly on the palm of his hand, waiting eagerly to bludgeon at their bodies. The first move would be crucial. Theobald's idea was to use Æthelfrith's great strength and speed in a quick counter. As his foe charged towards him, Æthelfrith suddenly doubted he could do it. The nearer he came, the more he realised that Gorthyn looked as big and agile as he was.

The two teams jolted to a halt as their shields clashed. Theobald was ready for Gorthyn's first strike, using one shield to ward off the blow and the edge of his second shield to momentarily trap the gnarled end of the cudgel onto the face of the first shield. It only took a heartbeat for Gorthyn to wrench it free but it was enough. As the blow was aimed, Æthelfrith had sprinted, head down from behind the safety of the wall, past Gorthyn, who was by then grappling to free his cudgel from the pincer of Theobald's shields. Swivelling hard round, Æthelfrith enveloped him from behind with steely arms and picked him off his feet. With a mighty shout, he dumped Gorthyn's flaying frame hard onto the ground. As his startled companions turned to face the attack to their rear, Theobald and Herin crashed their shields into their unprotected backs and Æthelfrith snatched Gorthyn's cudgel to strike at their startled faces. It was all over.

The speed of their victory seemed to take the audience by surprise. A stunned silence greeted the three victors as they stood arm in arm to claim the honours, but as appreciation of their bold tactics sank in amongst the crowd, a throaty roar rang loud around the festival field. Æthelfrith greeted their applause with a wave of his arm as he walked deliberately towards the high table where Mynyddog nodded his head in admiration of their feat.

'You have surprised our champions with your daring ploy. You are indeed worthy of a prize. But if you still wish to claim

Bebba, the captive who seems to have captivated you, you must first pay the price of entry into our festival.'

'Which is what?' Æthelfrith asked, catching his breath.

'Peace between our kingdoms. That's the price of taking part in our festivities and becoming a true northern king. If you take an oath to weave the threads of peace between our kin, you can take Bebba as your woman.'

Six

As Æthelfrith and his companions followed Aneirin through the gates of Din Eidyn, the shadow of the black rock above the fortress fell upon them and dampened their high spirits. Their lively chatter gave way to anxious glances as their eyes grew accustomed to the gloom of their surroundings. The cobbled courtyard that had stood almost empty when they had first arrived was now a hive of activity as servants dragged trestles and benches from the great hall and arranged them into rows that were rapidly filling the entire area. Competitors and spectators from the sporting events hurried between huts around the square to prepare themselves for the festivities that were to follow.

Aneirin approached a steward who was waving his arms, pointing and shouting seemingly at anyone who came near. He bent his ear to listen to Aneirin before eyeing the small group of Bernician warriors who stood awkwardly in the square trying to keep out of the way of the frantic preparations that swirled around them. Aneirin returned, smiling.

'It seems there is a lack of sleeping quarters. The main halls are already full to bursting, so they have given you a small hut to the rear. If you would like to follow me?'

Æthelfrith saw Theobald scowl as they were led past a pit of stinking waste to a small building. No doubt he was sensing danger at being lodged apart from the other warriors, but then he would probably see threats whatever the arrangements. It was good that his brother's caution did not extend to the battlefield, otherwise he might be a liability. But Æthelfrith knew that he would fight relentlessly without thought for his own safety once he was face to face with an enemy. He caught his brother's uneasy mood and nodded to one of his thegns to go through the door ahead of him.

The room was bare except for straw on the floor. The smell of fresh-cut pine and the green of the thatch told him that it was newly built, like the collection of buildings around it. The King of the Gododdin had been spending his fabled wealth on extending his estate, it seemed. But to what end?

As his men tried to make themselves comfortable in their sparse surroundings, Æthelfrith nodded to Herin and Theobald. 'A word outside, if you please.'

They gathered around the waste-pit as the only place that offered any privacy.

'I would like to know your thoughts on their offer.'

'I would take the woman and use the peace to enjoy her,' laughed Herin.

'And pay the price afterwards, you mean.' Theobald was looking hard at his brother. 'There must be several hundred men gathered here. Can it just be for mock fighting?'

'So your advice would be to return home empty-handed?' Æthelfrith broke a small stick that he had picked from the ground and threw it onto rotting pig-bones.

'Not so empty. I will have the happy memory of Gorthyn's face as you picked him off his feet and dumped him on the ground.' Theobald's smile quickly disappeared. 'But there is something very strange about the way they are treating us.

First, an enticing hostage, now peace and friendship. It's not like them.'

'So what are they going to do to us? Cut our throats?' asked Herin, shaking his head. 'They could have done that already. No, they've tried to drive us away and failed and now they realise they have to accept us. Maybe they have listened to their god who preaches peace and love. I say we should stay and enjoy their hospitality.'

Theobald could not contain his unease and raised his voice. 'No, that's the trap. Whilst we quaff their mead, they'll send warriors to take away our land. That's their intent, I'm sure of it.'

Æthelfrith rounded on his brother. 'Keep your voice down. Let's not tell all the world of our fears. I'll think on what you have said but so far I am of Herin's mind. Let's enjoy the hospitality – for the moment.'

*

The feast that night was beneath bright stars that shone down on the broad courtyard of the Gododdin citadel. When Æthelfrith saw the baying multitude seated at the benches under the fire-torches, he understood why the tables had been dragged outside. The hall could not possibly house that many warriors. He quickly estimated there were over three hundred men, drinking and shouting, throwing wheaten-bread at each other, impatient for proceedings to begin and the meat to be served. As he walked towards the high table behind Mynyddog, Owain, Rhydderch and Áedán, a throaty roar went up from the trestles as the assembly jumped to their feet, pumping fists and waving tankards in the air. He could not help feeling proud at being included in this tumultuous welcome for the Kings of the Old North.

When they had all taken their seats, a figure wearing a hooded tunic that fell to his feet came forward from the shadows and held up his hand. Æthelfrith nearly chuckled at the strange style of his hair that was shaved back from his scalp to the line of his ears. But he stopped when he realised that every last one of the noisy multitude, from white-haired warriors to half-bearded youths, had fallen silent and were bowing their heads.

'The Lord God has given us this bread to eat and this wine to drink through the generosity of his follower, King Mynyddog,' the priest said, lifting a loaf and a goblet from the table. 'So we give our thanks and loyalty to them both in equal measure, from the bottom of our hearts.'

'From the bottom of our hearts,' Æthelfrith heard them respond as they all stood to raise their wine and tear at the bread loaves.

There was no missing Mynyddog, who next pushed himself to his feet. The golden torc around his neck and the shimmering gown trimmed with fur that fell full length from his shoulders reflected the flames of the torches so that he seemed to glow like a candle. He waved a hand towards the priest.

'Thank you, Brother Rhun of Rheged, for offering us prayers tonight. You are especially welcome to guide us at this moment as we seek to live in peace with our neighbours following the words of our Lord in Heaven, Jesus Christ.'

His voice was so frail that those seated further away could not hear and Æthelfrith heard the whispers as his words were passed along the tables.

'With that intention in mind we have invited a guest to honour at our feast, a neighbour who until now has felt the wrath of our God rather than his compassion. I ask you to welcome King Æthelfrith, who has travelled from the land of Bernice to be with us. Not forgetting his followers who dine amongst you.' He waved his hand towards Theobald and his thegns, who sat on a lower table. The announcement was greeted with a muted cheer and tapping of wood as he continued.

'You watched Æthelfrith and his two companions win a notable war game today and he has asked to take a Brittonic wife as his reward. What greater prize could there be!' The old king cackled at his own words and he took a gulp from his goblet before continuing. 'Tonight we would drink from the oath-cup to confirm our commitment that he will be joined to Bebba, daughter of Áedán, King of Dál Riata.' A loud cheer went up from the tables, followed by the stamping of feet. 'This holy union between one man and one woman will be a sign of the coming together of all the men and women of Bernicia with the kingdoms of the Old North. We will henceforth live in peace and jointly seek to repel any enemies who seek to destroy us.'

Mynyddog clapped his hands and Æthelfrith was passed a drinking horn carved with entwined knots and filled with red wine to its silvered rim. 'Speak your oath and drink your fill from this pledge-binder,' Mynyddog said as Áedán leaned forward to watch carefully.

Æthelfrith raised the horn-cup with steady hands that did not spill a drop even when it was above his head for all to see.

'I, Æthelfrith, son of Æthelric, son of Ida, kings of the Bernice all, do give you, Áedán of Dál Riata my pledge to take your daughter, Bebba, as my wife. To you, Mynyddog of the Gododdin, and to you Owain of Rheged and to you Rhydderch of Strad Clud, I give my oath to point my spears away from your lands.'

He placed the great horn to his lips and began to drink as the feast-folk tapped on their tables in time to each gulp. He slowed, expecting a rush of wine as he drained the twisted end of the horn, knowing that a large spillage or failure to finish would ill fate his oath. With a flourish he upturned the horn on his head to signify that it was empty. The rhythmic beating broke into a climax of sporadic banging and cheering as Æthelfrith sat down. He wiped his mouth and clamped his teeth tight together as he desperately fought to keep down what he had just swallowed.

Mynyddog took back the horn and peered into the top. 'I see you like our wine as well as our women,' he said with a flicker of a smile. 'Let us hope you do not eat your words as well as your dinner.'

Æthelfrith watched closely as the horn was re-filled to well below the rim with thin-coloured mead. His host was obviously taking no chances of spilling dark liquid on his golden gown.

'I, Mynyddog Mwynfawr do accept the pledge given to me by Æthelfrith the Angle to accept a peace-weaver between our lands. The Almighty God above will surely strike him down if he dishonours his word.' He had no difficulty in swallowing the meagre draft and placing the drinking horn on his head, to wild stamping and banging from his followers. 'I now ask Áedán of Dál Riata as father of the intended bride to confirm the giving of Bebba as this man's wife.'

Áedán's hair was neatly tied at the back of his head, giving his face the fierce look of an eagle, and Æthelfrith could see no sign of his earlier unsteadiness as he rose. His accent was still heavy but his words were clear. 'I Áedán, son of Gabrán mac Domangairt, do give ma daughter Bebba to Æthelfrith of Bernice as a mark of peace between our clans.' The flaming torches lit up his face as he stared intensely towards Æthelfrith. 'And if you break ya oath, I will kill you.'

He grabbed the drinking horn one-handed from the maid who had refilled it to the brim with a deep coloured mead and steadily drank it dry without a pause, all the while glaring intently at Æthelfrith. He sat down carefully when he had finished and belched loudly. The hall erupted into shouting and stamping once again.

In turn, Owain and Rhydderch both drank from the horn and pledged to live in peace with the Bernicians. Unable to contain the churning of the strong wine in his stomach any longer, Æthelfrith rose unsteadily from his seat.

Mynyddog looked up, smiling wanly as he lurched away. 'Feeling queasy?' he asked.

'Just going for a piss,' Æthelfrith said, walking quickly around the back of the hall where he gagged and threw up.

Theobald came quietly round the corner, startling his brother, who was bent double against the wall. 'You never could take your drink,' Theobald said, wiping dribble from Æthelfrith's ashen face. 'Or was it the oaths that have sickened you?'

'Whatever the cause, I have managed to soil my tunic,' Æthelfrith said, trying to wipe the stain from his clothes. 'Could you see if there is straw to clean me up in the barn over there?' He pointed towards a high-eaved building nearby.

Theobald pulled and pushed at the door of the barn but it would not open. He peered through a crack beside the doorpost and whistled softly. 'Come take a look. No wonder the entrance is barred.'

Æthelfrith put his eye to the gap, expecting to see sacks of grain and land-tools. Instead he saw row upon row of saddles and riding tackle. He groaned and slumped to sit by the door, holding his head in his hands. Theobald peered through the crack once more, counting as he did.

'Enough gear to mount several hundred horses. Yet we have not seen any riding at these games,' he said.

'This is the equipment for a mounted warband, not for a festival. You were right, Theobald. They are preparing for conflict whilst pledging peace. We need to leave and protect our home.'

'And the oaths?'

Æthelfrith breathed out slowly. 'We cannot arouse their suspicion. So the oaths will have to stand. I will excuse our rapid departure by telling them I am impatient to return to my bride to be.'

'And I don't think you will have to lie about that, will you brother?' Theobald said, wiping at the dribble that still remained on Æthelfrith's tunic with some grass.

*

Æthelfrith was the first ashore when the longboat nudged into the harbour wall at the base of his fortress that towered above the sea. During the two-day journey home, he had thought deeply about their visit to the land of the Gododdin. Had he acted too hastily in taking a wife in return for an oath of peace with the Kings of the Old North? Theobald certainly thought so. He'd said they should not turn their backs on their fellow Angles if Mynyddog unleashed his warband on Deira – and that seemed the Gododdin king's most likely option if he kept to his pledge of peace with Bernicia.

As Æthelfrith took the first of the rocky steps that led up to his cliff-top home, a more immediate concern made him slow his ascent. How was he to tell Bebba that he had won her as a prize in a tournament? She might not believe him or resent being given away so lightly. The Picts were known for the strange ways of their women. He had heard that females fought with the warbands and that chiefs were chosen through the mother's rather than the father's bloodline. He suddenly wished there was someone else who could tell Bebba the news.

'Welcome home. I trust my kin treated you well?'

Hearing a woman's voice above him, Æthelfrith almost stumbled from his perch half way up the cliff. He looked up to see Bebba smiling down on him, red hair streaming across her face, hands on hips, her tunic billowing in the breeze to give him glimpses of her fine legs. Shaking with either excitement or fear – he could not tell which – he shot a glance downwards to see that his men were still in the harbour below. He had no choice but to go up and face her alone.

'Yes, most kindly, thank you,' he said, scrambling up the remaining steps, wondering why he could feel his heart banging hard against his ribs.

She held up a hand as he approached. 'Stay. I want to look you in the eye.' She walked calmly to the top of the steep footpath that was hewn into the hard rock. 'See, we are of equal height now.' She moved so close to him that her gown flapped against his body and her hand briefly touched his. 'What news? I sense you may have something important to tell me.'

Æthelfrith froze, unable to climb higher, mesmerised by the closeness of her soft green eyes.

'News? Yes there is some,' he heard himself saying. 'Shall we go inside, out of this… this breeze?' Her robes flew up above her knees and it was all he could do to stop himself swaying backwards off the steps.

She held down her dress. 'Tell me now or I will burst. Do I stay or do I return?'

Æthelfrith swallowed hard. Did she know already?

'No, no you can stay. For ever.'

Her lips parted into a broad smile and he thought she was about to throw herself at him.

'Then, my lord, walk me to my new home.' She took his hand to help him up the final step and led him through the narrow gate of the wooden palisade that ringed the promontory. Arm in arm they strolled up the gentle slope past the workshops where smithies and bakers gaped as they made their way towards the great hall that crowned the highest point of the fortress.

Seven

The tapping on the door of his hut grew louder but still Æthelfrith did not stir from the mattress. He rested on one elbow, admiring the sheath of shiny hair that lay like a sunset on the pillow next to him. He wanted to run his finger along the serpent tattooed around her waist and down her thigh as he had done during the night, but he did not want to wake her. He contented himself by counting the freckles dotted around her shoulders.

The tapping became a loud knocking and he heard his brother's voice.

'Æthelfrith, lord, I need to speak with you urgently. There is important news.'

He sighed, gently covering Bebba's bare body with a blanket before standing to pull a gown around his shoulders. He opened the door slightly and peered out. Theobald stood outside, frowning in the bright sunlight.

'At last, you are awake—' he began.

'I can assure you I have been awake most of the night, brother. Just not available.' Æthelfrith stepped outside, closing the door behind him. 'She is sleeping, so I have a few moments.'

Theobald was studying his neckline carefully. Æthelfrith hitched up his robe to cover the scratches that he knew ran from his neck all the way down his back.

'What is this news that cannot wait?'

Theobald shook the smirk from his face. 'Before you retired two days ago, you gave orders to heighten the earthworks inland, yet you didn't specify which ones. I set men to work to the north along the line of the Tweed towards Gala Water and the Catrael. Yet it occurred to me we have weaker defences to the south. Should we not also be building along the Swæle to the Tees to stop an incursion from that direction? There are rumours that the warriors of Elmet are gathering south of the wall, and of course Deira—'

Æthelfrith waved a hand to stop him. 'Yes, yes. Do what you think best. Take as many men as you need. And the news?'

Theobald raised his eyebrows, seeming surprised at his brother's lack of interest in the defence works.

'The news is born by a messenger from King Ælle who arrived yesterday from Eoferwic and insists on speaking only to you. He came with Guthlaf, the trader, who sails on the evening tide.'

Æthelfrith exhaled audibly. He felt the weight of kingship falling back onto his shoulders when all he wanted was to lose himself in the arms of the exotic woman who occupied his bed. Theobald did not move but stood impassively waiting for an answer.

'I will come in the afternoon to see him and we can discuss the defences further at the same time.' Æthelfrith turned to go.

'But it is the afternoon, brother.'

He whirled around. 'Then tell him to await me in the hall and I will see him presently,' he said through gritted teeth.

*

Quietly returning to his hut, Æthelfrith was surprised to see Bebba standing so close to the door that, when he opened it, it almost struck her. She wore only a short skirt, leaving her flowing hair to cover her upper body as best it could. He swallowed hard, knowing that he had to leave her for a while.

'Anything wrong?' she asked.

'No, just some messenger on a merchant ship who needs my attention.'

'A merchant ship! Perhaps they have garments to sell. I brought so little with me that I have nothing to wear.' She shook her hair so that it rippled around her naked body to illustrate her point. 'Can I meet this trader?'

Æthelfrith was about to reach for her but he stopped himself just in time and grabbed his boots instead. 'He sails very soon so you will have to hurry.'

Bebba was already snatching up her robe and making ready to leave.

*

Æthelfrith could not miss the disapproving look on Theobald's face when he re-emerged from his quarters followed by Bebba. He would have to teach his younger brother the virtues of a woman's company other than those in the crude jests of the mead hall.

'What news old friend? I believe you are keen to catch your tide,' Æthelfrith said to Guthlaf, who was waiting with Theobald at the doorway to the hall.

'Indeed I am. Tide and winds. They both change to my disadvantage shortly,' said Guthlaf, looking admiringly at Bebba.

'This is Lady Bebba from Dál Riata, who is keen to see any garments you have to offer,' Æthelfrith said.

Guthlaf bowed his head. 'Pleased to make your acquaintance, my lady. Alas, I have precious little clothing left and what I have, is promised at my next destination.'

'Which is where?' asked Bebba.

'I am headed for Din Eidyn.'

Bebba clapped her hands. 'Excellent! You can return Cynon to his home.' She turned to Æthelfrith. 'He's no longer needed here as a hostage is he? He can take our goods news back with him and ask for my possessions to be sent here.' She peered through the doorway. 'I think I see him inside. I will fetch him while you talk.'

The three men watched admiringly as she swayed past them into the hall to find Cynon, the Gododdin prince who had also been held as a guarantee for their safe passage to Din Eidyn.

Æthelfrith brought himself reluctantly back to the business in hand. 'Where's this messenger?'

Theobald pointed through the doorway of the hall to the high table where a young man sat polishing the buckle of a belt. 'There, awaiting your pleasure.'

Æthelfrith strode into the hall, nodding at the cooks who busied over pots on the central hearth and snapping his fingers at a dozing dog that jumped up and eagerly followed him to the high seat. As he sat and stroked the dog, he glanced into the far corner where Bebba was talking animatedly to Cynon, and fought to bring his attention to the young man who was scrambling to his feet by the bench.

'What's your business here?' he snapped.

Theobald took his place next to the king. 'He has a message from the court of Deira.'

'Indeed I do,' the young man said. 'My name is Forthhere, thegn-son in the service of King Ælle. He asked me to give you his greetings and a message.'

Æthelfrith waved distractedly towards Bebba, who had finished her conversation with Cynon and was chatting to one of the women at the hearth. 'Get on with it then.'

'My king asked me to repeat these precise words.' Forthhere closed his eyes for a moment before continuing in a rhythmic tone. 'I snap a spear in two and turn a sword to rust. Warriors always sleep and women never weep, when I become their lord.'

Æthelfrith held up his hand. 'What is this? Is your king so old he wishes to play games with me?'

'King Ælle has a habit of using riddles to disguise his messages in case they are overheard by his enemies,' Forthhere explained. 'There is a little more if you will permit.'

'Riddles? If we have to work with riddles, we need a woman's wit.' Æthelfrith stood and waved at Bebba to come over.

'I'm not sure that's a good idea—' Theobald began.

'Nonsense. You doubt your future queen?'

'Surely her ladyship will be bored with these matters of government, brother?' Theobald scowled as Bebba swept up to the high table.

'Try me. I'm rarely bored, am I, dear?' Bebba draped her arms around Æthelfrith.

'Nor boring,' Æthelfrith laughed. 'This young fellow has a riddle for us. Tell it again, Forthhere.'

Forthhere cleared his throat and shot a glance at Theobald, who was sitting with his head in his hands.

'Very well. The message starts: "I snap a spear in two and turn a sword to rust. Warriors always sleep and women never weep, when I become their lord." It continues: "I can be woven by a maiden, the daughter of a king. I await you at the sign of the wild boar." That's it my lord.'

'Women never weep? Woven by a maiden? Any ideas, my love?' Æthelfrith asked.

Bebba scanned the faces of all three men. 'No, none at all.'
She patted Æthelfrith's hand. 'Sorry, I don't understand your
kingly games. I will leave you to them and say my final farewell
to Cynon.' She rose from the bench and turned to go.

Æthelfrith stood in silent protest but she swept away
without a backward glance.

'Maybe you were right, Theobald. She is bored by matters
of government.'

'On the contrary, I think she is very interested,' Theobald
said. 'Can we speak in private, brother?' He moved closer to the
high chair as Forthhere bowed and made his exit. 'We seem to
have frightened off all our foes. Now it's King Ælle who wants
peace. What else breaks a spear or rusts a sword, but peace?'

'Or makes a warrior sleep. But what does he mean by the
weaving maiden?' asked Æthelfrith.

'He is offering you a peace-weaver between our kin, the
hand of his daughter in marriage.'

'Does he now? We'll just have to tell him I'm already taken.'

'Not so fast.' Theobald looked around to make sure that
they were not overheard. 'You may have sampled one dish, but
now there is another on the table. One that may be more to
our taste.'

Æthelfrith put his hands to his ears. 'Why is everyone
talking in riddles today? Speak plain.'

Theobald took a deep breath. 'Very well. If you marry the
daughter of the king of Deira, you and your children could
become rulers of that land as well Bernicia. That would create
a kingdom large enough to sweep away the British rulers that
now feign peace, once and for all. But if we sit and watch while
they defeat King Ælle, they will gain the wealth and strength
of his territory. We will be isolated, surrounded. Do you think
we will survive for long? You have not yet married Bebba. The
price for her is too high.'

'Spoken very plainly, brother. But, for me, the price for Bebba can never be too high.'

'Surely we cannot miss this chance to ally ourselves with Deira and become masters of the north? The last line of the riddle is an invitation to meet King Ælle at the town of the wild boar, which is Eoferwic. At least, talk with him.' Theobald looked desperate.

Æthelfrith grasped his brother hard by the arm and thrust his face close to his.

'I welcome your counsel, but not on women, especially this one. I will marry Bebba, and soon.' He released his grip and sat back in his high seat. 'But you are right about Deira. We cannot let it fall. Ælle must be desperate to ask for our help. You say Elmet is marching against him?' He reached down to stroke the dog sleeping at his feet as Theobald nodded. 'We are not sworn to peace with them. Take two boats to Eoferwic and help Ælle against the threat from the south. Then we will both be ready to face the Old North if they should turn against us.'

Theobald exhaled audibly and nodded. 'That's certainly better than doing nothing.' He glanced towards the entrance of the hall where Forthhere waited patiently. 'And Ælle's daughter? How do we deal with her?'

Æthelfrith threw back his head and laughed. 'You seem more worried about her than the British warriors. As you said, we cannot miss this chance. *You* must marry her.'

Eight

Acha threw the cloth irritably to the floor. She really did not want to spend her day making a garment when a slave-maid could do it perfectly well for her. Yet, if she was to be paraded before Æthelfrith the Awful, she wanted to appear as unattractive as possible by wearing ill-fitting, unflattering garments. A slave might be punished for making such clothes, so she had to do it herself. She scratched her cheeks with her nails, wondering if a reddened face would make her look less appealing. Trust her luck that she had no disfiguring spots just when she needed them.

There was a sharp tap on the door of her hut.

'Message for the Princess Acha from the king,' said a strangely deep voice that she half-recognised.

She threw open the door and burst into laughter. Lillan stood before her, shield and spear at his side.

'Why, your voice is changed, young sir. Is this another of your vulgar jokes?'

'I wish it was but I am on the king's business. He wants you to join the meeting of his council.'

Acha felt her heart pound. The moment she had been dreading had come. The king was about to announce his marriage plans for her, she knew it. And she had not yet plucked up the courage to tell Lillan.

'Sorry, I'm not feeling so well. Do you think I really have to—'

'He was quite insistent. I think it would be wise to come, unless you are very ill,' Lillan said, shifting his shield uncomfortably.

She wanted to throw herself into his arms and tell him to take her away to some place where they could live quietly together.

'Give me a moment to prepare myself,' she said.

*

King Ælle looked strained. A thick, ornate cloak hung from his shoulders even though the day was warm. Acha thought his face unusually grey as she slowly walked the length of the hall towards his high chair. His most senior thegns flanked him, all carefully displaying the silver and gold arm-rings, buckles and ornaments that their king had given them. Even Ælfric was there, regarding her sternly as she approached. Lillan hurried past to pull out a bench before her father and his advisors. Ælle indicated that she could sit.

'Welcome to this meeting of the Witan. There is one subject my council have been discussing which vitally concerns you and—'

A loud bang on the door interrupted the king, who glowered before nodding to the guard to admit whoever was outside. Two warriors burst in, bowing low.

'Forgive us, lord king, but your orders were to inform you immediately. We have taken prisoners as instructed,' one of them said.

Ælle was on his feet. 'Good. Bring them in. Are they from Elmet?'

'Yes, they were coming from that direction.'

Acha moved aside as a man and a boy, their hands bound, were dragged into the hall and shoved before the king, who had risen to inspect them. Ælle studied the man long and hard. He had a drooping moustache and shoulder-length hair and tried to move closer to the young lad, who was whimpering at his side. Ælle grasped the wooden cross that hung around the man's neck.

'You follow this god who preaches peace and forgiveness?'

'Yes, lord,' the man stammered.

Ælle pulled hard on the cross to bring the prisoner's head close to his own.

'So why were you following a warband who clearly are not intent on peace?'

'They came to our village and took us. Made us forage for food. I'm a farmer, not a fighter, lord.'

'I can see that.' Ælle dropped the cross and fumbled at the neck of his own tunic, pulling out a large gold medallion on a chain. He thrust it towards the prisoner.

'This is my god,' he said pointing to the embossed figure of a warrior on a horse flanked by two birds. 'Woden. He didn't die meekly on a cross like your god. He bargained for knowledge and got it by sacrificing his right eye. Now I need some knowledge from you, but I do not want to lose my sight, so I'm thinking I will offer you this boy's eye instead.'

Acha flinched and looked away as her father took a small knife from his belt and held the point onto the skin beneath the boy's eye. The boy's pupils rolled up towards his father in terror.

'Tell me all you know about this warband and this lad – your son, is he? – gets to keep his eye. Hold back and I will gouge it out to tempt you to talk.'

'No, no, you don't need to do that. I'll tell you what I know, but it's not much, honest,' the man pleaded.

'Who leads the warband, how many warriors are there and where are they going? That's the price of his eye.' Ælle circled the knife around the boy's eyeball.

The prisoner was trembling and gabbled out the information as fast as he could. 'Ceredig, the king himself, leads. We have to find enough food every day to feed a hall, like this one, brimful of warriors. Soon they will be joined by others, they said, so we have to find food to store as well. Each day, they march hard, to the north.'

'To the north?' Ælle looked inquiringly to the men who had brought in the prisoner. 'They are not moving east towards us?'

'No, lord. They travel on the old road that runs north,' one of the warriors replied.

Ælle stroked his beard, thoughtfully. 'You mean north on Deere Stræt that leads to the Wall and into Gododdin territory?' When the warrior nodded in agreement, Ælle turned to address his thegns, banging his fist on the table. 'I told you. The British kings will join forces somewhere along that road. Then they will turn towards us. This band from Elmet is no great threat on its own, but if their numbers are swelled by the men of Rheged, Gododdin and Strad Clud, we will be greatly outnumbered.'

Acha groaned inwardly as her uncle, Ælfric, rose to speak. 'If they have marched past us and continue north, surely it is to confront Bernicia that lies to the north? Why do we suppose they threaten us rather than Æthelfrith, their sworn enemy?'

Ælle once more pointed his knife towards the face of the son and growled a question at the father. 'When they are drinking and singing in the feast hall, who do they insult? Whose name do they spit upon and scorn?' The man looked confused, hesitating to answer. 'Come now,' the king encouraged. 'I will not punish you or your son for an honest answer, only for the lack of one.'

'It is King Ælle, lord, that they mostly mock.' Beads of sweat dripped from the man's brow as he answered.

Ælle roared triumphantly towards Ælfric. 'You hear that? We are the enemy. We have debated enough. We will defeat these rude men of Elmet before they can join up with their northern friends.'

Ælfric shook his head. 'I still say we should wait here where our defences are strongest. Why risk all by fighting beyond our boundaries? And what of the delegation from Bernicia who are on their way here?'

'No, we cannot allow their armies to join up. I will take my thegns to intercept them. You will take charge here in my absence,' Ælle said, pointing to his brother. 'And you, Lillan, will lead the thegn-sons who stay to guard the elders, women and children. I can only spare a few warriors so this is your time to stand with the spears.'

Acha watched with pride as Lillan straightened his back and took the king's arm to accept the promotion. But she shuffled along the bench, away from her father.

Maybe he has forgotten his plans for me.

Ælle stroked his beard thoughtfully as he briefed Lillan. 'I do not wish to spurn the Bernicians but every moment is precious. Tell Æthelfrith when he arrives that I have headed northwest on Deere Stræt to head off the Elmet army. Tell him to join me with all speed unless he wants to be overrun by the British kings. But make sure you introduce him to my daughter before he leaves.' He turned to look deliberately towards Acha. 'And see she behaves in the manner of his future wife.'

Acha's ears burned fiercely and she dare not meet Lillan's eyes once she had seen the look of shock and disbelief on his face.

'Yes lord,' she heard him say.

*

Acha sat with her chin in her hands at the high table of her father's hall in Eoferwic, waiting for the guests from Bernicia to arrive. Lillan, who had hardly spoken to her since the hurried departure of King Ælle the day before, stood by the door with a group of thegn-sons. Edwin fidgeted at her side, fingering the wooden sword he held under the table.

'How much longer do we have to wait?' he complained.

Acha heard feet stamping on the ground outside and saw Lillan grabbing at his spear and standing alert.

'No time at all, it seems.' Acha scrambled to her feet. 'Don't forget to be rude,' she whispered to Edwin as a group of warriors came through the door. She frowned as she saw Ælfric leading the way, but it was the man in a flowing blue cloak and tousled blonde hair in the centre of the delegation that caught her eye. He carried no spear or shield as the others did, just an ornate sword that hung from a belt on his shoulder over a gleaming shirt of chain mail. She assumed he must be the Bernician king and tried to pout and look miserable, sniffing like a common woman as she had planned. But she could not look away from his sparkling eyes that seemed to lighten her mood when they fell on her. He seemed little older than Lillan and – dare she think it – equally good-looking, if not more so. His disarming smile almost had her smiling in return.

Ælfric waved a hand towards the guests. 'My lady, the delegation from Bernicia has arrived.' Before he could speak further, the handsome young man in the blue cloak stepped forward.

'My greetings to your ladyship.' He inclined his head and held forward a wooden box. 'I offer you a small gift by way of apology for the absence of my brother, King Æthelfrith.'

Acha looked around, confused. *A gift?* Who was this charming man offering her a gift, if not the king?

'Apparently their king is detained elsewhere. This is his brother, Theobald,' Ælfric explained.

Acha looked to Ælfric for more guidance as to what she should do, but he offered her none. Edwin chirped up in a loud whisper that covered her confusion.

'Aren't you going to open the present?'

Acha reddened and fumbled at the lid. 'Thank you, Lord Theodore.' She picked a golden, disc-shaped brooch from the box, recognising it instantly from Guthlaf's collection of the latest ornaments from Frankia. 'This is most welcome. It is beautiful,' she said sincerely.

'Then it will match its new owner,' he said bowing towards her, adding in a whispered voice: 'It's Theobald, not Theodore.'

Acha put a hand to her mouth to stop herself giggling at her mistake and from the relief of meeting such a thoughtful man instead of the ogre she had been expecting.

'Is your brother… is he following you?' she asked.

'No, he is engaged elsewhere. I am here to replace him in whatever duties your father has in mind.' Theobald paused to turn towards Ælfric. 'Which I haven't had the opportunity to discuss with him as I believe he has departed to face the threat from the south?' When Ælfric nodded his confirmation, Theobald quickly added: 'In which case I must follow him immediately with my warriors as I am here as an ally.'

'Can you not stay for the refreshments we have prepared?' Acha asked.

'Time is of the essence in matters of war like this. We would gladly take some of your food with us, but we cannot stay.' He took her hand and gently brushed it with his lips. 'I will be back,' he said quietly and walked briskly from the hall.

Acha slumped back in her chair, trying to ignore Edwin, who ran behind the departing entourage waving his sword and shouting encouragement. She breathed deeply and reached for some berry juice to quench the dry feeling in her mouth, unexpectedly finding herself wishing for the safe and rapid return of the Bernician royal party.

Nine

Æthelfrith took Bebba's arm as they ambled across the courtyard towards the hall of his citadel. Sucking in a deep breath of the crisp air that blew in from the sea, he felt warmed by the woman at his side. His adult life had been spent almost exclusively in the company of men. Night after night, he had eaten and drunk himself silly with his warriors and slept next to them in tents or on benches in halls. By day, he had laboured with them, building defences, hunting wild boar and deer, practising combat skills or fighting side by side with them in a shield wall. The only time he had ever spent with the women of his kin was when they offered him a jug of beer or a plate of pork and then they did not presume to linger or speak with their king on social matters. That had changed. Today he had a woman to converse with. He had been surprised at how easy it was to share his thoughts with someone he had only just met. Unlike the men he knew, Bebba did not boast of her own exploits but asked after his life, his plans, his problems. He enjoyed men's company, of course, but it was always full of light-hearted banter and bawdy jesting. No man had ever asked about his innermost thoughts in the way that Bebba did. Theobald was the closest friend he had but they kept their discussions to practical matters. He had opened his heart more to Bebba in the few nights that they had spent together than he ever had to any man, including his brother.

As they sauntered along the cliff-top courtyard, Bebba paused at the circular stonewall of the citadel's well. 'Quite a miracle that you can pull fresh water up to such a rocky summit,' she said casually.

Æthelfrith proudly tapped one of the stout posts that supported the winch beam above the well.

'Nothing to do with miracles. This well was built by the hard labour of men. It was one of the first things I did when I became king.'

Bebba idly turned the handle so that the bucket began to descend. 'It must go down a long way to find water.'

'The height of twenty five men, much of it though solid rock.'

Bebba gently squeezed one of his biceps. 'Mm, you must be very strong to dig down so far through rock.'

'I did have some help. Mainly from that man there.' Æthelfrith pointed down the slope towards a building near the gateway where a stout figure was steadily beating a length of iron with his hammer.

'The smithy? How did he help?' Bebba leant forward to inspect the dark hole into which the bucket descended.

'He fired the rock to such a heat that it would crack and we could dig it out. It took all of one winter to complete.'

'Why not have slaves carry the water up from the streams below? Save your strength for more interesting things.' She twined her fingers into his blonde beard and ran a long fingernail over his cheek.

'We can't fetch water from outside of the palisade when we are surrounded by hostile armies sent by your northern kin, can we?' he said.

'But now you have me in return for peace.' A gust of wind blew wisps of her hair across his face as she nuzzled into him. 'All you have to do is to keep me happy so that I won't run away.'

'And how do I do that?'

'I'm not complaining so far. Your welcome has been most... most satisfying,' she said, suddenly moving away and turning her back on him. 'But I know that my mother was given a gift in return for allowing a man to enjoy her most valued possession.'

Æthelfrith felt himself redden with shame. He gave his warriors gifts of gold and silver, even land to the older ones, when they served him well. So why hadn't he done the same for this wonderful woman who had opened his eyes to pleasures he had never known?

'A gift? Yes of course, you can have anything, anything I have.' He made to put appeasing hands on her shoulders but she whirled around, smiling.

'Good. Where shall we start? What do you have that you value most?'

Æthelfrith's mind reeled. It would be his sword, but he had bent it so badly on an enemy shield that the smithy was making him a new one from patterned iron and steel, and that would take many moons to finish. He looked around him for inspiration.

'This citadel is what I value most. It's my home. You are most welcome to that.'

Bebba sucked through her teeth. 'That's a kind gesture, but not exactly a gift as I would have to share it, not just with you but also your sweaty warriors. And it's worthless without them as someone would soon take it away. But you could name it after me? That would be a start,' she said with a gleam in her eye.

Æthelfrith was taken aback. It was an unusual gift and one that would cost him nothing. He took both her hands in his. 'It would be an honour. We will name it Bebba's Fortress.'

She wrinkled her nose. 'That doesn't sound very homely and it needs a blend of British and Anglish to celebrate our union, don't you think? How about Bebbanburg? ' She brushed her lips on his as she spoke so that he could not reply. But inside his head, he was singing.

'Speaking of union,' she continued in a whisper. 'Isn't it time we were married? Unless you want your child to be born a bastard that is.'

'You are with child?'

'If I'm not, I soon will be. You have sewn enough seeds in me to make an army of child—'

She was interrupted by the clanging of the warning bell and the sentry's voice from the rampart.

'Riders coming in hard!'

Æthelfrith cursed and hurried Bebba towards his quarters before racing up the ladder to the earthen top of the wooden palisade. He followed the sentry's arm that pointed towards two riders crouching low over their mounts, pounding towards them from the hills to the northwest. As they neared, he recognised his own scouts and ran to the gate and down the steep steps to meet them.

'What tidings?' he demanded before they had even dismounted.

'The warband has left Din Eidyn. Three hundred riders heading south,' the scout shouted above the wind that whistled around the dunes.

Æthelfrith grabbed the halter of his horse. 'When exactly and what route?'

'Two days ago. They were heading down Deere Stræt to the Wall.'

'You have done well. Rest and I will see you in the hall at feast-time.'

As he climbed back up the path to the palisade, Æthelfrith silently cursed his decision to send Theobald to Ælle with a third of his men. It was as if the Gododdin king knew the very moment that he had divided his forces. Why, after months of feasting and games had Mynyddog sent forth his troops now? He would be outnumbered by two to one if they attacked him in Bernicia. On the other hand, if the British warriors skirted his territory and headed into Deira, Theobald would be caught in a pincer movement between the armies of Elmet to the south and the riders descending from the north. By the time he had reached his hut and fallen breathless into Bebba's arms, he had reluctantly decided what he would have to do. But first, he would marry.

*

Acha was walking amongst the ruins with her maid when she heard news of a second royal visit. She liked to walk around the crumbling walls and fallen buildings even though the thegn-sons no longer had sufficient time away from their duties to exercise there. It took her mind away from day-to-day concerns and back to a time when the giants had mingled on the earth with the gods. She felt more relaxed since Ælfric had been called away to his residence to attend his wife who had given birth to a son. Acha's daydreaming turned to the Bernician lord as she examined yet again the brief words he had spoken to her. What did he mean by the 'duties that her father has in mind'? Was he referring to military matters? Or maybe the proposed marriage between their kin? If so what—

'Acha, Acha come quick!' It was Edwin's unmistakable voice. 'It's the king. He's here.'

Acha clambered hurriedly over fallen masonry looking for her brother.

'Father has returned already?' she asked when he finally ran into view between a roofless arch.

'No, not that king. King Æthelfrith,' he spluttered, panting and pointing in the direction of the harbour. 'He's arrived with four ships.'

Acha's first instinct was fear. A rival leader with enough men to easily overwhelm their tiny force could mean danger. She grabbed at Edwin to take him into her arms.

He pulled away from her. 'He's going to join his brother but he wants to meet you before he leaves.'

'Where?'

'At the wharf. He's taking his ships up-river.'

'Who told you all this?'

'Lillan. He says you should come immediately.'

They ran together, skipping over the fallen stones until they reached the riverbank, which they followed to the harbour. Acha caught sight of a handsome face under a shock of tousled hair and thought that Theobald was back, until she realised this man was taller, much taller.

'There he is,' shouted Edwin. 'The big one.'

Æthelfrith towered over those around him and at the noise of their approach he turned his head quizzically in their direction. As his eyes fell on her, Acha realised that the unkempt appearance she had planned for his visit was how she must now look. She was not expecting visitors so she wore an old tunic that was covered with the dust of the ruins, and her thick hair was tousled from their running. The eyes that looked down on her did not seem as unkind as she expected from a man nicknamed 'the Ferocious'. They had the same softness as his brother's, yet she detected an intensity in them that Theobald's did not possess. She slowed to a more respectful walking pace, brushing at the grime on her tunic. Æthelfrith's eyes flicked from her to Edwin, who grasped Acha's hand tightly when he felt his powerful gaze.

A group of thegn-sons ran to usher them into the king's presence. Lillan, she noted, stood at Æthelfrith's side, talking seriously and pointing up the river. Edwin cowered behind her, silenced by the presence of this giant of a king. Lillan introduced them without once meeting her eyes.

'How old are you, boy?' Æthelfrith's voice resounded around the harbour, silencing all those who stood nearby. Acha squeezed Edwin's hand to reassure him, but he buried his head in her robe and put a thumb to his mouth.

'This will be his tenth summer, lord,' Acha replied.

'Does he have no voice?' Æthelfrith asked.

'Oh yes, he has plenty of voice but he can be timid before strangers.'

Æthelfrith crouched low and thrust his large head in front of Edwin's. 'Soon it will be your turn to stand with the spears against enemies who will most likely be strangers to you, just as I am. You can't be timid before them. You cannot expect others to follow you if you are faint-hearted like this.'

He stood and turned to look at Acha. 'Was my brother, Theobald, to your liking?'

It was Acha's turn to freeze, uncertain of how to reply, especially as Lillan had now fixed his eyes on her.

'He was kind enough to give me a small gift, lord.' It was all she could think to say. Æthelfrith threw back his head and chuckled loudly.

'My brother's very clever. He'll make you a good husband, you'll see.'

Acha felt her cheeks burn.

'Now I must take my leave of you. If I don't reach your father before the Gododdin do, Edwin here may find himself king before his time, faint-hearted or not.'

Acha bowed her head and nearly tripped over Edwin as she tried to reverse away from Æthelfrith's towering presence.

*

That evening, Acha did not take much pleasure from her position on the top table in the absence of her father and his fighting men. The mood was unusually sombre as those gathered in the feast hall digested the news that warbands were converging on their forces from the north as well as from the south. Edwin sat at her side slurping the barley broth. He pushed his bowl away and spoke to her for the first time since their encounter with the Bernician king.

'What does faint-hearted mean?' he asked.

Acha thought for a moment, searching for comforting words but Edwin continued.

'It means I'm afraid, doesn't it? He said I was too afraid to stand with the spears.'

'No, he didn't mean—' Acha began.

'Well I'll show him. I will stand with the spears and I will kill him,' he said.

Ten

Æthelfrith widened his stance to steady himself in the prow of the longboat as twenty oarsmen powered it through the water. Night was falling and he was in a hurry. Satisfied that the other boats had left the wharf in close formation behind his, Æthelfrith turned his attention upwards. He needed a clear sky if the half-light of dusk was not to fade into complete darkness. A full moon was rising over his shoulder as the sun set, and he prayed that it would light his way through the shadowy waters ahead. He made a silent promise to Tiw, the one-handed war-god, that he would kill a wolf in revenge for the beast that had taken the god's hand, so long as he blew away the clouds that were gathering on the horizon. But Tiw did not listen and as the four vessels pulled away from the glow of Eoferwic's fires, the cloudbank gradually snuffed out the moon's light and Æthelfrith led his warriors, unsighted, into the blackness of the river.

Lillan, the young Deiran thegn, had assured him that there was sufficient draught to take his boats up-river to where the army of Elmet had last been sighted. The flat-keeled craft were made for the tidal mudflats around his castle so they could navigate shallow rivers like the Ouse and the Ure. But unlike the sea, these inland waterways did not provide straight lines of travel. They meandered along the valley floor in never-ending twists and turns, and his boats could easily run aground on the sharp bends if they were over hasty, which made night travel particularly perilous. Yet he knew that it should still be quicker and less tiring than marching over the hilly countryside, and he could not afford to stop even for one night. Not if he was to catch up with the British and Angle armies that were circling each other for a final confrontation somewhere out there in the gloom.

'Hard on the starboard oars,' he heard the bow lookout yell as the steersman threw his weight on the tiller to send their boat lurching around a horseshoe bend. His captains had no experience of this river and Æthelfrith looked anxiously behind to make sure the following boats had seen the course. He missed Theobald most of all at times like this: his sharp eyes and mind were ideal to guide them in such manoeuvrings. Lillan had agreed to come with him as he knew the terrain, but even he was not much use in the pitch-black.

'Back down the oars, hard!' the bow lookout yelled and their boat slewed awkwardly across the river that had taken an unexpected turn.

Æthelfrith turned to see the following boat loom out of the darkness towards them.

'Look out behind!' His warning was too late: the snarling animal head on an upturned prow crashed into their side, smashing blades and wooden planking. An oarsman screamed as his legs were pinned beneath the heavy oak bow that was now wedged into the side of their boat. The moon finally appeared between the clouds to show a gaping tear in the planking where water was pouring through. Æthelfrith had no choice.

'Beach our boat, steersman,' he shouted above the confusion. 'We will abandon it and cram as many into the other boats as we can. The remainder will have to march.'

He was more concerned by the delay than by the loss of one boat. Maybe it would be quicker on foot. No, he would stick to his decision and continue by river. The British seemed to love their horses but he always preferred to travel by boat. Boats didn't need hay and some men could rest whilst the others rowed. His mind went back to the moment when he had discovered the riding gear in the barn at Din Eidyn. He had puzzled ever since why the British would want to mount an entire army. He had been told that the men of Elmet were skilled at fighting on horseback. Apparently, they had learned it from their forefathers who had been taught by the soldiers who manned the Wall. But the Gododdin did not fight on horseback. Some used mounts to arrive at the battlefield but once there, they dismounted for combat. No, the reason they were on horse was to spring their cunning trap – the trap that Theobald had foretold if only he had listened. The Kings of the Old North had offered him peace in return for a rapid, unchallenged passage past his territory and into Deira. Ælle would be crushed between the army of Elmet from the south and the Gododdin and their allies arriving suddenly on horse from the north. That is, if he didn't manage to find them first.

The three remaining boats were soon gliding quickly along a straighter stretch of the waterway, his men straining at the oars to make up for lost time. He just hoped that the absence of the twenty men he had put ashore to make their way on foot would not prove vital.

'Back oars! Stop ahead! Stop!' the bowman cried pointing ahead to a silhouette of low arches where a bridge crossed the river.

As they bobbed to a halt, Æthelfrith's immediate instinct was to order his men to pull the wooden structure down so that they could pass, but Lillan came forward and pointed out the jagged rocks spreading through the water beyond.

'We've reached the end,' he called over the shouting of the steersmen and the grunting of rowers as they strained to control the boats that had congregated in the shallow basin. 'The river is not navigable beyond this point. Not for these craft.'

'Where are we?' demanded Æthelfrith, looking anxiously around at the shadowy shapes of bushes and trees that lined the river.

'Some call it Hripis after the people that settled here. The Elmet army were last seen nearby. We can look for them at first light.'

'No,' said Æthelfrith. 'We can better find them now, by their light. They are bound to have fires. We will camp here but you and I will go in search of King Ceredig and his men.'

*

Æthelfrith was proved right. It was relatively easy to find Ceredig's encampment once he, Lillan and the two other warriors that accompanied them had climbed clear of the woodland that surrounded the river. Tiw had woken and blew drowsily at the cloud cover so that the moon suddenly appeared to spread its light over the land and vanished as quickly again. Lillan managed to find a narrow track through thick undergrowth that snagged at their jerkins as they stumbled up from the valley floor. As the woods gave way to more open scrubland, Lillan stopped at the top of a ridge and pointed ahead to a circular earthen-work that lay in their path.

'An ancient hillfort of the Brigantes who lived here before the giants came,' he explained.

'Does it always glow at night?' asked Æthelfrith. 'Or are there fires within those mounds?'

They were both staring so hard at the grassy enclosure that they were almost taken by surprise when two riders emerged from a dip in the land. Fortunately, they seemed so engrossed in conversation that they did not notice even the tall figure of Æthelfrith as he flattened himself on the ground to slide into the shadows of the bushy hillside with his companions.

'A patrol speaking the Brittonic tongue. I think we have found our foe,' Lillan whispered.

'I need to get closer but that will be difficult.' Æthelfrith indicated the bright moonlight that now lit up the field between where they lay and the banks of the hillfort. 'Unless we borrow their horses.'

He signalled to his two warriors to follow him and they crept as close as they could to the mounted guards. Just as the clouds plunged the hillside into darkness again, Æthelfrith stood and groaned loudly, stumbling from the bushes, clutching his stomach and making retching noises. One of the guards backed away as his horse shied at the commotion, but the other laughed and thrust his spear towards the bent figure before him.

'Can't hold your ale, soldier? You should be in camp,' the guard said, kicking his mount forward.

Æthelfrith waited until he could grab the shaft of his spear with one hand and the halter of the horse in the other. He yanked the rider from his mount with such speed that the man could only mutter a choked warning as Æthelfrith's giant hand covered his mouth. The second rider had little time to react as the two warriors jumped up from the shadows to drag him from his horse.

'Cut their windpipes so there's no noise,' Æthelfrith ordered. 'And keep the horses calm.'

Soon after, he and Lillan rode casually around one side of the circular enclosure, keeping a watchful eye on other guards who were patrolling the hillfort in the distance. Gradually they made their way to a gap that served as the entryway between the mounds so that they could see into the encampment. Æthelfrith caught his breath at the numbers of animal-hide tents crammed into the circular space. When he saw not just one but two bright banners waving in the centre of the camp, he immediately understood why the warband was so numerous. He was expecting to see only the image of an owl, the crest of King Ceredig of Elmet on the flags, but a fiery red dragon, the symbol of the warriors of Gwynedd, the mountainous kingdom to the southwest, also fluttered in the breeze. The addition of those fierce fighters meant he could not attack such a stronghold without reinforcements.

'How far away is King Ælle, would you say?' he asked Lillan.

'He cannot be far. Probably less than a day's march to the north. We are close to Deere Stræt, which was the road he took from Eoferwic,' he replied.

'Deere Stræt is the road the Gododdin are coming down. We must deal with this warband quickly before the two armies can join together.'

'What do you propose, lord?' asked Lillan.

Æthelfrith fingered his moustache, wondering where his brother was. No matter. There was only one course of action.

'Take these horses and one of my men and ride until you find your king. Tell him to bring his army quickly towards us here. I will position myself to the south of Ceredig and will strike from that direction once Ælle has attacked from the north. Urge him to move the moment you arrive so that we can finish with Elmet and Gwynedd before the Gododdin and their friends arrive. Understood?'

'Yes, my lord.'

He looked hard at the thegn-son, trying to assess his temperament. He would have to do. 'Do not fail in this.'

'I will not my lord.'

'One other thing. Find out what happened to my brother.'

'He should be with King Ælle by now,' Lillan said.

'In which case bring him too.'

*

Æthelfrith was woken where he lay on the boards of his boat by a sharp tap on the shoulder. He sat up quickly, blinking in the daylight, his hand automatically gripping his sword. The warrior who bent over him had served his father and had the scars on his face to show for it.

'Sorry, lord, but you said to wake you if anything changes.'

'And?' Æthelfrith growled.

'Something has changed.'

'Well, what is it?' Æthelfrith scrambled to his feet, nearly knocking the warrior over in his impatience.

'Our scouts report tents are coming down and they've begun to move out.'

'Well don't just stand there,' snapped Æthelfrith. 'Line up the men. We need to follow them.'

They trailed the British warriors as if they were stalking deer. Their prey marched northwards, two or three abreast in a long column along Deere Stræt, the road made by the giants. The route offered little cover for Æthelfrith and his men, who had to conceal themselves in the contours of the hills and the woody thickets away from the ancient trail. To make his warband less conspicuous, Æthelfrith had divided it into smaller groups that followed each other at a distance, advancing only when the scouts signalled that it was safe to do so. As he scrambled up a rocky incline, Æthelfrith tried once again to estimate the odds. If only he knew when the Gododdin cavalry would arrive. He realised that Ceredig would not have left the safety of his fortified enclosure unless he knew that his meeting with his allies was imminent. He just had to hope that King Ælle would arrive in time for them to deal with the army he now trailed, before they had to turn their attention to the mounted force from the north. The sun was already sinking towards the horizon, so he knew the chances were growing slimmer. When he saw his scout raise his hand to stop their advance, he prayed to Tiw that it was because he had seen the Deiran army. Quickly joining him on the ridge, he had to shelter his eyes from the low sun before he realised that the enemy had left their route along Deere Stræt and were making for the same rocky knoll on which he now stood.

'Have they seen us?' he asked the scout.

'I think not, lord. They are heading for the stream further ahead. I think they intend to rest and water their horses. They've had a warm journey with little shade.'

Æthelfrith held his hand up between the sun and the horizon, estimating the remaining hours of daylight. 'Mmm. Probably camping for the night.'

'I would say so, lord.'

'In the name of Thunor, where are the Deirans? We can't afford to waste another night before we attack. Can we surprise them?'

The scout looked thoughtfully at the progress of the enemy line. 'They seem to have planted their banners by that stream,' he said pointing to the base of the hill. 'If they camp there, we can come down on them through the trees.'

'Yes, but first let's see what's happened to our ally. Make your way north along this ridge and find King Ælle and his men. They must be close.'

As the scout went quietly forward, Æthelfrith watched the opposing army pitch camp, wondering what his brother would advise in this situation. He would tell him to be patient because he could not afford to lose men in an attack where he was outnumbered. He would say that the advantage of surprise would not outweigh the odds of two men against every one of his. But then he wasn't Theobald. He could not wait any longer. His men were worth three of every one of the British warriors.

*

The light on the wooded hillside was fading fast by the time he had gathered his forces for the assault. The disposition of the enemy camp had made up his mind for him. They had split their forces conveniently into two camps, one on each side of the stream. The owl of Elmet flew from the far bank whilst the dragon of Gwynedd fluttered on his side of the stream. He would have equal numbers against the dragon until the owls could cross the stream, time enough for him to wreak havoc amongst the men of Gwynedd, who must be tired from the long march from their home. He had hoped his scout would return with news of the Deirans but, as the sun set, his patience snapped. He would do it on his own. As lines of his warriors began to inch down the hill, he heard a hoot, the lookout's warning signal. It was followed by scuffling noises and a muffled shout.

'Wait. We've news.'

His scout escorted Lillan into the clearing, looking tired and bedraggled.

'Where have you been and where is your king?' Æthelfrith asked in an angry whisper.

It took Lillan a moment to recover his breath before he could reply. 'It was hard to find you. King Ælle is ready to attack at sunrise.'

'Why not tonight if he is near?'

'He said tomorrow at sunrise. The night is short so it will make only a small difference,' Lillan said.

Æthelfrith glanced anxiously towards the enemy camp, where the dying rays of the sun illuminated their banners. 'But a small difference could be all-important. What news of the Gododdin?'

'There was no sign of them when we left the encampment this morning. Lord Theobald remained behind to hold them up should they arrive before we have finished here.'

Æthelfrith was relieved to have news of his brother, although he was surprised that Theobald's small force had been left to face the Gododdin alone, if only for a short time.

Lillan must have seen the concern in Æthelfrith's face. 'There are stone defences there.'

'Let's hope he doesn't need them. We had best rest for the night.'

*

Æthelfrith squatted to relieve himself in the undergrowth before the darkness of night became the greyness of dawn. He liked to attend to his bowels before battle as they could empty themselves unexpectedly if he did not. He knew what he had to do that day, but as always before a fight, he suddenly doubted he could do it. They not only had to win but they had to do it quickly and consolidate their forces before the next opponent arrived. All depended on timing. Should he attack before Ælle arrived and catch the enemy off-guard in their camp? Or should he wait until they had formed up against the Deirans, when he could surprise them from the rear? Once again he heard his brother's voice urging him to be patient and wait for Ælle.

He agreed with the advice, but still he did not follow it. It was he who was caught by surprise.

His warriors were lined up at dawn, twenty men across and five deep, the metal of their spears and battle-axes hidden behind their jerkins so as not to give away their position by reflecting light towards the enemy below. They did not speak but yawned and fidgeted with their equipment, straightening their arm rings and touching the charms around their necks. Æthelfrith took up position slightly ahead of his men with a handful of his most trusted thegns on either side. His stomach churned with anxiety as he cursed the King of Deira for his lateness. Men were already stirring by the stream below, making ready to break camp and continue their journey.

He heard a rustle in the undergrowth and thought he saw a movement in the trees below. A young deer wandered into view. The creature must have picked up their scent at that moment for it paused, seemingly aware of possible danger. Its eyes widened as it sensed their presence and it quickly broke cover in the trees and raced down to the open field and the stream. The enemy camp below shouted with surprise, then hooted with glee when they saw the animal splash through the water. Men jumped on horses to head it off and others ran after it, yelling and whooping, many without weapons or clothes. They had little chance of catching the deer, but it was a moment of fun to break the monotony of marching to war. As he watched their ill-disciplined cavorting, Æthelfrith recognised his opportunity and waved his men forward.

They came out of the woods as quietly as warriors running hard in full battle gear can possibly be. The men of Gwynedd had given up chasing the deer and were light-heartedly playing catch amongst themselves. A guard finally saw the danger and shouted in alarm. It was the signal for Æthelfrith to begin his throaty battle roar that was taken up by his men as they poured down on the ill-prepared foe. His long legs took him a pace ahead of his warriors but he did not care anymore. The red mist had risen through his body and he was driven on by instinctive forces to do what he did best. He became a ferocious killer. His men said that the spirit of Tiw was in him when he fought and he took on the god's form, except that he had two hands and the war-god had only one. Once he was in the thick of battle, Æthelfrith sensed that the action around him slowed down so that he could see precisely what to do. His warriors were trained to form a shield wall that protected them as they fought as one unit. He preferred to fight out front, hurling his enormous frame against whoever stood in his way, smashing down their defences, slashing at their bodies and moving forward with such speed that he caught his opponents off their guard.

He was soon embroiled in a knot of warriors thrusting spears and swinging long swords at him as the Britons tried to regroup. Somehow he danced his way through them and turned to slash one to the ground. Two horsemen, returning from the deer chase, sensed a moment of glory and rode hard at the giant king. As the first horse pounded towards him, Æthelfrith swayed to one side, stopping the rider's spear with his shield and slicing at the steed's flanks with his sword as it passed. The horse stumbled, throwing its rider, and Æthelfrith was on to the man in a flash, thrusting his sword into his belly as he rolled clear of his mount.

A spear whistled past his head, thrown by one of Æthelfrith's personal guards, who were desperately struggling to catch up with him. It spiked the second rider in the leg, but the horseman ignored his wound and still bore down on the king, swinging his war axe towards Æthelfrith's exposed back. Ripping his sword out of the guts of the first rider, Æthelfrith swung it upwards to deflect the descending axe and sideways to catch the rider's waist. He did not wait to see him sway from his saddle, but leapt into a group that had formed a small shield wall ahead of him. As two of his men joined him he crashed his shield into their flank, pushing a defender around until his side was exposed so that he could chop into his neck. The man slithered and slipped on his own blood as Æthelfrith pushed him aside to get at the next warrior in the wall.

The Bernician thegns had formed a long line that advanced steadily, pushing the enemy back towards the stream. On reaching the bank, the Gwynedd fighters splashed into the water to join forces with the men of Elmet on the other side, where King Ceredig had roused his troops to form a shield wall. As the last of the Gwynedd forces fled across the stream, Æthelfrith remembered the wise words that had come to him earlier: the element of surprise does not last for long. The army that now confronted them still outnumbered their own and they would have to cross the slippery rocks of a stream to reach them.

He soon became aware of another problem: Ceredig had called forward archers, who were bending bows in their direction.

'Shields!' Æthelfrith yelled as a dozen arrows hissed towards them from close range. He felt the jolt as one struck his shield and he saw the barb appear menacingly through the cracked wood. His own archers were with Theobald, so he knew that he would either have to withdraw out of range or go forward across the stream. When Tiw was in him, he knew only one way.

'Forward,' he shouted and plunged into the stream, followed by his men. The fast flowing water came up to their knees, so they had to push hard to move at speed over the slimy stones. The enemy realised their weakness and leapt forward to jab at them from the bank with long spears. A thegn cried in pain as a lance was thrust through his leather jerkin and Æthelfrith saw the water turn red. It only served to spur him on and he snatched angrily at a spear, pulling its owner towards him so that he could smash him aside with his shield as he clambered up the bank. Making dry land, he expected to be surrounded by enemy fighters, but they were melting away. He checked his urge to chase after them, waiting until his warriors had scrambled up out of the water behind him, wondering why their crossing was now unchallenged.

'Look lord,' one of his thegns said, pointing into the bright sun ahead of them. 'The army of Deira is arriving.'

Shielding the morning light from his eyes with his hand, he recognised the banner of the boar's head. King Ælle's force was moving rapidly towards them in the shape of several wedges as the men of Elmet and Gwynedd desperately tried to reach the protection of higher ground.

*

The last phase of a battle was always the messiest and took longest. Æthelfrith normally gloried in the hacking down of defeated men. It was as well to thoroughly eliminate a generation of rival warriors so that their kin could not seek revenge. Yet this was a victory he wanted to complete as fast as possible and he soon became irritated at Ælle's diligence in seeking out every last one of the defeated army. Ceredig and his close companions had escaped on horse, but the Deiran king wanted the rest of his army accounted for. Some fled into the woods but most fought on in desperate groups until they dropped from their wounds.

Æthelfrith drew aside to rest with some of his thegns. Nearby, Ælle was assessing a prisoner who held tenaciously onto the silver cross around his neck. Evidently his wounds were too severe to render him valuable as a slave or for ransom because the Deiran king drew fingers across his throat to indicate his fate. As a warrior raised his sword to strike at the man's neck, Æthelfrith could wait no longer.

'I think our business here is done,' he called, striding towards his fellow king. 'We should regroup our forces for the next assault.'

As he approached Ælle, he could not help but notice how his appearance had changed. Æthelfrith had been just a lad, too young to stand with the spears, when his father had first taken him to the Deiran court. The powerful, upright leader he had admired that day had turned into the stooped, grey-bearded figure before him who no longer filled the boar-skin jacket on his shoulders.

Ælle eyed him with surprise. 'Æthelfrith, it is good that you came. But you attacked too early and now you would leave too soon. Savour our success. There is time enough to win a second battle and our men need to rest.'

Æthelfrith felt like grabbing the old king by the throat and dragging him from the field.

'This is too open a place to be caught by an army on horse and the Gododdin will be here any moment.'

'So I have heard. But I left your brother, Theobald, to warn us of their approach.'

'Where exactly is he?'

'A short march to the north, in the ruins of a stone fortress. Easy enough to defend from cavalry. Why don't you join him there if you are anxious? It's a good place to trap the Gododdin. They call it Catræth.'

Eleven

As he marched his warband rapidly along Deere Stræt, Æthelfrith wondered at the industry of the giants who had laid down the hard foundation beneath his feet. It was less comfortable than travelling on grassy tracks, but faster, and he desperately wanted to find his brother and reunite his armies before nightfall. He had lost several men in the battle by the stream, but thankfully those he had set ashore from the damaged boat had managed to find them to reinforce their numbers. He would need to be at full strength to deal with the Gododdin, especially as King Ælle seemed agonisingly slow to join any fray. Maybe he had become over cautious with age, or his mind was addled.

'Scouts returning, lord,' his lead thegn shouted.

Æthelfrith peered ahead, curious to see three men returning when he had sent only two to scout. When he recognised one of his brother's thegns splattered with mud and blood, he knew why.

'You have news from Theobald?'

'Yes lord.' The man tried to straighten up but staggered and held onto the shoulder of his companion for support. 'He says to bring all your forces to his position at Catræth as soon as you are able. He says he cannot hold the Gododdin there much longer, nor can he withdraw.'

'When did they arrive?'

'This morning. They made as if to ignore us and ride on past our defences, but Lord Theobald made a sortie that persuaded them otherwise. Now he is surrounded most likely. He sent us out before they closed the ring around him.'

'Us? There were more of you?'

'Three, lord. One to get killed, one to get captured and one to make it through. That's how he joked about it before he asked for volunteers and that's how it's turned out. Except no one was captured.'

Æthelfrith waved his arm for the column to advance more urgently. His young brother had deliberately provoked a mounted warband three hundred strong to attack his own force of sixty foot soldiers. There was only one reason why a cautious leader like Theobald would do that: in order to delay his opponents and keep their armies divided. Whether or not Theobald lived to tell the tale, it was a glorious sacrifice that the bards would praise in feast halls around the land. He quickly despatched a messenger to Ælle, to plead with him to make haste, and urged his men to move even faster to relieve the trapped cohort.

*

They saw the horses before they saw the army. They were in a field, tethered on long ropes, drinking water brought up in buckets by youths from the nearby stream. Æthelfrith did not want to go too close and alert the enemy to their presence, but he could not mistake the wearer of the brightly coloured, flapping cloak who stood in the midst of a group of monks squatting by the river. It was Aneirin.

Still writing poetic lies about his masters, no doubt. Soon, he will be praising how they died.

At that moment, a sound like a crash of thunder hit his ears. He instantly recognised the clatter of metal on wood and the maddened shouts of warriors as they struggled in close combat. It was the beginning of a battle his brother could not win without him. He yelled at his men to follow as he raced towards the noise. When he made the top of the rise, he could make out the ruins of a stone fort and wiped the sweat from his eyes to assess the situation in the fading light. He could see men grappling in the gaps between crumbling walls, not in one line of battle but in several desperate fights as the defenders used what remained of the ruins to break up the attackers' advance. The shields of one group of defenders collapsed under the weight of the attackers, who roared as they streamed forward through the gap. Æthelfrith plunged after them, waving at his thegns to follow him into the fort.

Time slowed for him as it always did in battle and he closed on a Gododdin warrior ahead, just managing to carve his sword into the man's neck before he could thrust his spear into a retreating defender. He saw surprise and terror in equal measure on the faces of the Britons who turned to see his long sword slashing at their exposed backs. His thegns were with him now, hacking their way through the enemy to protect Theobald's men. Outside the walled enclosure, the rest of his army had fallen on the rear of the British attackers, who now found themselves wedged between two lines of Bernician warriors.

'Re-form! Inside the walls, now!'

Æthelfrith heard the command from a familiar voice and swivelled to see Theobald, pointing and waving through one of the gaps in the wall. Æthelfrith's smile of pleasure at finding his brother still alive was short lived as he saw the shadowy forms of horsemen charging towards the backs of his warriors who were still outside the walls. He leapt into one of the gaps to try and break the deadlock before the cavalry could cut his men down from behind. The fighting was so confused now, with layer upon layer of attackers and defenders, that he almost found himself slicing at one of his own soldiers. The Gododdin horsemen arrived before all of his warriors could break through into the fort, leaving them exposed to thrusting spears from behind. He screamed in anger as he saw his men lanced and trampled, unable to reach them through the swaying mass of foot soldiers in close combat. His warband had wreaked great havoc by falling on the enemy rear and now it was their turn to suffer, except their attackers sat out of reach on horses' backs, stabbing with long lances and chopping down with axes.

'To me! To me! Inside this way.' Theobald's voice thundered again, this time from the one gap in the wall that had been breached and was temporarily empty of fighting men. Æthelfrith scrambled over heaped bodies of the dead and dying to join him outside of the wall just as the Gododdin cavalry turned their attention that way. Theobald planted a spear in the earth and twisted to avoid the charging horse that crashed to the ground as it took the blade in its ribcage. Æthelfrith arrived in time to run his sword into the belly of the fallen rider before fending off the spear of a second horseman and slashing open his leg as he rode past, screaming in agony. The Bernician forces outside the wall were now cutting their way through to where their leaders stood and streamed through the gap into the protection of the fort.

The deep sound of a horn brought the battle gradually to a halt as the Gododdin cavalry escorted their foot soldiers to safety away from the walls. Æthelfrith clasped Theobald's arm and patted his back, breathing heavily, unable to speak.

'Good to see you, brother,' said Theobald. 'Even if you were a little late.'

Æthelfrith grunted at the rebuke. 'I was trying to persuade our ally to leave the last battlefield.'

'Yes, where is King Ælle?' Theobald looked around at their surviving forces inside the fort. 'We won't last here much longer without him.'

'He's become very measured in his old age. He will not hurry, even to battle.'

'I think it's his cunning, not his age,' Theobald said, taking his brother's arm and pointing at the bloodied bodies that covered the ground around them. 'There's a sight to please any Deiran king. The dead of his two most feared enemies and not one of his own warriors amongst them.'

Æthelfrith felt his mouth go dry. 'You think he won't come?'

'Oh, he will come alright. He will want the Gododdin defeated so they cannot challenge him. But he wants us mightily weakened as well. So he will sit and watch as we fight ourselves to a standstill and then he will march in to claim victory. He'll come but we may not live to see it.'

They dragged corpses to plug the gaps in the walls. The badly wounded were sent on their journey to the next world with a quick cut of the knife, and those worth saving were comforted with incantations and herbal poultices. Having organised the guards and honed the blades of his weapons, Æthelfrith slumped down to rest next to Theobald.

'They'll sing of this battle in the mead halls for generations, brother,' he said, wriggling his body to make the hard earth more comfortable.

'I hope we live to hear it.'

'Don't worry, we will. Woden has sent his birds to watch over us. I saw them as we marched here, two kestrels hovering over the moors. He never lost a battle and nor have we. And I don't intend starting now. Not now that... ' He paused wondering if he should talk about such things to his younger brother. He never had before.

'Now that what?' asked Theobald, propping his head on his arm to look at him.

Æthelfrith saw the first stars appear through the dark mist overhead. 'Now that I have something to live for, other than feasting and fighting.'

'You mean your woman?'

'Yes, Bebba. Did I mention that we married before I left?'

'No you didn't.'

'Yes, we took an oath before Frigg, although Bebba insists our goddess of love is not as powerful as her Christ god who rules over all men's affairs. I can't imagine how one god can be responsible for both love and war, but she insists we will have another ceremony with her priests when I return. She may be with child and we wanted to make sure he would not be born a bastard if... well, if anything should happen to me. For the first time that I can remember, I am looking forward to going home.'

'Home? I'm not sure where that is,' said Theobald, pulling his cloak up to his chin. 'We spend little enough time in one place, always on the move, seeing to our defences, collecting our dues.'

'You're right, we wear ourselves down for the sake of our kin. I sometimes wonder if I shouldn't have been born a farmer. They seem happy enough, living in comfortable huts with their families, protected by us. They just have to look after cattle and cut corn, not face charging cavalry.'

Theobald laughed. 'Until their nasty king arrives to take half their crops as his render and kick their backsides for being lazy. No, give me the mead hall over a farmstead any day. Your woman has made you soft, brother.'

Æthelfrith sat up and gave Theobald a friendly punch. 'We'll see how soft I am tomorrow when the Gododdin arrive. Anyway, I heard that Frigg was whispering in your ear when you met Ælle's daughter and you gave her a gift. Was she to your liking?'

Theobald paused, as if choosing his words carefully. 'We met very briefly, as I had to hurry after her father, who had already left to cut off the Elmet warband. Even so, I could see that she would make a very acceptable companion.'

Æthelfrith rocked back to the ground, chuckling. 'What an enchanter you are! A very acceptable companion, is she? I shall tell her that's how you described her.'

Theobald picked up some earth and threw it into his brother's face.

*

Æthelfrith did not sleep for long before he was woken by the sound of a guard's challenge and steps coming in his direction. He recognised Lillan's voice before he could make out his face in the darkness.

'Says he has a message from the King of Deira, lord,' the guard said, gruffly.

Æthelfrith shook Theobald awake and stood to greet the thegn-son.

'An urgent one, my lord,' said Lillan, looking apologetic as the Bernician king stretched his tall frame before him.

'I hope your king is close by and ready for the fray tomorrow,' said Æthelfrith.

'Indeed, he is most anxious to coordinate our advances on the enemy,' said Lillan.

'Advances? If I am not mistaken we are trapped here and cannot advance without tripping over the enemy.'

'King Ælle suggests you surprise them by attacking their camp from the north whilst he approaches from the south to encircle them. Fewer will escape if we come at them from both sides.'

Theobald stumbled to his feet, smoothing his unkempt hair. 'Where exactly do you think the Gododdin are?' he asked.

'By the stream. I saw their fires as I came.'

'Exactly. We would have to leave the protection of these barricades if we attack first,' Theobald said.

'He knows of your reputation,' Lillan said, glancing at Æthelfrith. 'You are famed for your ferocious sorties.'

Theobald snorted scornfully. 'Your king would flatter us into a dangerous mission when he knows very well he could attack first before we leave the safety of our fort to fall upon their rear.'

Lillan shook his head. 'King Ælle insists we must encourage the British leaders to keep to their false belief that it is their allies who lie to the south, not their enemies. That way, they will turn at your attack, not knowing that they expose their backs to us. If we attack before you, they know of your position and so will retreat by a different route. My king argues that his forces should remain hidden until the last moment.'

'Whilst we bear the brunt of the fighting,' said Theobald.

Æthelfrith pointed to the corpses piled between the walls. 'Tell your king we have suffered heavy losses. We are still outnumbered and cannot engage their forces for long. If he delays again in joining the battle, I fear the Gododdin may overrun us and make their escape to the north. He must attack at dawn this time.'

'Ah, he asked me to clarify that point,' Lillan replied. 'Last time, you attacked at dawn but he had agreed to strike at sunrise.'

Æthelfrith and Theobald looked at each other, eyebrows raised. 'And what does he propose this time?' asked Theobald.

'King Ælle proposes that, as sunrise is the more precise moment to determine, we should use that as our signal. The sun will rise over the flatlands to the east and so will not be long after the first light of dawn.'

'Providing there is no cloud to obscure the sky. You will hear our attack. Come then,' said Theobald.

Æthelfrith put a hand on Lillan's shoulder. 'You have argued well, young man, but my brother is right. Tell your king to be ready at dawn and move as soon as he hears us engage the enemy.'

*

Æthelfrith embraced his brother by the shadowy walls of the fort and watched as he led a small band of warriors armed with bows and spears stealthily towards the stream where the Gododdin had tethered their horses. Theobald had reasoned that cavalry would give the enemy an advantage in open territory and that they should therefore try to deprive them of their horses by stampeding them. It would also provide a diversion to their attack as the sun rose. As Theobald and his men disappeared, Æthelfrith anxiously climbed on some fallen rocks of the wall to improve his view. Glimpsing his brother crouching by bushes, he signalled to his men to file out of the fort and line up ready to advance.

Moonlight swept across the field where the horses had been kept, and his heart skipped a beat. All had gone. At first he thought they must have been moved to find better grass, but as his eyes searched the nearby pastures, he saw shadowy figures vanishing in the distance. The Gododdin army was awake and on the move.

'They've broken camp. Let's get after them,' Æthelfrith shouted, scrambling from the wall to position himself at the head of his warriors as they stretched tired limbs and picked up their shields and weapons. He had lost sight of Theobald and his band but he had no time to find them. His priority was to keep the enemy in view in case they disappeared into the moors and escaped.

They caught up with the Gododdin by the river. Æthelfrith later discovered it was named the Swæle and ran into the Ouse. He also learned that Ælle had ordered his warriors to ford its fast running waters just as the British warband appeared. It must have been the first time that the Gododdin realised that they had enemy forces ahead of them as well as behind, and he could imagine the consternation it must have caused in their ranks. But Owain, their leader, had reacted quickly by ordering his forces to attack the Deirans in the river, realising that this was his best chance of breaking though their lines. Just as Æthelfrith's force had been exposed to the men of Elmet as they waded a stream, so the army of Deira was vulnerable to the Gododdin as it crossed the river. The difference was that the Deirans hesitated mid-crossing and the river was wider and deeper than the stream.

When Æthelfrith crested the incline above the valley floor, he heard the shouts as the two forces clashed below him. The Gododdin were picking off Ælle's men as they clambered out of the water and causing havoc with spears and arrows amongst those who floundered behind.

Adding their own throaty cries to the screams of the men who were being cut down in the river, the Bernician warband raced towards the conflict. As he ran, Æthelfrith assessed his tactics. This was not the moment to call for a deliberate, slow-moving shield wall. Their advantage lay in a swift, surprise assault on the rear of the Gododdin, who were using the advantage of the riverbank to slaughter the Deirans in the treacherous waters.

'Spread wide! Into the river with them,' he yelled, sprinting ahead of his men to throw himself on the Gododdin warriors clustered around the banner of a stag. As they turned in alarm, he instantly recognised the distinctive scarred face of the King of Rheged.

'Owain, you treacherous turd, did you wager on me coming this time?' he mocked, quickly hurling his spear at his exposed side. A tall warrior next to Owain moved sharply sideways to protect his king and took the spear in the shoulder. Æthelfrith drew his sword, smashing his shield into the wounded warrior, knocking him to the ground.

Owain growled at Æthelfrith as he parried his sword thrust. 'No but I bet that bitch Bebba is opening her thighs for someone right now. Just as she once did for me.' His blade flashed above Æthelfrith's shield, aimed at his neck.

Æthelfrith knew that warriors taunted each other as they fought, to distract attention from their blows. He did it often enough himself. But he had never felt an insult so keenly as he did at that moment. Blinded by Owain's smirking face, he did not see the fallen warrior beneath him draw a short knife, nor did he hear the warning shout from one of his own thegns who was desperately trying to reach the skirmish. He just raised his shield so that Owain's blade glanced harmlessly away.

'Bebba the Bed-hopper, we call her.' Æthelfrith heard Owain's taunt at the very moment he felt the stab in the back of his leg. Roaring with anger and pain, he slumped backwards, unable to stand, desperately fending off Owain's swinging sword as he went down onto one knee. He'd often wondered what it was like to be wounded in battle; he had only ever caused injury, never received it. A savage blow from Owain's shield knocked him breathless onto his back, unable to stop the descent of the sword that he saw above him. The blade seemed to slow whilst his mind raced with unanswered questions. Would they sing his praises in the mead hall? What would Bebba tell her unborn child about the father he never met? The steel edge glinted enticingly in the sunlight, beckoning him to another world.

Something hit his ribcage like a rock to shatter the hypnotic moment and return the action to its frantic pace. The descending sword bit into an arm that was not his own and he felt the warm blood on his face and the weight of a screaming body on his chest. Æthelfrith heaved hard at the convulsing frame on top of him and rolled to one side. Trying to stand, he could only sprawl when his wounded leg gave way. Again he watched, powerless to move, as Owain freed his sword from Æthelfrith's loyal thegn who had thrown himself on top of his king, and drew it back to strike again.

'Pray on your knees, you slippery son of Satan, that you will be forgiven for—' Owain's words stuck in his throat as an arrow thumped high into his chest. He yelled and fell on the riverbank where he writhed and shrieked some more. Æthelfrith did not turn to see who had fired but quickly crawled forwards.

'You're the one who should be praying,' he snarled as he drew his blade firmly across Owain's throat. 'For my wife's forgiveness.'

'Shields around the king!' The familiar sound of his brother's voice made Æthelfrith breath in relief. 'Bind his leg and bring forward a horse.' Theobald was quickly organising a group of thegns to protect their fallen king. Æthelfrith noticed he was carrying his bow; he might have known that it would be his arrow that had felled Owain. Feeling the full pain in his leg for the first time, he tried not to grimace whilst an older thegn applied a mossy poultice. Once the soldier-healer had stemmed the flow of blood, he helped his king onto the back of a horse from where he could survey the battle raging before him.

Theobald had ordered a long shield wall to form and push the Gododdin down the slippery riverbank and into the fast-flowing water. Some of Ælle's forces remained there to engage them in desperate hand-to-hand fights, slithering and sliding on the shale-stones and mud of the riverbed. Without their king to instruct them, the Gododdin were frantically trying to fight their way out on either side of the soggy battleground. Their mounts were of little use to them now; their riders had dismounted as the horses shied on the banks or slipped in the water to be stabbed by the spears that bristled on either side of the river. Æthelfrith recognised some of the warriors from the festival in Din Eidyn as they tried all manner of ways to climb out of the watery trap.

One was Gorthyn, his brawny opponent in the sport of three on three. He now formed the apex of a wedge of warriors who were steadily battering their way towards a gravel shelf formed by a bend in the river. King Ælle saw the danger and ordered archers forward to rain arrows down on them, forcing them to raise their shields whilst spearmen lanced at their exposed bodies. At the same time, Theobald's group of bowmen shot at them from the other side, making the enemy twist and turn to try and avoid the missiles. When the last of his band fell, Gorthyn made a desperate attempt to climb up the sodden bank, but for once his great bulk worked against him. He grabbed at a bush to help him scramble out but it broke under his weight. As he staggered back, off balance and off guard, a spear thumped into his waist and another struck his shoulder. Gorthyn threw back his head and roared like a rutting stag, tearing the blades from his body and hurling the spears back at the taunting soldiers on the bank, before slumping to his knees and clasping his hands together. Æthelfrith watched in respect as the mighty warrior muttered prayers while the life force flowed in a red torrent from his wounds, until finally he toppled, face down into the water.

Deiran and Bernician warriors controlled both banks, jeering and yelling above the cries of pain and anguish as body after body joined those that floated and bobbed in the reddened waters. Æthelfrith looked on in a daze, unable to do anything but watch as the remaining Gododdin warriors chose to honour their oath to their leader and die on the battleground around him. Unable to overcome the handicap of the slippery riverbed and the high, muddy banks, every last one was systematically chopped down until the river was choked with the bodies of men and horses.

Twelve

Acha tugged hard at Edwin's hand, trying to drag him through the door into the great hall.

'I want to be outside with my friends. Do I have to go in there with the women?' Edwin whined.

'Yes you do. I need a remedy from the healers. And anyway, your friends, as you call them, are all working hard. The thegn-sons are too busy to look after you.'

'Forthhere said they would be training in the ruins after midday and he would show me some shield moves,' Edwin said, pulling his hand away.

'Did he? Then perhaps I should remind him that we are relying on him and his companions for our defences now that the thegns are away. He should be out on a proper patrol, not playing battles with you.'

Edwin relented and stomped into the hall behind Acha. She crouched down beside a group of older women who sat around the central hearth. A slave accidently disturbed the ash as he was blowing at the fire with bellows to rekindle the flame.

'You clumsy oaf!' one of the healers known as Hilda shouted. 'Is that how you greet the king's daughter – with a face full of embers?'

The slave scurried to brush the ash from Acha's tunic whilst Edwin chuckled, idly kicking at a burned-out log at the edge of the fire to make even more mess.

'Edwin! Behave. I need a remedy for an ache in the head and all you can do is to make it worse,' Acha said between clenched teeth.

'And I need a remedy against women's chatter and all you have done is to make it worse by bringing me here. Are there no menfolk I can talk to?'

The women all turned to stare at them in silence. 'Perhaps your ladyship and the ætheling have not heard the news?' Hilda finally said.

Acha felt her heart beat faster. It must be news from the war front. Surely she would have been told already if anything had happened to her father? Maybe it was Lillan, or even her new suitor, Theobald? She was desperate to hear the news but the women just sat passively watching her without a word.

'What news would that be?' she managed to say in a calm voice. 'There is so much at present.'

'Your Uncle Ælfric's wife has died. They could not stem the flow of blood after the birth of her son,' Hilda said.

'Shouldn't have happened,' the woman sitting next to her muttered. 'Must have used the wrong bog-moss.'

'We will offer her ashes to the gods when the Lord Ælfric brings her urn to us,' said Hilda searching Acha's eyes with a worried look. 'The ashes disturbed from the fire may be a sign for you. You have an ailment?'

'I have a slight ache in my head. It's nothing really,' Acha said, aware of the old woman's intense stare. The healer began to rock gently on her heels, gazing at Acha's head and then into the fire. Acha dare not move as the other women gathered closer around her. Edwin rolled up his eyes and wandered off to play with a hunting dog.

It seemed like an age before Hilda spoke again. 'I see elves and goblins at work on you and your family. You must protect yourself with a remedy of wormwood and deadnettle that I will prepare. For the headache, take crosswort.' Finally, she pointed towards Edwin with a toothy grin. 'And tell the ætheling that if he cannot bear women's chatter, he should eat a radish at night,' she cackled, and the other women sniggered.

Acha felt relieved by their mirth. However the news was still worrying. She was not so much bothered by the elves, but she sensed that a newly bereaved Ælfric could only spell trouble.

*

From the shade of a hastily erected tent, the two kings watched the grim work of dragging bodies out of the river. Warriors were making their fallen comrades ready for the funeral pyre and eagerly searching for anything of value amongst the enemy dead. King Ælle pointed towards the long row of lifeless soldiers and shook his head.

'What a cost I have paid to beat these British neighbours of yours,' he said to Æthelfrith, pounding a fist into his hand. 'Whilst you have a scratch on your leg and your men live to strip silver and gold from the foe, my brave warriors lay cold on the ground. Why did you not attack before they came upon me as we had arranged?'

'I told you. I went to their camp at sunrise but they had already moved out.' Æthelfrith felt the rage rising within him at Ælle's ranting, his mood not helped by the throbbing in his leg.

'Did your scouts not alert you to their movements? Why did you not send someone ahead to warn me so I was not ambushed in the river?'

Before he could reply, guards appeared at their tent, holding a prisoner, a dishevelled figure wearing a flapping gown that Æthelfrith knew all too well.

'Aneirin, I thought you avoided battles,' Æthelfrith snorted. 'But I see you've survived this one whilst those you would praise have not.'

'How I wish that I had not!' Aneirin wailed, tears running down both cheeks. 'I would gladly join them to be spared the sight of so many ashen faces.'

'That can be arranged very easily,' Ælle snapped, his hand on the hilt of his sword.

'Wait,' interrupted Æthelfrith. 'This man is famed amongst the Britons. He will tell the tale of this most famous victory and keep a generation of would-be warriors in awe of our prowess. They need to know who to fear.'

Aneirin fell to his knees and raised his hands as if in prayer. 'You are right, my lord, let me perform this one task for my fallen comrades. I have been a bystander until this moment. Now my work must begin. This slaughter will serve no purpose unless I record the deeds.'

'So long as you record who truly won the battle and who looked on from afar,' Ælle said pointedly.

Æthelfrith gripped onto the tent post in irritation at Ælle's slur. Would this old king never stop his moaning? He had to get away from him before he did something rash. Signalling for a guard to help him hobble outside to inspect the corpses, he nodded to Aneirin.

'Let us look on your dead. You can name some of them for me. You bards have a habit of inventing heroes who were not even present at the battles you sing about.'

Aneirin scurried alongside him, wringing his hands. 'Would that they could name themselves and not have me do it for them. Let us start by the banner where the king lies.' He indicated the flag painted with the image of a giant stag that still fluttered gently on the riverbank.

Owain's body lay almost naked in the centre of a ghostly pile of thegns, his face serene despite the red gore that matted his beard. He had been stripped of everything: headgear, body armour, ornaments, clothes; all except his sodden, blood-soaked leggings that clung tightly to his legs. Aneirin knelt beside him.

'Beloved friend, it should be me, not you, that lies here as food for the ravens,' he wailed.

Æthelfrith was reliving with some satisfaction the expression on Owain's face as the arrow had struck him. 'He met a warrior's death, mocking my new wife as he died.'

'He would have preferred this bloody end to a nuptial feast, that's for sure. He always favoured fighting over praying,' Aneirin said, placing gentle fingers on Owain's eyes. 'Farewell, friend. I will make sure you are not forgotten in my eulogy. I was never amongst your enemies.'

'He was unpopular?' asked Æthelfrith.

'It's hard to avoid jealousy when you lead an army of Britons.' Aneirin wiped the bloodstains from his fingers on the grass. 'Look around and you will not find a man from Dál Riata or Pictland. They would not follow Owain. If they had, it would probably be you lying here, not him. Nor this brave thegn beside him. Tydfych the Tall they called him.'

Æthelfrith recognised the face of the warrior who had taken his spear to protect Owain. 'He's the one I have to thank for my wounded leg.'

'Then you are lucky to live. He has slaughtered many of your kin far and wide.'

'There is one other of your kinsmen I would respect. The giant we fought in the festival who met a brave end in the river.'

'You mean Gorthyn the Great, a huge, happy bear of a man who could down more mead in one gulp than I could drink all night. We will all weep on his grave.'

A shout attracted Æthelfrith's attention. He was surprised to see a second prisoner being dragged towards the tent. It was the thegn-son who had been a hostage in his fortress. Aware that King Ælle was showing no mercy to survivors, he hobbled quickly to meet him.

'Cynon, how in the name of Tiw did you get here? The last time I saw you, you were sailing north,' he said.

Cynon hung his head, avoiding eye contact. 'Yes lord, Guthlaf had favourable winds and took me to Din Eidyn just in time to join the Gododdin cavalry.'

Ælle was hovering close by, listening carefully. 'Guthlaf? Does he mean Guthlaf the Frisian? Did this lad travel on the same boat as my messenger to you?' he asked.

'Same boat, but not at the same time,' Æthelfrith said.

Ælle glanced suspiciously at one then the other, like a fox coming out of its lair. 'But they must at least have overlapped in your harbour. I have been wondering why Mynyddog chose to unleash his dogs at the very moment we were vulnerable in the field. His timing seemed too good to be an accident.' He moved closer to Cynon and grasped him by the throat. 'Tell me this, boy, before your bard over there adds you to his catalogue of the dead. What message did you take to your masters in Din Eidyn?'

Cynon struggled to breath. 'Only the happy message that King Æthelfrith was to marry one of their daughters,' he gasped.

Ælle glared at Æthelfrith, letting his hand drop from Cynon's throat. 'Is that true? You married into the kin of our enemies?'

When Æthelfrith did not deny it, he waved an angry finger under his nose. 'That would explain everything. I wondered how the Gododdin cavalry could ride this far south without challenge and how they came upon my forces at the very moment we were fording a river. Now I know. You arranged it all!'

Closing his eyes and clenching his fists, Æthelfrith felt the red rage swirl inside his head. 'Nonsense, you old fool. Why did I come so swiftly to your rescue if I arranged the attack against you?'

Ælle's eyes narrowed. 'Who did you marry?'

'Bebba, daughter of Áedán of the Dál Riata.'

Ælle threw back his head and exploded with laughter. 'I should have guessed. Her father has used her before as a whore-band when his warband cannot win. She wove her spells on King Rhydderch's thegns. The slut of the Strad Clud they called her then. No wonder we were betrayed. She must have spied on you and sent word with this youth to Din Eidyn.'

Æthelfrith looked hard at Cynon, his head spinning, his throat tightening so he could hardly speak. 'Is this true? Did you take such messages?' he asked.

'No, lord. I knew nothing of your plans, so I could not betray them,' Cynon said.

Æthelfrith snarled angrily at the guards. 'Take him outside and bind him.'

He turned towards Ælle, who now stood alone with him in the tented shelter, still glowering and muttering. Æthelfrith's temper was worsened by the thought that the bitter king before him had even made him doubt his own wife.

'You heard what he said. Take back your slur on Bebba's name.'

'Her name *is* a slur. Bebba means beautiful traitor in the tongue of the Gaels. Or didn't she mention that?'

Ælle's words inflamed the rage burning inside Æthelfrith like a smithy's bellows igniting a furnace. He shut his eyes to rid himself of the taunting vision of the old king's face, but when he reopened them it was Owain who swirled before him, shouting insults and striking at him once more with his sword. Æthelfrith stumbled on his aching leg, unable to reach for a weapon to protect himself. Grasping at the tent post for support, he swung his fist hard at the mocking head. His arm jarred with pain as his hand struck bone above the ear. The colour drained from the face before him and the body crashed to the ground like a felled tree, the head rebounding when it hit the hard earth.

A guard rushed in at the commotion, followed by another, both staring at the inert figure of King Ælle, unsure of what to do. When Æthelfrith saw them approach, his mind quickly cleared.

'Call for a healer. The king has had a seizure,' he shouted.

*

News of the victory over Elmet and Gwynedd reached Eoferwic on the morning of the funeral of Ælfric's wife, adding excitement and expectation to an otherwise gloomy day. Forthhere recounted the briefest of details to Acha and Edwin as they crouched outside the main hall eating the morning bread and broth. The weather was dry and warm, so the cooking fires had been lit outside the hall for once. Ælfric's retinue of companion-thegns and servants swelled the numbers taking food that day as they had all travelled from his nearby estates to see the ashes of their lady laid to rest in the royal burial ground.

Acha watched disdainfully as Ælfric flitted everywhere, reassuring the elders and the healers, encouraging the thegn-sons and the younglings, chiding the servants and the slaves, leaving no one in doubt who was in charge that day. He bowed his closely cropped head when offered sympathy for the loss of his wife and puffed out his chest knowledgeably when the talk turned to the war campaign, as if he was leading it from afar. He paid particular attention to Acha, admiring her grey robe trimmed with white and asking after Edwin's welfare. When the procession finally moved off towards the old wall, he insisted she walk by his side with her brother. After all, there were very few members of the royal family left, he reminded her. Behind them, the wet nurse cradled the small baby who had survived the birth that killed his mother.

Acha could not believe how frugal Ælfric had been in selecting items to be buried with his wife. She knew that she had prized jewellery above all else and had an extensive collection of gold and silver brooches and bracelets. Yet all that Ælfric put in the grave for her afterlife was a string of amber beads and an ugly dress-fastener over a simple brown robe, together with a set of iron keys and a girdle-hanger to signify that she had once been head of a household.

The priest was wailing incantations and waving scented smoke from his bronzed burner over the grave when they heard the pounding of hooves on the old road from the north. All eyes flicked that way and a few risked the wrath of the gods and raised their heads, Edwin amongst them. He soon poked Acha in the ribs.

'It's Lillan,' he murmured as three horsemen pulled up by the wall, tethered their mounts and walked purposefully towards the funeral party.

Ælfric could hardly wait for the priest to finish his work and bounded across to talk to the riders whilst the earth was still being shovelled into the grave. Although Acha strained to catch their words and could hear little, their serious expressions were enough. Something was wrong. Ælfric was nodding and pointing to some of the elders as he debated with the riders. Finally, he held up his hands for attention.

'On this saddest of days, we have been struck another blow. Our forces have prevailed over the Gododdin. But our king has fallen under a spell of sleep, it seems. He breathes but does not wake.'

Acha hugged Edwin tightly in disbelief. Someone must have paid gold to the elves to put a curse on her father. And top of her list of suspects was the odious uncle who was now giving instructions to Hilda and the healers to ride to the king.

'Wait here,' she said to Edwin and ran over to Lillan, tugging at his sleeve to pull him away from the gaggle around Ælfric.

'What happened?' she asked.

Lillan hesitated but stepped aside. 'Your father mysteriously collapsed after the battle and cannot be woken,' he whispered.

'Will he live?'

Lillan shrugged. 'I saw him only briefly before we were ordered to ride for help. There was much confusion but they decided it would take too long to carry the king to the healers, so they sent for them instead.'

'I want to be with my father. Will you take me?'

'Our camp is not the safest of places. There's unrest between the two armies because Æthelfrith was alone with our king when he fell asleep.'

'You suspect him?'

'Many do. You must protect Edwin. He will be under threat if the king does not wake,' Lillan replied, his eyebrows indicating Ælfric, who was still gesticulating and giving orders.

Acha turned to look at Edwin who stood forlornly by the grave, anxiously looking in their direction. 'You're right. I should stay.'

At that moment, Hilda broke away from Ælfric's impromptu council and scurried over to Acha.

'When I fetch my potions for the king, I will leave one for you and the ætheling. Beware the elves. They will try and take you too,' she hissed.

Thirteen

Torches flickered in the gusty wind as Æthelfrith faced the Deiran thegns. He realised that the words he was about to speak would be some of the most important of his life. In the front line of his audience stood Ælle's personal band of companions, warriors toughened by years of constant campaigning, their unsmiling faces silhouetted against the skyline by the torchlight. They wanted to know exactly what had happened to their king. Æthelfrith straightened his back and stretched up his shoulders, jamming back his wounded leg so that he could stand unaided. These warriors respected only the most dominant of men and had no time for weakness. Theobald and his own thegns flanked him on either side, ready for any trouble, but they did not want a fight. The inevitable losses would be high on both sides, whoever won. The two brothers had discussed long and hard what to do, once they had sent fast riders to fetch healers for the unconscious king. Now he had to carry out the first part of their plan and it was not going to be easy from the look on the thegns' faces. The only sound was the jingling of metal from sword belts and arm rings as they watched expectantly, waiting for him to begin.

'Men of Deira and Bernicia, together we have won a victory so famous that it will be told in the mead halls by our children and our children's children for generation after generation. Your names will never be forgotten!'

A gust of wind blew sparks up from the fires and the warriors nodded, some half-heartedly raising their cups.

'Nor will the names of those who lie atop the pyres that we will shortly light. What better memorial could a man have than the renown they have gained? I for one would not wish for a more fitting end to my warrior's life than the great battle we have just won together. Yet the god's have spared us to fight another day. They have chosen us to live whilst our brave brothers lie cold awaiting the heat of the funeral fires. Why us?'

Æthelfrith paused and glanced at Theobald, who raised his eyebrows in encouragement. He knew it was the moment.

'The gods have another purpose for us, that is why. Tiw, Woden and Thunor have seen how we fight together and they know we are ready for their next, most glorious of tasks. We must now fully subjugate the British kings that have defied us. We cannot spend time in celebration, nor in recrimination, whilst they regroup their forces, as we have done in the past. Now is the moment to lay our hands firmly on the lands of our enemies. Elmet, Rheged, Gwynedd, Strad Clud, Gododdin, all must now bow before us and pay tribute.'

Again Æthelfrith paused and looked around him. He felt no pain at that moment, only elation. The heads of the battle-hardened warriors had begun to nod. They were with him – thus far.

'We can only do this together. We have fought and won a great campaign, together, which we would have lost if we had stood alone. The gods know that if we are to complete the task they have given us, we must have unity between our two kinfolk. Which is why they have put your king to sleep so that we follow only one sword. Yes, it was not the elves as some have said, but the gods who have given him rest. Whilst your king sleeps, the gods ask that you give your loyalty to me. Do that, and they know I will lead you to victories so great that you will be revered and honoured forever. Do that, and I will reward you with riches beyond your imagination.'

He bent low and scooped dusty soil into his hand, holding it high and allowing it to drift through his fingers.

'Our forefathers did not prize earth like this when they first came to this island. They wanted to take gold and silver back home across the sea. But now we know that the land here is more precious than any metal. It is so fertile that farmers can harvest much more than they need for their families. They can produce enough to pay large renders to the warriors who protect them – warriors who will not in future be sent by British leaders, for they lie rotting over there.' He pointed to the dark, decaying mounds by the river.

'No, if we act together, the warriors who next collect the dues from these lush lands will be you!'

He knew that would start a buzz of conversation amongst the thegns and it did. He crossed his arms and looked expectantly at his audience. Finally, a grizzled warrior whose beard showed flecks of grey stepped forward.

'Lord, I am Leax, son of Hrothgar, leader of King Ælle's hearth-companions. I thank you for your words. We do not doubt your renown in battle. You have the might of many men. We would gladly follow your sword and accept the rewards for doing so, especially if you would offer us land. But we have given our oath to our king, and while he still breathes we cannot give it to any other man.'

Those around him nodded and rumbled their agreement.

Æthelfrith was ready for this. 'I would never ask such brave and loyal thegns to break any oath they have freely given. I would instead ask your king to recognise me as overlord. That way you can rightly follow me to glory.'

Leax stepped forward once again. 'So you intend to wait until our king wakes?'

'No, when we return to Eoferwic, I intend to ask his council to use their authority on his behalf until such time as he wakes,' Æthelfrith said as Theobald nodded firmly alongside him. 'In the meantime, let us live in unison, honour our dead and celebrate our victory!'

He raised his tankard to the sky to a great roar and stamping of feet. He breathed a long sigh of relief. That was the first part of the plan in place. The next would be harder. He knew that a young warrior king like him would not so easily sway Ælle's elderly council.

*

Acha gingerly removed the lid from the pot that Hilda the healer had left for her. She recoiled at the sight of the greasy fat floating on the surface of the liquid balm and the pungent smell of garlic and hops that it gave off. Did she really have to rub this on her face and over her eyes? Hilda had been most insistent that both she and Edwin had to do so: her aching head and her father's long sleep were sure signs of elves at work. Glancing at her brother, who was sitting on the bed watching her, she knew she had to be brave. He would never apply it if he saw her wince.

'Why did the elves put father to sleep?' Edwin asked. He had hardly spoken since she had briefly told him what had happened to the king.

'It may not be elves. Some people sleep for a long time because they are very tired,' she said, gingerly putting a finger into the balm.

'Uncle Ælfric says that the elves are so angry with father that he may never wake again.'

'Uncle Ælfric's just guessing. We'll know more when the healers return.' Acha rubbed some of the balm gently onto her cheek, pleasantly surprised by the tingling sensation.

'Does it hurt?'

'Not at all. Try some,' she said, rinsing her hands in the washbasin.

Just as Edwin sat on Acha's knee, screwing up his eyes for the first application, there was a sharp knock and Forthhere's voice sounded through the door.

'Message for her ladyship.'

Edwin gleefully wriggled from Acha's lap and grabbed at Forthhere as soon as he came into the hut.

'Lord Ælfric asks to see my lady,' Forthhere said, ruffling Edwin's hair.

Acha's eyes widened in alarm. Why did he want to see her and why so late? The sun had set long ago. Surely he should be drinking with his thegns in memory of his wife.

'Is he in the hall?' she asked.

'No, he asks that you meet him in the king's quarters. He says it is important.'

'He's moved into my father's hut? I won't meet him there. Tell him I'm in bed.'

'He said I was to insist. He forbade me to return without you.'

Acha sighed, knowing that to disobey would bring her uncle's wrath down on the thegn-son's head and that would be unfair.

'Then you must come too, Forthhere. To bed, Edwin. I will be back shortly. We will call a guard to stand by your door.'

It was a warm evening so Acha did not take a cloak, a decision she came to regret.

When she entered the royal quarters, she was struck by a sweet smell that had not been there when her father had been in residence. Nor had the tall candles that fluttered in the breeze as they opened the door and cast shadows that danced on the walls. As her eyes adjusted to the shimmering light, they were drawn to a bench on which Ælfric lay, face down, whilst two young slave girls rubbed at his naked back and thighs.

'Sorry, Uncle. You're busy. I'll come back tomorrow,' Acha said, averting her eyes from the sight of his flabby flesh.

'No, no, stay,' he said, heaving himself up into a sitting position as the girls wrapped him in a robe. He flicked the bejewelled fingers of one hand towards Forthhere. 'But you can go. This a private, family matter.'

Acha folded her arms nervously as Forthhere left, giving her a nod of apology and encouragement. She tried not to watch as the slaves dressed Ælfric in a gaudy tunic and combed his neat beard and what was left of his hair. He did not have the air of a husband in mourning, she thought. What was he up to now?

'You must be disturbed by the news of your father,' he said, fingering the large garnet ring on his middle finger.

'And you by your sad loss,' she said.

'Quite so, but I will recover from my wife's death. If your father dies that will be another matter.'

'You think he is dying?'

'I am told he hit his head hard on the ground when he fell. I have seen others fall asleep after such a blow and they do not often wake. Those that do are seldom the same. We have to guard against such an eventuality. The ravens are already circling overhead, waiting and watching.'

Acha was suddenly attentive. 'Which ravens?'

'Ruthless men who would take away your brother's birth right.'

To Acha's mind, the person who best fitted that description was sitting right in front of her. 'And what do you suggest I do about these ravenous ravens?' she asked.

He chuckled, standing to put a hand on her shoulder and guide her towards the stool next to her father's old seat. 'Don't worry. I would hardly ask a young girl like you to consider such a problem if I had not already thought of the solution. If we stand together we can resist the ravens.'

He sat in the king's high-backed chair, just as her father had done when she had last visited him in this residence. 'We? You mean my father's thegns?'

'No, I count some of them amongst the ravens. It is you and I who must protect Edwin.'

'And what exactly do you think *we* can do? A girl and… ' she hesitated, searching for words that were not too insulting.

'An ageing uncle? Is that what you are trying to say?' Ælfric interjected.

Not exactly but it will do.

'It's true, I am no longer young enough to be a warrior,' he continued. 'So we have to use a different strategy to protect ourselves. You and I must marry.'

Acha felt like being sick all over his finely sewn shoes. Had he been eating magic mushrooms from the forest? Neither her father nor his council would ever countenance such a thing. More to the point, nor would she.

'But you're my uncle,' was all she could say.

'Ah, I thought you would mention that. Actually it is only half true. Not many know this so take care who you tell. I have the same father as my brother, Ælle, but not the same mother. Mine died giving birth to me. Luckily the priests decided her death was the punishment of the gods for my father's disrespect for his wife. So he had to atone for his behaviour by caring for me as a son. That makes me your half-uncle, which means we can marry. And for Edwin's sake we must.'

'How could such an unnatural union possibly help Edwin?' Acha's nausea was turning to anger at such a foolish idea.

'Don't you see? When your father departs this life, you will attract the attention of all those who would be king. Whoever marries you will have a legitimate case to succeed while Edwin is still too young.'

'Does that not include you, Uncle? Sorry, half-uncle. You would not suggest marrying me unless you could also gain from it, would you?' Acha stood and turned her back on him, her mind racing.

Ælfric grabbed Acha by the shoulder and spun her round, slapping her on the face.

'Take care for your tongue, young lady. You need to show me more respect.'

The blow shocked Acha more than it hurt. Until that moment she had regarded him as more of an inconvenience than a threat. As she held her hand to her stinging cheek, she saw the cunning malevolence in his eyes as he spat out his words.

'What I propose is for the good of our family, not me. I will ask the council to honour Ælle's wishes for Edwin to succeed him, but whilst he grows into the spears, I will act as king in his place. But if you marry one of his rivals for the kingship, I will not be able to protect him for long.'

She shook her head, squaring her shoulders to look her uncle firmly in the eye. His cowardly blow would not subdue her.

'Then I will marry a humble thegn-son who has no pretentions to rule.'

Ælfric wore his tunic over one shoulder so that the well-oiled skin of the naked half of his chest gleamed in the candlelight. She could not bear the thought of that wrinkled body touching hers. He gave her his special smile that showed off his full set of gleaming teeth. Why he was so proud of them when most warriors boasted about the gaps in their mouth and how they had come about them in one fight or another, she could not imagine.

'You mean Lillan, I presume?' Ælfric said. 'His father, Leax, is a powerful warrior and no one's fool. Do not expect him to remain a humble thegn once you have married his son. He would soon promote a claim to rule. No, you cannot be safely married to anyone but me. The council meets tomorrow when I will ask for their blessing.'

Acha's mind whirled in panic. She realised he would have already seeded his idea to the elders of the council and she would be helpless to stop this madness. Perspiration prickled her brow.

'But my father wanted me to marry King Æthelfrith. His judgment still counts whilst he lives,' she gabbled.

'Æthelfrith has already married and if you marry Theobald, his brother, Edwin can say goodbye to his king's seat for ever.' He tried to put a reassuring hand on her but she shrugged him away. 'Look this must have come as a shock. But it will be for the best, you'll see. Here, I have a present for you.'

He picked up a garment from the bench. 'Here is a dress for you to wear tomorrow when we become betrothed. I can see you are growing into an attractive woman. There will be much more finery like this when you are the first lady of the kin. Try it on. Let me see some of the beauty that is bursting upon you like new fruit on a tree.' He thrust the gown towards her.

Acha stared at him, realising her nightmare had just become worse. She was wearing nothing under her tunic and no cloak over it, and there was no private place where she could change. She crossed her arms, aware that he was examining her breasts. If he was thinking he could pluck her like fruit from a tree, he would have to think again.

'I will try it on in my hut.' She snatched the dress and tried to flee through the door. His over-fed body was quicker than she imagined and he darted in front of her, ushering her back into the room.

'No, no. I want to see you wear it now. My girls will take care of you' He snapped his fingers and the slave-maids emerged from the shadows of the hut. They led Acha into a corner where they unfolded the new dress and tugged at her tunic to pull it over her shoulders. She slapped the hand of one of the girls to stop her haste as she sensed her uncle's prying eyes examining every inch of her body.

'Blankets!' she shouted at them. 'Hold up some blankets.' Arms crossed, her clothes intact, she waited until one of the slaves had hoisted a large bed cover to give her the privacy she needed to whip off one tunic and quickly pull on the other.

'There,' she said, emerging from her makeshift changing-room, nervous that the low neckline and tightness of the dress might be displaying too much of her curves.

Ælfric licked his lips and stepped forward to brush at an imaginary crease. She stopped his arm. 'I am sure the council would like to know I have not been violated in any way when you make your proposal tomorrow,' she said.

He backed away. 'Quite so. The robe will do fine, will it not?'

'Yes, Uncle, I will wear it home so I can be prepared tomorrow.' She picked up her old tunic and stomped through the door.

The guard outside her hut looked surprised to see her running towards him, holding up the hem of the long dress so she did not trip.

'Don't let anyone in,' she gasped. 'Except Forthhere. Bring him to me. Immediately.'

Fourteen

Æthelfrith stretched out on the decking of the longboat that twisted and turned through the meanderings of the river. He was glad of the chance to rest his aching leg after the ride back to Hripis where he had left his boats guarded by a few men. Little did he think he would be sharing the return journey to Eoferwic with the lifeless, but living, body of the King of Deira, who was lying in the bows. Ælle was wrapped in a furry skin even though it was a warm summer's day, his head coddled by woollen blankets, eyes closed, mouth open. Two healer-women watched over him, one occasionally shifting his legs and arms to keep him comfortable, the other regularly leaning in close to his face to feel the slight movement of air from his mouth, the only sign that he was still alive. Six Deiran thegns guarded their king, sweating in full war gear, keeping a watchful eye on the riverbanks and on Æthelfrith and the Bernician warriors who rowed the boat. The number of oarsmen had been reduced to accommodate the king's retinue, so progress was slow as they laboured under the weight of their passengers. The crews of all the boats were made up of a mixture of Bernician and Deiran warriors to minimise any perceived threat on either side. As

Theobald had said as he had marched off with the main armies south along Deere Stræt to Eoferwick, trust between warbands that had fought each other for generations would take a while to establish.

Looking up at the sky, Æthelfrith caught sight of a kestrel hovering over long grass, patiently searching for prey, biding its time before striking. His brother said he should act more like a bird of prey. Instead, he had charged like a wild boar into the centre of the Gododdin forces and got himself injured. Maybe he should have gritted his teeth and ignored Ælle's insults and not hit the king. He looked guiltily at the healers. They could pluck a man's thoughts from his head. He had to be more careful about what he was thinking.

But despite his rashness, things had not turned out too badly, he realised. He and Theobald had agreed that recent events had given them an exceptional chance to establish supremacy over their British neighbours by uniting the two Angle kingdoms. All that remained was to get the Deiran council to agree to his leadership of their joint forces and to seal their union with Theobald's marriage to Ælle's daughter. Once that was done, he could go confidently around the British kings demanding their submission to his overlordship. He had begun his reign contained in a small, coastal fortress and now he was close to controlling all of the lands north of the Humbris, from the east coast to the west.

The Deiran thegns seemed to be on his side. It had been a desperately close thing to convince them that he had played no part in the injury to their king. After the battle, they had of course quizzed their king's own guards but fortunately they had been occupied with the two prisoners and so had seen nothing, although they did claim to hear a noise. Æthelfrith suspected that some disbelieved his story but dared not challenge him and seek revenge for their king. No individual warrior wanted to pick a fight with Æthelfrith the Ferocious, and the Deiran warband had suffered such heavy losses that they were now outnumbered by the Bernicians. Besides, they had no leader for any conflict.

The kestrel dropped like a stone into the moorland but quickly reappeared with nothing to show for its strike. Mynyddog must be feeling equally frustrated, Æthelfrith thought. He had waited patiently for the moment to attack, plotting a truce with him to gain passage to an enemy he judged to be weak, to no avail. Had he sent Bebba to spy on him? He had tried not to think about that, not wanting to give any credence to the slanders made about her by Owain and Ælle. With only the rocking of the boat and the occasional shout from the tillerman to interrupt his reflections, he could no longer avoid the thought. But he still could not believe that she had been sent to him as a deliberate bait to take the path of peace, as Theobald maintained. After all, he had been the one to ask for her as the prize in their mock combat. Mynyddog was not that clever. He surely could not have calculated the attraction between them in advance of their meeting. It was the goddess Frigg who had smiled on him when the old king had chosen which hostages to send. She had rewarded him and he would gladly accept her gift. There were no warriors from Dál Riata or Pictland in the enemy warbands so he had not fought Bebba's immediate kin, only her neighbours, and her father had frequently quarrelled with them. Besides, there was no going back: they were already married. How could he ever forget the picture of loveliness she had made in a clinging gown garlanded with summer flowers, standing solemnly in the temple of Din Guari? He smiled, remembering he must now call it Bebbanburg. He had left Herin behind to guard the fortress with only a small force. With its strengthened defences it could hold out for many moons, giving Æthelfrith time to relieve any siege. He wished he were there now, lying in bed with Bebba instead of on the hard deck of a slow-moving boat with a near-corpse for company.

'Hard on the starboard blades!' The command of the steersman interrupted his thoughts as they rounded a particularly tight bend. The bank was lower at this point, so Æthelfrith could see workers in the field who had stopped scything the barleycorn to apprehensively watch their approach. Did he really once wish he could be a farmer like them, with only the harvest to worry about? No, he would keep the promise he had made at his grandfather's grave. He would be the one to fulfil Ida's dream. He would unite the Old North, and more, under Angle leadership. With Bebba, his queen, by his side.

Loosening his cloak in the bright sunlight, he chuckled to himself when he remembered his lucky escape. If he hadn't met Bebba, he probably would have married the scruffy daughter of the Deiran king. He could see her startled face as she stared up at him in amazement when they had first met. Imagine a slim thing like that in bed with him. One good thrust and he would likely split her in two. That would be his brother's problem now.

Figures appeared on the bank in the distance, shimmering like apparitions. He shook his head to clear his mind of his reverie. Glancing around he saw the ruins of giant stone buildings and walls. They were arriving in Eoferwic. He had been daydreaming longer than he thought. Recognising two of the people waiting on the quayside, he rubbed his eyes to make sure he was not still dreaming. One was Acha, the Deiran princess. The second was his brother.

What is he doing here ahead of me?

*

Acha strained anxiously to see which of the boats approaching the harbour carried her father. She needed him more than she had ever done before. And she needed him awake. She instantly recognised the unmistakable frame of Æthelfrith, the Bernician king as he heaved himself to his feet in the stern of one of the ships. As the boat drew nearer, she could make out the healers in the bow of his boat and the thing she had been dreading most: a still body stretched out on the decking. She moaned and ran to the jetty as ropes were thrown ashore amidst shouts of command from the sea captain. A Deiran thegn took her outstretched hand and helped her to scramble aboard. Brushing aside Hilda and her companion, she knelt beside her father and put a cheek towards his face, placing it almost onto his lips. She felt nothing. She was too late. Her own heart seemed to falter as she looked forlornly towards the healers. Was that a slight movement of air on her cheek? Yes, he still breathed!

Laying her head on his chest, she began to sob uncontrollably. Hilda gently rubbed her back, and her tears gradually subsided until she could kneel up to look into his bearded, grey face and mutter a prayer to the gods to defeat the elves who had taken him. He was her last hope. As she watched, she thought she saw an eye flicker. Or was it a shaft of sunlight tricking her? Her prayers were fast becoming a scream inside her head as he continued to lie motionless on the deck.

Wake up father! You need to sort out your bastard brother. Please, please help me.

She wanted to beat him on the chest or pinch him. Anything to take that serene look from his face and get him to wake.

After Ælfric's absurd proposal, she had ridden out at first light with Forthhere in search of the one man who could help: her father. Galloping along Deere Stræt in the hope that King Ælle had recovered enough to ride with his army, she had found Theobald with the warriors, but no king. Theobald had told her that her father was travelling by river and offered to ride with her to the harbour to meet the boat, ahead of the main army.

The boat rocked and she turned to see Æthelfrith stepping onto the shore to embrace his brother. No doubt, Theobald would tell him the news of Ælfric's plot. Not that they could do anything about it. Whilst her father slept, the council of elders would be entitled to make decisions such as royal marriages, and they were meeting right now, no doubt agreeing to her future with a loathsome, lecherous uncle. And the only man who could stop it was under a spell of sleep. She fell forward onto his chest, hugging him tightly, despite Hilda's protests.

*

Theobald whispered in Æthelfrith's ear as the two embraced on the quayside.

'There is immediate work to be done, brother. We need to pay a visit to Ælle's great hall, now.' He quickly explained what Acha had told him about Ælfric's plans to marry her.

Æthelfrith had not foreseen a challenge from someone who seemed to prefer fine clothes to fighting, but it seemed that what Ælfric lacked on the battlefield, he made up for in intrigue in the royal compound. They had to act swiftly to forestall him. The thegns were disembarking from the boats, stretching their legs, pleased to be back on firm ground. Amongst them was Leax, head of Ælle's hearth-companions, who had spoken out at the meeting after the battle. Æthelfrith pulled him aside.

'I believe your council is meeting now to deliberate what is to be done if your king remains asleep. I intend to ask for their agreement to my overlordship in matters of war, as we discussed. Will you support me on behalf of the king's companions?'

Leax scratched at his beard. 'It is strange they are debating without our views. So yes, I will come and speak of our resolve to extend our oath to you.'

They quickly ordered their men to form into marching order and set off for the royal encampment. Æthelfrith looked back at the boat where King Ælle lay. His daughter was still with him, now hugging the healers, now looking forlornly in his direction. She must be wondering what life married to an old lecher like her uncle would be like. It would be a waste of her young life that was for sure. And inconvenient to their plans. Theobald seemed unusually angry about it. He had even encouraged Æthelfrith to be bold in his words with the council. Theobald urging him to be bold! That was a first. Maybe he had taken a shine to the girl.

When they arrived at the hall, the door was shut. Leax stepped forward.

'Open it,' he ordered. 'We have news for the council that cannot wait.'

Æthelfrith and Leax ordered their men to surround the mead hall and ducked through the doorframe to the chinking of chainmail and swords as soldiers ran to obey. The wizened heads of the council members turned as one in their direction, their conversation abruptly ending. Ælfric looked up in surprise from the king's chair, fiddling anxiously with the rings on his fingers. From the smell of stale sweat that hung in the air, Æthelfrith reckoned they had been closeted in the hall, blathering, for some time.

'Why do you debate here when you should be attending your king, who is disembarking in the harbour at this very moment?' he asked, striding forward to glower at the assembled elders before pointing a finger at Ælfric. 'And why do you already sit in his chair?'

Ælfric stood shakily. 'The king lives? The gods be praised. We were merely discussing—'

'How to usurp his powers whilst he lies sick in a boat in your harbour?' Æthelfrith snarled.

Ælfric held up his hands, shrugging innocently. 'We were merely debating mundane matters which I am sure need not trouble him,' he said.

'Matters such as the marriage of his daughter? That is of great concern to him. And we know the king's wishes on that matter, don't we?' Æthelfrith looked pointedly into the eyes of each of the seven council members in turn.

Ælfric glowered, his face ashen. 'Does the King of Bernicia seek to tell this council what to do with its royal family?'

Æthelfrith spread both hands onto the table and leaned his formidable frame towards Ælfric so that his forehead almost touched his skull.

'No, I will tell you what your own king would do with his royal family.' Without taking his eyes from Ælfric, he uttered a command to those behind him. 'Fetch Forthhere.'

It took only a moment for Theobald to beckon Forthhere from the place by the door where he had stationed him. At his nod, warriors began banging on their shields so the council could be in no doubt they were there.

The menacing drumming filled every corner of the hall, and Æthelfrith saw the fear in the elders' eyes. He waited until the din had subsided before he waved Forthhere forward.

'This fine thegn-son of yours was sent recently to Bernicia by King Ælle to propose a new strategy between our kin. He coded it in a riddle. Tell it again now, Forthhere.'

Forthhere cleared his throat. 'This is the message that King Ælle instructed me to take to King Æthelfrith, my lords: "I snap a spear in two and turn a sword to rust. Warriors always sleep and women never weep, when I become their lord. I can be woven by a maiden, the daughter of a king. I await you at the sign of the wild boar."'

The council members whispered furtively amongst themselves whilst Ælfric squirmed uncomfortably in the king's chair. When Æthelfrith heard the words 'peace' and 'peace-weaver' mentioned, he held up his hands.

'I see you are clever enough to understand your king's meaning. Yes, he proposed peace between us signified by the marriage of his daughter as a peace-weaver to our kin. We must honour his wishes. Particularly when we can now see that the gods had a hand in his message. "Warriors always sleep", he said to indicate the peace he sought between us. Which is how he now lies – in sleep. He has fought all his life and now he sleeps so that a peace can exist between us. It is the gods not the elves who have muted him to show us the way to unite our kin and defeat our common enemies once and for all.'

Ælfric seemed to have regained his composure and nodded as if in agreement.

'A unity which has indeed achieved its purpose in victory over those enemies, and we are grateful for your part in that. King Ælle did, of course, discuss this plan with us before the messenger was sent. He clearly intended the offer of marriage for you, lord Æthelfrith. Unfortunately you could not accept it could you? Perhaps because you were already married? Which leaves us free to arrange her marriage to someone else, as we have just done, does it not?'

Æthelfrith wanted to hit him hard between the eyes for being so clever. He glanced at Theobald, who gave him one of his 'control-yourself-brother' looks.

'Not so fast. Your thegns and I have agreed that whilst your king sleeps, I will have their allegiance for a joint campaign to secure the full submission of our enemies. Is that not so, Leax?'

The Deiran thegn cleared his throat. 'Yes, lord. Although we remain loyal to our king, we firmly ask that this council agrees to such an arrangement so we can strengthen our authority over the British kings.'

'In turn, I accept that the ætheling Edwin will succeed his father when the time comes,' Æthelfrith continued. 'And the princess Acha will marry my brother, Theobald, to secure a lasting accord between our kin.'

He banged his fist hard onto the oaken table so that the drinking cups jumped and trembled.

'This is how it is to be.'

No one dared to speak for what seemed like an age. The council elders looked furtively at each other, hoping that someone else would respond. Some glanced through the open door to where warriors of both armies stood together, spears at the ready.

Ælfric swallowed hard and wiped at his brow. 'I am sure we all admire your firmness of purpose.' He stood slowly, and managed a smile. 'But, believing that King Ælle is no longer fit to rule even though he is still alive, this council has decreed this very day, that I will serve as his regent until such time as he either recovers or his son Edwin can rule in his place. So we have the authority to decide matters such as the marriage of the royal princess. And, to prevent possible rivalry within our own kin during this uncertain time, we have decided that I will marry Acha.'

Æthelfrith felt Theobald's eyes burning into his back and shot him a glance. His brother waved him closer to whisper in his ear, and the two retreated towards the door where they held a hasty conversation whilst the entire hall strained to overhear their words. Finally, Æthelfrith puffed out his cheeks and returned to stand, hands on hips, before the council.

'I assume by your words that you agree to my overlordship whilst your king sleeps so that we can defeat our common enemies?'

Ælfric looked around the council and, seeing them all hastily nod, he also signalled his agreement.

'Good, in which case we recognise you as regent whilst the king sleeps and whilst Edwin is not old enough to be king.'

Æthelfrith paused and glowered at each of the council members one more time.

'As is our normal practice, we will seal this agreement by an exchange of hostages. I will send you my cousin Herin to reside here in this court. In return, we will take the princess Acha to live under our protection in Bernicia to avoid the possible intrigue of which you have spoken. The question of her marriage will be decided later when she fully attains her womanhood.'

Once again his fist descended to reverberate on the table.

'This is how it is,' he repeated.

This time there were no dissenting voices.

*

Acha was sitting by her father, who had been returned to his old quarters to lie motionless on the bed, when Forthhere gave her the news. She hugged him when he told her that she would not be marrying her uncle, not yet anyway. When he hesitantly explained that she was to be a hostage in Bernicia, she sat in shock, head in hands, wondering how her little brother, Edwin, would survive without her.

PART TWO

Degsa's Stone

– AD 603 –

Fifteen

The crash of sword on shield accompanied by shouts of pain and triumph echoed around the ruined walls of Eoferwic. The thegns and their young king dripped with sweat as they trained energetically on a hot day. Edwin used his growing strength to trap his opponent's shield with his own and hacked hard at the exposed shoulder.

'My strike!' he cried as the hardwood blade crunched into bone.

'Alright, but try not to cripple me.' Lillan dropped his sword and clutched his arm. 'I want to be in one piece for a real battle.'

Edwin pointed his blade towards a figure running towards them from the direction of the village. 'That looks like Forthhere coming to join us. I'll try him if you have lost your appetite for the fight.'

'He is Ælfric's duty captain today, so I doubt he is here for battle practice.' Lillan picked up his sword and they walked together to meet Forthhere.

'Ælfric has visitors. He says to come urgently and meet them.' Forthhere panted, pointing back the way he had run.

'Ælfric spends all his time talking to toadying guests. They can wait. Training is more important than meetings. Come and join us for a while.' Edwin said.

'I think this is a meeting you should not miss, lord. Whoever has come, has arrived discreetly by boat and awaits away from the village. I have directions to take you there.'

'If we must,' Edwin sighed and scrabbled amongst the rubble that surrounded them, grasping a heavy stone slab, grunting with the effort of picking it up and cradling it in his arms. 'But we will use it as a drill to build our muscles.'

Forthhere was resting on the remains of an old wall and raised his eyebrows towards Lillan. 'As you command, sire. We take the path to the river, then follow it downstream.'

'Race you there.' Edwin set off at a trot, scrambling over stones through a gap in the wall to take a shortcut towards the river that meandered across the meadow in the distance. His body had grown noticeably in the three years since his father had died so that he was almost the height of a fully-grown man and his rigorous daily exercise was rapidly putting muscle on his long limbs. But he had picked a heavy slab, and the soggy soil of the meadow sucked at his feet, making running even more difficult. Staggering, he was almost ready to drop his load and rest. Instead he did what he often did at moments of tiredness like this: he brought to mind the image of his sister, Acha, as she was led away from the royal settlement by King Æthelfrith and his warriors.

He hadn't liked that man from the moment he'd first met him. When he had taken away the sister who had cared for him like a mother, he began to hate him. And when he'd found out that Æthelfrith had almost certainly killed his father, he had set his mind on revenge. He dared not speak of it even now, but Hilda the healer had whispered the truth into his ear as he had knelt by his father's corpse to say his farewell. It had taken two blows to kill King Ælle, she'd said, and she had furtively shown him two bruises to prove it. One large ruddy patch on his right temple where he had hit the ground was obvious, but the second mark was concealed beneath his hairline on the left. That could not have been made by the fall. It was a compact bruise, the sort left by the pommel of a sword, or a fist. It could have been caused during the battle, but none of the king's companions who were close to him throughout the fighting had reported any strikes on their leader when they were questioned. Only one person had spent any time close to Ælle after the battle before his fall: Æthelfric. He must have delivered the blow that caused the king to fall. From that moment on, Edwin had no doubt that he was duty-bound to seek revenge. Hilda had warned him not to tell a soul about their suspicions until he was ready. To do so would invite his own early death.

Slowing to a walk, he turned to see Lillan and Forthhere catching him up. He had told his secret only to these two faithful companions and they had agreed with Hilda's advice. No point in dying as a troublesome ætheling. Say nothing but build his strength until he was ready to strike. He wrenched his foot from the sodden earth and ran on towards the river.

A guard emerged from a copse of trees as he panted through the undergrowth following Forthhere's directions. Tossing the slab onto the ground, he looked around him.

'Where is this meeting I must attend?' Edwin said, brushing the debris from his hands.

More guards appeared at the noise and led them towards a hollow surrounded by shrubs and trees. As he parted the brushwood, Edwin stared open-mouthed at the sight before him. Four people stood huddled in a ring. Herin, cousin to Æthelfrith, was next to Ælfric. This did not surprise Edwin as Herin had increasingly joined in Ælfric's deliberations. It was the two strangers that caused him to gawk. One was dressed in the long brown robes of a monk; the other was a giant hairy warrior whose head seemed level with the tips of the trees.

Ælfric looked up at the sound of his approach. 'Ah, Edwin, I was hoping you would take time away from your exercise to meet our visitors.' He indicated the two men who turned to greet Edwin. 'This is Rhun, brother of Owain, the King of Rheged who was so cruelly killed at Catræth. When his lands were overrun by King Æthelfrith, he joined the monastery of Bangor in Gwynedd and now advises the king of that region.'

Edwin looked curiously at Rhun's hair that had been cropped from the front half of his scalp yet hung full and long at the back. He had heard of these strange holy men who lived together and worshipped the god on the cross, but he had never before met one.

'May God be with you, King Edwin.' Rhun spoke softly but his eyes were sharp and flicked from Edwin to his two companions. 'And with your thegns.'

'This is Lillan and Forthhere… ' Edwin began.

'Who will be leaving us. We have urgent royal affairs to discuss,' Ælfric said, waving them away.

'I would rather… '

'Private matters are for a king, not his companions,' Ælfric insisted.

Edwin eyed the huge warrior who stood at Rhun's side. He was shrouded in a thick, woollen cloak even though the day was hot.

'But Rhun has a companion.'

Rhun smiled. 'No one to worry you, my lord. He is a friend.'

Edwin could see no weapons hanging from the belt around the man's checked trousers, so he nodded to Lillan and Forthhere. 'Wait by the river.'

Rhun paused until they had been escorted away by the guard before he continued. 'This is Maelumai mac Baetan, known as Maelumai the Fierce, a king's champion who is undefeated throughout all Ireland. He has come from the land of the Gaels to offer you the support of himself and the warband he leads.'

Ælfric cast his eyes around the trees to make sure they were alone. 'Rhun and his ally have come to us with interesting information.'

Maelumai grinned at Edwin and idly ripped bark from the trunk of a nearby tree as if he were skinning a deer.

Ælfric cleared his throat. 'Before we begin, I should say that we are meeting in this spot, away from prying eyes, for a reason. If we agree to follow the path we will outline, our lives will hang together as one. We cannot tell anyone else of this discussion unless we all consent. Is that agreed?'

Edwin looked carefully at the men who all had their attention on him. What was his uncle up to now? When his father had died, he knew he was too young to become king in anything but name and so he had to let Ælfric take over. It all sounded very tedious anyway: calculating which farmer owed what and collecting it when it was due; ordering repairs to royal buildings; keeping thegns fed and equipped. He enjoyed the hunting and the feasting, of course, and most of all, the battle practice. Put a sword and shield in his hands and he was one happy ætheling. Ælfric could do the boring bits of ruling whilst he built himself into a formidable warrior so that he could stand with the spears and, one day soon, avenge his father's death.

He nodded and they all put forward an open hand to place on each other's to signify their agreement.

Ælfric lowered his voice. 'I will be short. King Áedán of the Dál Riata has offered us an alliance because he is increasingly concerned at the power base of Æthelfrith of Benicia, who is now overlord of most of the British kingdoms of the Old North since his victory at Catræth.'

Edwin strained to hear above the rustling of the trees. 'What do you mean by alliance?'

Ælfric rubbed his temples and turned to Rhun. 'Excuse us, brother,' he said quietly. 'Our king is in his formative years, despite his stature.' He smiled weakly towards Edwin. 'This is very confidential, my lord. You must not speak of it even to your trusted thegns. Herin, perhaps you can explain the background for our king.'

Since his arrival three years ago, Herin had become a popular figure, particularly amongst the womenfolk of the Deiran court. But Edwin and his thegns had never particularly taken to him: for a warrior, his beard was too neatly trimmed and his clothes were cut too tight; besides he seemed to share many of Ælfric's tastes, including for young slave girls. Herin cleared his throat, obviously about to make the most of his opportunity to speak.

'When Æthelfrith left to fight the Gododdin, he put me in charge of the remaining forces in Bernicia. I travelled to Dál Riata at the request of his wife, Bebba, who said she had to collect clothing and other private goods and needed my protection on the journey. It was obviously something of a pretence as, once I was there, she made sure I talked to her father, King Áedán, and his sons about political matters. I have kept in touch with them ever since. As Ælfric has said, they are very concerned about the growing power of Æthelfrith, who has subjugated their British neighbours and will turn on them next, they believe. Once they received my intelligence that they were not alone in their concerns, they invoked their ties with the Gaels, their original kin in Ireland. They are formidable warriors and have agreed to join Áedán in his challenge to Æthelfrith. Hence Maelumai's visit here. If we can guarantee sufficient support, he will bring his warband to join us.'

Edwin was very attentive now. The plotting was happening very fast; perhaps too fast for his purpose. He was not yet ready to take his place in a shield wall and he wanted to be there for the final confrontation.

Ælfric took up the story. 'So we took contact with Rhun here to see what appetite the British kingdoms to the south have for a further fight.'

Edwin was beginning to wonder why he had not been consulted over these plans, and it must have shown in his face because Rhun turned to him with a friendly smile.

'My son, I see you may not have followed all this diplomacy between our kingdoms. Rest assured it is all designed to keep you safe and secure as king in your own land. To do that, we must remove the one who sees you as a rival and will never allow you to breed the children who can threaten his dynasty.'

Edwin was not reassured by the strange priest. 'My sister said your god was good at forgiving, not fighting.'

'You are right, my God does forgive. Lend me your palm,' Rhun said taking Edwin's hand. 'Can you imagine the pain of a nail driven through your flesh, just here? And a nail through your other hand and others hammered through your feet? It would hurt, wouldn't it, and to make things worse, think of these nails taking all of your weight as you are suspended high up on a wooden cross. There you slowly starve and bleed to death, mocked by the sentries who guard you. That is what happened to our lord Jesus, the son of the God who rules over us all. Yet he did not seek vengeance on the soldiers who had knocked those nails so cruelly into his body. Jesus asked for their forgiveness because they knew not what they did. They were just following orders. That was a moment to forgive. Yet there is an enemy of our God called Satan, the devil. He seeks to undo the good things our God has done. When we see this devil in action, we must oppose him to prevent his evil spreading. Æthelfrith has given himself to Satan, enslaving the followers of Christ who live in your lands and in your neighbours' lands. That we cannot forgive. He must be stopped by force.'

Edwin felt reassured by the monk's words. His God's wishes were in accord with his own, it seemed, but he still had doubts. Ælfric took up the thread of the discussion and talked of a grand alliance of the Dál Riata to the north, Gwynedd to the south and Ireland to the west, all to defeat Æthelfrith, the evil king who worked for Satan, the devil.

When Ælfric paused, Edwin blurted out: 'I don't worship this Jesus-god, so am I following Satan too?'

Maelumai groaned and spoke for the first time.

'Enough of this talk of God and the devil.' His growl resonated around the hollow like an angry bear in a cave. 'I will fight this king, evil or not, in return for land. Just as Áedán's forefathers did generations ago, I will bring my warband here to find good land. Can you promise me that?'

Rhun inclined his head. 'That is not for a monk to say.'

Edwin felt like stamping his foot to make them listen to him for once.

'It is for a king to give land. If you bring warriors, we will give you land,' he said quickly but reddened under Ælfric's stern gaze. 'Isn't that right, Uncle?'

Ælfric nodded. 'Yes, we need your men, so we will give you land. Herin, tell them the plan you agreed in Dál Riata.'

Herin smoothed his hair and gave Edwin a lofty look as he replied.

'I have met with King Áedán on several occasions and discussed strategy in some detail. And I know my cousin, Æthelfrith, only too well, of course. I believe there is one way to defeat him. His army is now too large to match in pitched battle. He has the oath not just of his own warriors but also of those he has defeated, and he can deploy soldiers from the British kingdoms as well as Bernicia and Deira. But therein lies his weakness. Many of his men live apart, in their own halls, many days march from each other. To defeat him, we must keep them apart and make sure he does not unite them into one army.'

'How?' asked Edwin. He often talked with Lillan and Forthhere about the tactics of war, so he felt more at ease with this discussion.

Herin wagged his finger assertively. 'By creating small diversions and raids that keep his men busy on all fronts. He won't realise a bigger army is behind the trouble until it is too late and we have er... let us say, removed him from power.'

Edwin looked hard at Herin. 'You mean to kill him?'

'Yes, quite so. He must die.' Herin's lips flickered into a thin smile.

For a heartbeat or two no one spoke, and Edwin felt his mouth go dry.

'How will you do that?' he asked finally.

'It is almost impossible to invade Bernicia,' Herin replied. 'Theobald has made sure that trenches and earthworks defend all the approaches into their territory. So we must trap him in the borderlands between our lands. That is where I come in.' He turned to Maelumai. 'I can show you hidden trails that go around their defences.'

Edwin's brow wrinkled. 'So who will rule after Æthelfrith?' he asked.

'I will rule Bernicia. But I will not claim overlordship over Deira. We will be equal neighbours,' Herin said.

Edwin studied him carefully, his eyes falling on his delicate, slender hands. Could he trust someone with such finely trimmed fingernails?

'What about my sister, Acha? What happens to her?' Edwin asked.

Ælfric raised a finger. 'I was coming to that. You see, we agreed she would live in Bernicia until the time came when she could marry. That was three years ago, and she is obviously now of a marrying age. Æthelfrith has demanded once again that she become wife to his brother, Theobald.'

'But she wanted to marry Lillan. She told me so herself,' Edwin said.

'Yes, and the king's counsel decided she should marry me,' said Ælfric.

That did it. Edwin knew this was the moment to assert his authority. 'It is for a king to decide who his sister is to marry.'

'This is a very delicate matter which we have to handle—' Ælfric began.

'No, I will meet Æthelfrith to discuss who Acha will marry.' As he spoke, another thought struck him and he turned to Herin. 'That might also give us the chance to ambush him, mightn't it?'

Herin lightly tapped his fingers, one on the other and looked thoughtful.

'It might, indeed it might. Áedán is planning to waylay him but it would be prudent to have another arrow to our bow. Bebba reports that Theobald, the king's brother, should also be eliminated. He thinks before he acts, unlike his brother. They are both formidable fighters but we have their match, don't we, Maelumai?'

The giant warrior rubbed his hands. 'Yes, you can leave them to me.'

'They hold my sister hostage, so we must make sure we can free her and that she comes to no harm,' Edwin said, pleased that someone had listened to his ideas for once. He saw Ælfric almost smile, and he looked about to speak, but something made him think better of it and for once he kept quiet.

Sixteen

Acha skipped along the pathway at the base of the rocky citadel that she had learned to call home. It led to dunes covered in marrow-grass where sandy bays could hide her from her pursuer. She loved the excitement of lying on the soft sand, her eyes closed, knowing that he was near, desperately trying not to make a sound until the moment when he would discover her. She had yearned to play more of these games when she was young, but it had taken until now, when she was in her sixteenth year and a prisoner of sorts in Bebbanburg, for her to feel free enough to run and play.

When she had first arrived she had been quite miserable. The memory of Edwin's bitter crying as she had ridden away from Eoferwic haunted her and she missed Lillan and her other friends. Gradually, she had learned to numb the pain of exile by exploring the area where she now lived. The unexpected joy of living by the sea, riding across mud flats at low tide and searching for oysters and shells in hidden coves, helped free her mind from the past. But it was the attention of the man who was now chasing her through the dunes that made the greatest difference to her mood.

A pair of gulls flew up, cawing loudly at the intruder. He was near. Trying not to giggle, she wriggled into the sand, knowing that he would soon find her. At first, he had acted more like a father figure, comforting her when she had been torn from her family home. News of the death of her father, King Ælle, who had never recovered from his fall, had been a particularly difficult moment, coming as it did almost as soon as she had arrived in Bebbanburg.

She heard him growl gently, like a soft bear.

'Ah! I smell the scent of sweet honey. I will take it in my paws and eat it.'

Acha shrieked and scrambled to her feet as Theobald appeared over the top of the dune.

'Oh no, big bear! I have no honey.'

Theobald licked his lips. 'You lie. I can see honey aplenty.' He grabbed at her and she pummelled him briefly with her fists before collapsing into laughter as he licked her neck and cheeks.

'Mmm. Nectar indeed,' he said, drawing his mouth onto her lips.

They stood, their arms locked around each other, wisps of their hair entangling in the sea breeze.

Theobald stood back, suddenly serious. 'We have to go. Æthelfrith wants to see us.'

'Us? The king wants to see me as well? He normally ignores me.'

Theobald smoothed tassels of hair from her face. 'Don't take it personally. He has a lot to think about.'

'Like what?'

'Nothing to worry you. Just a lot of incidents around our borders. And Bebba seems to have disappeared.'

'Disappeared? Where?'

'You remember she went home to visit her family in Dál Riata?'

'Well, I remember the shouting,' said Acha. 'She wanted to take their son, Eanfrith, because he is in his second summer and never seen his grandfather or uncles. And Æthelfrith refused because he said it was too dangerous. But she had her way as usual. Why do you say she has disappeared?'

'She was due back some time ago but there has been no word from her. Æthelfrith is worried sick. Raiders have been burning crops and farms close to our own borders, and he thinks she may have been caught up in the troubles.'

'So why does he want to see me?'

Theobald looked at his bare feet as he wriggled them in the sand. 'You remember the agreement with your father's counsel in Deira that they would postpone the decision about who you were to marry until… '

Acha looked alarmed. 'Don't tell me Æthelfrith is going back on his promise?'

Theobald grabbed her wrists and looked into her eyes.

'No, of course not. But we can hardly pretend you are not yet of a marrying age, can we? Just look at you!' He swept his eyes over the curves of her body.

'No, don't look at me, especially that way. Not until you promise that you and your brother won't let Ælfric force me to marry him, do you hear?'

'I've told you, you cannot marry Ælfric or anyone else for that matter, because you are to marry me. That's what I want and I hope you do too.'

She nodded. 'I might have wished for a more romantic proposal, but it will do. I accept. So why does Æthelfrith want to see us?'

'Let's go and find out shall we?' He took her hand and they walked side by side up to the fortress on the rock.

*

From his viewpoint high up on the wooden ramparts that encircled the stronghold, Æthelfrith caught sight of the two figures approaching from below.

About time the lovebirds returned.

When the grumpy girl had first arrived, he had been surprised that Theobald had been so taken with her. More recently, he had begun to realise his brother had made a fine catch. The dowdy fledgling had turned into an eye-catching adult with a quick wit and easy smile. She seemed to grow more appealing by the day. Unlike Bebba, his wife who had lost her fine figure after the birth of their child and who had become increasingly irritable. The fun seemed to have gone from her. When they'd first met, they laughed a lot together. Now they just argued.

He looked into the steely eyes of the falcon whose talons gripped the leather thong around his arm.

'You don't smile much either do you,' he muttered to the bird. 'But at least you come back to me.' He unclasped the chain on his wrist and released the bird towards a flock of gulls mewing overhead. 'Go get 'em, girl.'

He had decided that the warm weather was a chance to eat in the open air, so he had ordered the cooks to bring the fires outside to the cobbled courtyard in front of the hall to bake the mackerel and herrings that were in plentiful supply. That had caught the attention of the gulls that had soon arrived in force to sample the fish that a slave had unwittingly left unguarded on a table. Cursing the unfortunate slave girl, Æthelfrith had sent for his favourite falcon. He would benefit from the mishap with a spot of hunting.

He watched in admiration as his bird wheeled above the flock of gulls, and wondered what it would be like to fly. He would definitely prefer to soar as a solitary predator like a hawk than flap about with the senseless gulls that spent their days mewing and feeding from scraps. His falcon suddenly dived into the flock to scatter the gulls back towards the sea, protesting loudly. That's how he would deal with the raiders on his borders: a fast, aggressive attack to frighten them away. And if he found any harm had come to Bebba or his son, he would slaughter every one. His stomach churned to think about it. Why had she gone? It wasn't as if he hadn't warned her of the dangers; but she was so headstrong, he couldn't think of a way of stopping her going to Dál Riata with his son, short of imprisoning her.

One of the cooks shouted and flapped a cloth at a lone gull that had evaded the falcon and had darted back towards the food on the table. His bird was quick and powerful but it could not be everywhere.

Like me.

He heard the sound of greetings from the northern sea gate below and watched as Theobald and Acha emerged through the palisade to stroll on the grass of the lower enclosure. They walked up the ramp towards the paved courtyard around the mead hall, at the highest point of the citadel, where the servants were lighting fires for the feast. As the pair passed by the well, he remembered the day when he and Bebba had paused there and she had asked him many detailed questions about why it had been made and how it worked. It was strange for a woman to be interested in the water supply of a fortress, but then Bebba was an unusual woman. As he opened the cage to return his falcon to her perch, he could not help but notice Acha's well-formed figure out of the corner of his eye.

'Find anything of interest in the dunes?' he shouted, smiling when she jumped at the sound of his voice, a hint of blush to her cheeks.

Theobald spun around. 'Fresh air and sea spray, brother. It makes you feel good. You should try it.'

'Perhaps I should. There is something that doesn't make me feel good right now, that's for sure,' Æthelfrith replied. 'Let's find a quiet place where I can tell you both about it, shall we?'

Acha glanced anxiously at Theobald. If she was needed for the discussion it could only mean one thing: her marriage. Æthelfrith looked more strained than she had ever seen him. When she had first arrived at his court, he was not at all how she'd imagined him from the stories she'd been told. He was full of life and fun like his younger brother; noisy and domineering as well, but then he was the king. He had had no hesitation in allowing her into the mead hall in the evening, so she had seen at first hand how he and Theobald joked and told stories with their warriors, who seemed to dote on their every word. Not that Æthelfrith stayed there late. After eating with the women, Bebba would stand, pushing her chair back noisily and looking hard in his direction. He would nod to acknowledge her departure and follow her soon after, as if she was tugging him by an invisible cord to their quarters. Things had begun to change when Bebba's belly swelled with their child. At first, Æthelfrith would escort his wife out of the hall, but return soon after to rejoin the merry-making and storytelling. That had stopped as she had neared her birthing time when he seemed to catch his wife's irritable mood. Acha had kept out of his way as much as possible after that. Luckily, she had Theobald to distract her. Poor Æthelfrith had nearly missed his son's birthing as he was touring some new territory, extracting dues from farmers, when Bebba had begun her labour. He had ridden through the night and arrived only moments before his son had appeared. Acha heard that Bebba was furious. Maybe she'd never forgiven him. She always seemed to be scolding him after that, and Æthelfrith's face had become drawn and unsmiling. The two brothers, once so alike each other except in height, suddenly appeared very different.

Theobald routinely wore a friendly smile; Æthelfrith a deep frown.

'What's the bad news?' Theobald asked once Æthelfrith had shooed away the servants and dogs so they could sit privately around the high table.

'Ælfric has sent a message to say that Edwin wants to talk with us about his sister's future.' When he saw Acha's expression, he quickly added: 'Sorry my dear but I have to go through the formality of getting his agreement for you to marry Theobald. He and Ælfric have been very submissive until now, but they seem to have caught the disease of discontent from the British kings.'

'They will soon change their minds when you arrive with your thegns,' said Theobald.

'That's the problem. I can't go.'

'Why not?' asked Theobald.

'I must go to Strad Clud, find my wife and deal with the thieves who are now looting farms on our side of the border. You can take warriors to meet Edwin. He has offered to meet us north of the Wall.'

Theobald did not seem pleased. 'That would mean dividing our forces and we swore we would never do that again. Not after Catræth.'

'But our forces are much larger now. We can divide them between the two of us and still outnumber whoever is opposing us.' Æthelfrith rubbed his eyes with his fingers. To Acha, he looked as though he had not slept much.

'So long as they haven't found reinforcements from elsewhere. There are reports that Saxon kings in East Anglia and Mercia are increasingly concerned by our power, not to mention the Picts to the north,' argued Theobald.

Æthelfrith blew air from his cheeks. 'You are always seeing threats from everywhere. I need to find my wife. You need to claim yours. Let there be an end to it.' Æthelfrith was close to shouting.

Acha feared the brothers would soon be arguing heatedly as they sometimes did, but Theobald stood to pace up and down, deep in thought.

'A better solution would be to take one large army into the field and camp it in a central position,' he said finally. 'Hide it somewhere whilst you and I each take a smaller force to deal with our particular problems. If we find there is a larger warband opposing us, we can retreat back to the main army for reinforcements and surprise our opponents.'

Æthelfrith thought for a few moments before his face cracked into a grin. He clapped Theobald on the shoulders.

'I knew you would find an answer. You always do.' He turned to Acha. 'Take this bothersome brother of mine and make him a happy man. You two will be wed when you return and we will celebrate with a feast to be remembered.'

Acha felt reassured by his words. Maybe everything could happen just as she dreamed. Theobald was planning a separate homestead outside of Bebbanburg and, once they were married, she would ask Edwin to come and live with them until he was old enough to be king in his own right.

But Theobald was far from satisfied. 'When you said, "you two", did you mean that Acha is to come with me to meet Edwin?'

'Yes I did. Edwin is asking to see her,' said Æthelfrith

'How kind of him,' Acha said, heartened to believe that her little brother was still thinking of her.

'Where shall we position our army?' asked Æthelfrith.

Theobald looked thoughtful. 'We need somewhere close to our border with the Strad Clud for your mission. How about Degsa's Stone? That's well known so that all our men can gather there, and there are wooded hills above the valley where they can conceal themselves. It's not far from the Wall and the old north road so that I can meet Edwin nearby.'

'We are agreed then? Let's muster an army and organise our wives!' Æthelfrith slapped the palm of his hand on the table in resolution.

'Agreed,' said Theobald. 'But I would like to say that this bothersome brother of yours is still bothered. They are deceiving us somehow, I know it. Pull back to the Stone if you run into trouble. No brave sorties.'

Seventeen

The misty rain swept across the moor into Edwin's face
as he peered into the haze. He could see little but the
rump of the horse ahead of him and the sodden back
of its rider. His own cape was so wet that he could feel the
dampness of his mail-coat and tunic on his skin and he had to
grit his teeth to stop himself shivering. He had not expected
that going to war would be a comfortable affair, but this was
miserable beyond imagination. He just wished they could find
the enemy so that the fighting could begin. Not that he had
ever been in a real battle. He had never held his shield against
a warrior who actually wanted to harm him, only against loyal
thegns who were training him. They'd sometimes hurt him but
never struck to kill. That would soon change. He fidgeted with
the war hat that his father had bought for him from Guthlaf,
the trader. He wanted to wear it in memory of the dead king
when he saw Æthelfrith die.

'Hold up! Riders approaching.' He heard the shout from
the leader of the column and quickly pulled up his mount as
the horses ahead skidded to a halt in the mud.

'What is it?' he asked, desperate to see through the foggy
downpour.

Lillan was the rider in front of him and he turned, drips falling from his leather helmet. 'Wait here and I will find out.'

'No, I'm coming too,' said Edwin digging his heels into his horse's flanks. He signalled to Rhun, who rode behind him with a cohort of warriors, and trotted ahead with Lillan.

He recognised the distinctive figure of Herin, who sat on his mount with a back as straight as a spear, his boar-crested helmet gleaming through the grey mist as if the weather was of no concern to him. He had left them several days before to meet Maelumai's warband and had evidently returned to brief Forthhere, who led their column.

'Our scouts report that Theobald and a band of about fifty warriors are just ahead of you,' Herin said, talking loudly to make himself heard above the wind, and pointing to the east.

'And where are Maelumai's forces?' asked Forthhere.

'To the west, less than a day's march. If you can keep Theobald talking, we can catch them like sheep in a pen.'

Lillan thrust his horse forward so that he could join the conversation. 'Surely he will retreat east when his scouts see you coming.'

Herin smiled smugly. 'I know a trail around the defences so we'll surprise them from the rear. The weather will help keep us hidden.'

Forthhere conferred briefly with Lillan before nodding to Herin. 'We will keep them talking as long as we can, but you will need to attack tomorrow at the latest. They will be suspicious by then.'

Herin held his head even higher. 'We will be there by midday. You would do well to keep out of the way when the Gaels attack. They can be easily excited and may not differentiate friend from foe.'

Edwin barged his way forward between the horses. 'Wait! My sister should be with them. She is not to be harmed in any way, do you hear?'

Herin nodded. 'I will order Maelumai to watch out for the girl, but you would do well to keep her away from the fighting even so.'

Herin flicked his reigns and galloped off into the mist.

*

Acha crouched by the smouldering logs in the entrance of the animal-skin shelter that Theobald's men had erected for her. She looked out towards the warriors guarding the curved, grassy mound ahead, wishing that the rain would let up even for an instant so that she could peer over and see what was happening in the valley on the other side. They were talking about her, deciding her future, she knew that, but why were they taking so long? Surely, Edwin should've agreed by now. She had asked to go with Theobald, but he had forbidden it until he had made sure it was safe.

A shout from the guard brought her to her feet and, despite the rain, she ran forward to see for herself what was happening.

Thank the gods. He's returning at last.

With a shiver, she hurried back to the shelter and waited impatiently as Theobald and his companions rode into the camp. As soon as he had dismounted, she heard him shouting orders and his men began scurrying everywhere. He waved to her.

'Pack up your things,' he called.

She raised her arms in a puzzled look and mouthed a question that was carried away, unheard, on the wind. He ran over quickly.

'We're moving out,' he said. 'Something's wrong.'

'Like what?'

'Like your brother Edwin is making strange demands.'

'What sort of strange demands?'

Theobald grabbed one of the covers of the shelter that had begun flapping in the rising wind. 'Like you should marry Lillan? At least its not Ælfric anymore, but why Lillan? I think they are trying to delay us for some reason. My scouts have reported movements in the forests. It smells like a trap to me.'

Acha breathed a sigh of relief. 'No, no, it's my silly brother. Lillan was my childhood sweetheart. Edwin thinks I still want to marry him. He's just trying to look after me, the sweet boy. It will be fine when I tell him I want to marry you.'

'I'm not sure it that's simple. Ælfric may have manipulated Edwin into spinning this story to his own ends,' Theobald said, waving her inside the tent where they stood huddled together.

Acha brushed droplets from her gown. 'I am sure if I just met Edwin and explained, it would all be fine. Why not invite him over to talk to me? It needn't delay us much. You could still prepare to leave.'

Theobald looked out into the fine rain that still persisted, watching his men pack supplies into bags to throw over the horses.

'Alright, providing he comes immediately. Any more delays and I'll know it's an ambush.'

*

Edwin was stripping off wet clothes in his tent when Lillan and Forthhere burst through the flap.

'Don't be too hasty in disrobing,' said Lillan. 'Acha has agreed to see you.'

Edwin had gazed at the earth mounds up the valley for some time that day, knowing his sister was probably camped behind them, wondering what she was like after all this time. If their plan worked, she would soon be free from her captors and all the more happy to see him.

'Right now?' he asked.

'I think Theobald senses something is wrong. I saw it in his face today. The more we talked, the more uncomfortable and suspicious he looked. I think he will leave if we don't have this meeting very soon,' Lillan said.

'I say it's too dangerous to send our king into their camp. They could hold him hostage, or worse,' said Forthhere.

'You're right. We will insist on meeting in the open. You will have to play her along for a while but it will soon be midday. Herin promised they would attack by then,' said Lillan.

*

Theobald's men had taken down all the tents except one when the messenger arrived. Acha was perched on a bag in the remaining shelter, straining to see what was happening but not wishing to get her last set of dry clothes wet before the journey back to the base camp of the main army. Theobald waved to a group of his thegns and walked briskly towards her.

'They have agreed you can meet but in an open space, not this enclosure. Edwin will be accompanied by Lillan and Forthhere. They claim you know them well. We can take the same number on our side.'

Acha breathed a sigh of relief. She would be amongst old friends whom she could trust. It would be hard talking of her love for Theobald in front of Lillan, but he would understand after all this time.

'I'm sure I can make Edwin see sense,' she said.

'I will be coming too. I'm not letting you go out there alone. But if it's a way of getting the bride I want, then let's do it and go home. I will be watching you every step of the way,' Theobald said, taking her hand.

*

Edwin desperately wanted the rain to stop so that he could see his sister more clearly. She was riding down from the earthen fortification into the valley towards him, flanked by her guards. He blinked, thinking he may have seen Æthelfrith. He turned quickly to Lillan and pointed. Lillan squinted, trying to make out the figures.

'It's Theobald with your sister, sire.'

Edwin suddenly felt that he could not carry out his role. Theobald had a reputation for cleverness as well as skill as a warrior. What if—

A distant roll of thunder interrupted his thoughts.

The gods are watching. If Rhun's god is on my side, I can kill the devil king and save my sister.

He nudged his horse ahead, urging Lillan and Forthhere to follow. The fine droplets turned to pelting rain, and he saw Acha pull her headpiece more firmly around her face so he could hardly make out her features.

'No further,' the man they thought was Theobald shouted to them from twenty paces. 'Keep your hands from your swords if you wish to talk.'

'What do we do next?' Edwin whispered to Lillan.

'Just do what comes natural, for the moment,' Lillan replied.

'Is that you, A… ?' Edwin unexpectedly choked on her name and he felt tears as he stared at what he could see of the face before him. He knew it was her just from her eyes.

Acha leaned forward in her saddle. 'Are you really the scrawny little brother I left behind?'

'And are you the bossy sister I once had?' Edwin chuckled. 'I know, I'll test you with a riddle.' He watched as Acha glanced towards Theobald, who was shifting uncomfortably by her side. 'How about this one? I grow very tall, erect in my bed, and a girl grabs me, peels back my skin and puts me in her pantry. What am I?'

Acha put her hand towards her mouth, and Edwin knew that beneath the woollen wrap, she was giggling.

'You're an onion and you're making my eyes water,' Acha said, dabbing at her face.

Edwin slid quickly from his horse and strode towards Acha, hands outstretched. 'Walk with me so I can see your face. I want to see if your spots are all gone.'

Theobald moved his horse closer to Acha. 'No! Don't go,' he shouted.

It was too late. Acha was already dismounting, running into her brother's arms.

'Sorry, Lord Theobald,' Edwin called over as they embraced, 'I think you have sent an imposter. I can't believe this good-looking lady is my sister.'

Acha stepped back to admire her brother. 'Look at you, you have grown so tall and strong.' Her foot slipped in the mud and he grabbed her wrist to steady her.

'Let's shelter under those trees where we can talk without getting so wet, ' Edwin said, keeping a firm grip on her arm.

Theobald looked alarmed and urged his horse towards them as they scuttled through the rain towards a group of trees at the edge of the valley.

'It's alright, Theo dear,' Acha called. 'I'll be safe enough.'

Theobald reigned back. 'Be quick then. It's not the moment for pleasantries.'

Edwin pulled her under some low branches. 'What's with this "Theo dear"? Do you like this man?'

'That's what I have to tell you. I love this man. I want to marry him. I will be his wife. You have to agree to it.'

Edwin laughed. 'You haven't changed after all. You're still my bossy sister, always telling me what to do.' He glanced up the valley towards the mound, hoping the warband would arrive and end this pretence, but all he could see was the rain. He looked back into his sister's face, his laughter gone. Her eyes told him she was serious about Theobald. She was going to be upset when the Gaels came.

Acha followed his gaze towards the mound, wondering what he was looking for.

'I'm certainly not the one who tells you what to do these days,' she said. 'I hear that Ælfric does that.'

'Oh, I let him do the boring things like collecting taxes. But I make the big decisions. Like who a royal princess is to marry.' Edwin could feel the pleading in her eyes. He glanced at Theobald, who was watching them intently and felt the possessiveness in his look. Was this what adults called love?

'Don't worry. I won't let them marry you to Ælfric.' It was the best he could do, but he could see she was not happy.

'No, I will not marry Ælfric, nor anyone else, except Theobald. You must agree to that, or—' Acha hesitated. She did not want to threaten him. He had grown up from the child she knew. He was already taller than she was.

I can't tell him what to do anymore.

'One day, I hope you will feel for a woman as I do for Theobald and then you will know what I am talking about. But anyway, it makes sense for our two families to be united, I'm sure you know that.'

Edwin suddenly felt the urge to tell her who had killed their father. That should persuade her that the kin she wanted to unite could never be joined together. But he stopped himself from blurting it out, remembering that he had to hide his hatred for Æthelfrith. Instead, he chuckled at a memory that flashed into his mind of watching his sister brush her hair while he played in his bath for as long as he could.

'You always wanted me to go to bed early so you could go out to meet Lillan. What happened to your feelings for him?' he asked.

Acha glanced over to Lillan's tall, slim figure as he sat unmoving on his horse, his attention on the fortifications up the valley. Why did they all keep looking up there?

'Yes, I was fond of Lillan but he was just a childhood sweetheart. Do you know what I mean? Do you have a girlfriend yourself?'

Edwin thought of the slave girls his uncle had sent to him on a number of occasions. 'Yes, lots.'

'But you wouldn't want to marry one of them, would you?'

Edwin laughed and shook his head as Acha continued. 'That's the difference between a temporary urge for someone and something that lasts much longer. Like us. I will always love you, Edwin, however big and ugly you might become. It's the same with Theobald.' Acha felt a flush to her cheeks even in the cold rain that dripped from the leaves above her head. It wasn't easy being so frank with him. He seemed such a stranger to her now. But she had to make him understand.

'You love him like a brother?' he asked.

'Yes and no. It's different but the same.'

'What if you have to choose between the two?'

Acha swallowed hard. She had not expected that question. This was more difficult than she expected. Theobald was right: something was wrong. Edwin was glancing up at the earthwork fortifications again.

'It's not a choice between you and Theobald,' she said. 'Quite the opposite. I was hoping you would come and live with us for a while before you finally stand with the spears.'

She was looking at him so earnestly that he almost wanted to cry out and stop the attack that would destroy her dream at any moment. But he knew the full story of Æthelfrith's treachery. She didn't.

'Do you believe in the devil?' he asked.

She looked puzzled, then chuckled. 'Now you do sound like my little brother. Always asking questions. What devil is this?'

'The devil Satan that the Christian god is always fighting against. One of their priests told me that... ' Edwin's voice faded, realising that he was about to say more than he should about the evil king. 'He told me that some people who work for the devil have to be killed.'

Acha felt a sense of panic rising through her body. Was he trying to warn her?

'What's wrong, Edwin? Has Ælfric made you do something you don't want to?' She looked around, sensing danger but seeing nothing but rain and the sodden figures on horseback who watched them intently. She waved to Theobald and began to edge back towards him, but Edwin grabbed her hand.

'No, you will be safer here with me,' he said tightening his grip.

'What do you mean?' she asked, but Edwin was gazing up the valley. She saw a hard look in his face that she had never seen before.

'God is coming for the devil,' he said as a bellow of voices from the earthworks above reached their ears.

She had heard that sound before when she had watched battle training. When she looked up to see figures brandishing weapons on top of the earthworks, she realised they were fighting for real.

'Edwin, what have you done? Let me go!' She wanted to get back to Theobald, but Edwin just tightened his grip on her wrist and grabbed her other arm, drawing her close to his body.

She could see the disbelief in Theobald's face as he stared first at his warriors, who were desperately defending themselves against the surprise attack up on the mound, and then towards her, hesitating between rejoining his men and rescuing her. Lillan and Forthhere moved their horses forward, barring his way.

'She will be safe with us, Theobald,' Edwin shouted. 'Look to your attackers and we will look after her.'

Acha saw that Theobald's men were beginning to stream over the earthworks, into the ditch and down the valley towards them. They were in full retreat from a howling hoard that poured over the ridge after them. The fortifications were designed to repel an attack up from the valley floor, not from the other side. Where had this enemy come from? Their warriors were unlike any she had seen before. They carried only light shields and wore no helmets, their red hair and checked cloaks streaming in the wind as they came over the crest of the mound like a deluge. One of Theobald's men stumbled and slipped on the wet grass. They were on him in a flash, thrusting spears into his back and slashing short swords at his body as he fell screaming in the mud.

Theobald hesitated no longer.

'Guard her well or you will have me to answer to,' he shouted to Edwin and urged his horse up the slope towards his retreating men.

'To me! Shield wall! Shield wall!' he cried as he leapt from his horse.

Acha stared in disbelief as she watched Theobald urging his retreating men to turn and face the enemy. They managed to form a straggling line and took the impact of the first ferocious assault, crouching behind their shields as men running full pelt down the hill fell upon them. More men joined Theobald's wall, but they were soon forced into a tight circle by the agile foot soldiers who danced around them, jabbing and hurling spears, all the while keening a strange, high-pitched battle-cry. The wall held but Acha could see heavily armed men and archers following the more mobile warriors. In their centre was a mountain of a man whose head stood out above the rest. He was growling orders, and a bank of archers ran forward as the first wave of attackers fell back. Soon arrows were whistling into the wall, thumping into the wooden shields or arching up to fall on top of Theobald's small band. Acha closed her eyes at the sight of a thegn who stumbled forward clutching at a shaft that quivered in the top of his skull.

'Where are your warriors? Call them to help,' she shouted at Edwin, waving towards the men behind him in their camp who stood watching the battle unfold. He appeared not to hear her above the tumult but tightened his grip on her arms. She winced as she heard the crunch of a huge blow from the giant leader, who had waved the archers away so that more heavily armed troops could throw themselves at the desperate defenders. Acha tugged at her wrists to try to free herself but he held firm. Forthhere and Lillan dismounted and ran to where they stood. She turned to appeal to them.

'Aren't you going to help them? I thought we were allies.'

Forthhere held out a rope 'Shall we bind her, lord?'

'Forthhere, what are you taking about? You're still sworn to protect me,' she shouted above the tumult.

'That's what I am trying to do, m'lady,' he replied.

Acha felt as though the blood was draining from her body as Edwin snatched the rope and tried to bind her wrists. The wetness made it difficult and she pulled a hand free and slapped him hard on the face.

'How dare you! I'm not your prisoner!'

She kicked him hard on the shins, tugged her other hand free and fled as fast as she could towards Theobald. Screaming attackers had engulfed the shield wall and all she could see of his small band were the wounded scrabbling in the mud and the red stain of their blood on the grass.

It was Lillan who caught her, throwing his arms around her and knocking her to the ground. She kicked and pummelled at him, desperate to see Theobald. Forthhere helped pin her to the ground before they carried her back to where Edwin stood. When she could struggle no more she stood and stared at the battle, hoping it was all a bad dream. She began to shiver and sob. Edwin shook his head when Lillan offered him the rope once more, but wrapped her in his cloak instead. When she looked at him, she saw a stranger, not her brother, and she felt cold, very cold.

Theobald was still standing with a handful of his thegns, and the enemy had pulled back to taunt them before the next assault. There was still time to save him.

'I'll marry whoever you want me to, if you stop the fighting!' she shouted.

At that moment, Acha heard the chant of 'Maelumai, Maelumai', as the Irish soldiers fell back from the remnants of the shield wall. The rain had eased into a fine mist but black clouds still loomed on the horizon as they chanted and made a semicircle, into which first their giant leader and then Theobald stepped.

Forthhere waved his hand towards the two men who stood facing each other. 'The Irish custom is to offer single combat. He has a chance to live if he can beat their champion.'

She could see that Theobald was dragging his leg as he tried to keep his distance from the giant who dwarfed him.

'Stop the fight and I will even marry Ælfric if that's what you want!' she screamed.

Her words were almost lost in the din as Theobald beat away the first swing of Maelumai's heavy sword that clattered against his shield. She turned to Edwin, who was straining to see what was happening in the ring.

'Do something. You're the king!'

Edwin was sweating, although the weather was cold. He had heard his sister's pleas to save the man she loved. It would not serve them to kill Theobald. If Áedán's ambush failed, Æthelfrith would come to avenge his brother. He watched Theobald duck under a huge swing of Maelumai's sword but take a glancing blow from his shield as he recovered his balance. Theobald seemed skilled in weaving away from the lunges of the Gael, but Edwin had seen the hesitation when he moved off his right foot. That leg had probably taken a wound in the early fighting and it would not be long before Maelumai's strength and long reach proved decisive. He winced as Theobald was driven down on one knee by another hammering strike that he only just managed to fend away. He realised his resistance could not last much longer. His sister was shouting at him again to do something.

He glanced at Lillan and Forthhere, who were looking towards him, questioning looks on their faces. Theobald cleverly used his opponent's weight to deflect Maelumai past him into a patch of mud where the big man slipped and stumbled, snarling like an angry boar. Theobald sucked in great gulps of air, unable to use his advantage as Maelumai found his feet. Both men paused, eyeing each other warily.

'Stop the fight!' Edwin used the lull to run forward. 'Enough! Lay down your weapons! Stand clear there!' he shouted, pushing past the onlookers.

Theobald turned at the sound of the young king's voice as he barged his way into the makeshift arena. Maelumai later claimed that he did not understand Edwin's accent and mistook the order. Whatever the truth of the matter, he picked that precise moment to make one more scything sweep of his long sword towards his opponent. Edwin's order distracted Theobald for only a heartbeat but that was all it took for his defences to be too slow to fully stop the savage swing. Maelumai's blade glanced up from the metal rim of Theobald's shield and bit hard into the unprotected flesh between his helmet and leather jerkin.

Edwin burst into the ring of warriors just as blood spurted from the cut, and Theobald's head flew back as he screamed to the skies.

'Stop I say!' Edwin yelled, and Maelumai finally paused, but not before he had used his blade like a saw to rip deeper into the neck.

*

Acha's heart skipped a beat when Edwin ran forward to stop the fight. Finally her little brother had seen sense and had come to their aid. No one tried to stop her as she followed him, stumbling across the wet grass, desperately hoping that he would be in time. What she saw when she burst into the semicircle of soldiers was something she would see again and again in her mind until the day she died: the giant blade whirring through the air, chinking off his shield, crunching into his skin; his pitiful cry as he slumped to his knees, clutching his neck, eyes wide in disbelief as they met her own.

Then the words, his final words: 'Warn Æthelfr... Herin.' It happened so fast, she did not have time for grief, even as she held his body to hers until his breathing suddenly stopped. How could a life be ended so quickly? It seemed only moments earlier that he'd sat on his horse watching her, protecting her. Now he was—

She wanted to scream and sob but there was no time for that. With his final breath, he had given her an order and she would follow it. Warn Æthelfrith. She could see her horse munching grass close by. She fumbled at the belt around Theobald's tunic as she carefully laid his limp body onto the ground, found the seax knife that he always carried and quickly put it into the pouch of her robe.

'You will be with me for ever, Theo,' she whispered, kissing his cheek.

Looking furtively around, she saw that the disorder was spreading. Edwin was shouting at Maelumai, who was breathing hard, resting his head on the pommel of his sword, its dreadful blade thrust into the earth. The remnants of Theobald's thegns still crouched behind their shields, looking in disbelief towards their dead leader. Forthhere was shouting orders to his men who were scurrying forward to join the melee. Amidst the confusion, she slipped quietly past the ranks of Irish soldiers who were still cheering Maelumai's victory. No one stopped her as she walked trance-like towards her grazing pony. Whispering soft encouragements to her mount, she took the reigns and jumped up on its back.

'Where are you going?' A man in a monk's habit had spotted her and was running over.

'Home,' she said, galloping past. 'And you and your god would do well to let me go.'

Eighteen

Thunder rolled around the sky and the misty rain turned into a downpour as Æthelfrith took his leave of Degsa's Stone. He touched the smooth grey rock wondering what magical powers, if any, it possessed. It was not quite the height of a grown man and he could almost put his arms around it, yet it stood immovable, tilted to the north-west, the direction in which he would be heading with a cohort of riders to repel the raiders and look for his family. The ancients had worshipped here for generations and human bones had been found in shallow ground around the stone, the remains of young children sacrificed to their gods, they said. Theobald had dismissed the stone as just another old rock before he had departed down the valley to the south-west. Æthelfrith wasn't so sure. The place was too well known. One of his British warriors told him that the stone pointed to certain stars where ancient gods lived. He'd laughed at that because he knew that no one lived in the stars. Stars were just fires kept burning by the gods to light their way around the heavens, and clever men had worked out how to use them to navigate around the earth. He closed his eyes and asked the spirit of the stone to give him the guidance he needed to find Bebba and his son.

He also asked the gods to keep his army well concealed in the wooded valley around the stone. Over two hundred warriors were spread through the hillsides above him and he could not see one of them when he scanned the trees. The omens were good. It was time to go.

He took thirty companion thegns, his elite warriors, all mounted and well-armed, wearing leather helmets and thick jerkins over their mail shirts. They were likely to meet only ill-equipped robbers, but he was in no mood to give them any quarter. And he was in a hurry: he wanted to put a stop to the raiding, find Bebba and return swiftly to make sure that Theobald could deal with the intrigues of the Deirans.

His spirits rose as a fresh breeze swept the rain away to leave clearer skies. The wooded slopes had given way to rolling, open countryside and the rhythmic pounding of the horses' hooves invigorated him. At last, he was doing something about his problems, not brooding on them in his fortress. It was a difficult ride along twisting trails but, before midday, he saw wisps of smoke on the crest of the hilltop ahead. He sent scouts to reconnoitre while he rested his troops. There was nothing worse than going into a skirmish, however small, with tired horses and men. When the scouts reported a burning farmstead in the valley below, he was not surprised: it was precisely raids like this that he had come to investigate. But when Æthelfrith led his men over the hillock and down into a vale, what he found puzzled him. A handful of huts had been torched and their thatched roofs were burning brightly, but there was no sign of inhabitants, dead or alive. Yet he could see cattle still grazing in the nearby field, pigs snuffling in the mud of an enclosure and ducks waddling at the edge of the stream that ran alongside the hamlet. Why hadn't the raiders taken the livestock, which surely they would have valued more highly than a handful of peasant farmers?

'Perhaps they saw us coming, lord,' one of his thegns offered.

'So why make a fire to show us where they were before they had even rounded up the cattle? Why take the villagers, who would slow them down? Something's wrong,' Æthelfrith muttered, scanning the wooded sides of the valley for signs of movement.

'Over there, sire!' Someone was pointing further down the valley to where more dark smoke had begun to billow towards the skies.

'Let's go,' yelled Æthelfrith, urging his mount forward. They might be able to catch whoever had lit that fire.

And they did. But it was not the small band of thieves they were expecting.

As they rode nearer, Æthelfrith began to make out the tops of spears and the waving banners of a warband, an army that was rapidly forming into a shield wall that stretched across the narrow valley floor.

'What the—' he cursed, reigning in his horse and holding up his hand to stop their onward dash. He strained to see the markings on the banners but they were unfamiliar to him. He quickly estimated that nearly a hundred men were blocking his way, but they were not from Strad Clud, whose territory they were entering, he was fairly certain of that. Their shields looked too small, their headgear and clothing strange to his eye. As he stared at this unexpected foe, he felt the skin at the back of his neck crawl with an unknown fear. The burning thatches had acted as beacons leading him to this encounter, he now realised, but for what reason?

He saw the shields part and horsemen make their way through the wall and ride towards him: no doubt a delegation to explain their purpose. Maybe they knew the whereabouts of his wife. The thegn to his right seemed agitated and edged his horse towards him.

'Look , lord, up in the trees. Movement.'

Æthelfrith squinted into the glare of white clouds above the darkened woods. He saw nothing except trees, but he heard the faintest of clinks and clunks, sounds he knew well: the sound of metal armbands jingling and hard shields and spears brushing through undergrowth. He shuddered, remembering Theobald's repeated warnings. It was an ambush. The delegation was a decoy to keep them there while they surrounded them.

'Turn around,' he said calmly to his men. 'It's a trap. We need to lead them back to the Stone.' He wheeled his horse around and broke into a trot back up the valley the way they had come. He never liked to retreat, but when he heard the shouts from both sides of the valley as soldiers ran from the trees towards them, he knew he had made the right decision. They had nearly fallen for the trick and tarried too long.

Then he saw something that made him realise that he had left it too late. Warriors were running in front of the smouldering buildings of the first village to block his path out of the valley.

He slowed his men to assess the situation, looking left and right to find an escape route. Shield walls to the front and to the rear, foot soldiers and bowmen running towards them from both sides. They were surrounded. They had to break through the net that was tightening around them. Where was the weakest point? Probably to the flanks where archers were running forward to get within range. If only Theobald was here; he would work out the best option in a heartbeat.

Æthelfrith remembered his words: *pull back to the Stone if you run into trouble. No brave sorties.*

He had no choice. They had to charge the shields ahead and return to Degsa's Stone, whatever the cost.

As he drew his sword to point the way, he knew his men would not like the choice he had made. They preferred to fight on their own feet, not on the back of a horse. Their mounts had little protection, and archers and spearmen would target them as they charged. Falling from a horse could leave you injured and isolated, easy pickings for soldiers with spears and shields. But to punch a hole in the wall of warriors ahead, thirty horsemen would make more impact than thirty foot soldiers. The cost would be high and he would have to sacrifice many of his men, but he had to survive to lead his hidden army against these invaders.

He tried to make out the banner of the force ahead. It was a white cross on a blue flag, different to the one that was now behind him. He knew that emblem well. It belonged to Áedán mac Gabráin, King of Dál Riata, father of Bebba, grandfather to his son. No wonder his wife had not returned. She could have alerted him to the preparations her father was making to invade his lands, so Áedán would have kept her in Dunadd, the royal stronghold of Dál Riata.

Which side will she be cheering, his or mine?

'Form into three groups. One to attack there, and one there.' He pointed to two points of the shield wall separated by a few paces. 'Your aim is to make a hole in that wall. The third group will stay with me, awaiting your breakthrough. When you see me make it through, follow me back to the Stone.'

His men all nodded. Their faces told Æthelfrith that they knew not many would survive to follow him. They would make the sacrifice that their oaths demanded and try to save their king with their lives.

*

As she urged her pony towards a thicket of trees up the valley, Acha did not dare glance around to see if anyone was raising the alarm. The monk did not run after her. Edwin was still arguing with Maelumai as they stood over Theobald. Her eyes brimmed with tears at the thought of his beautiful, bloodied body lying abandoned, without a friend to watch over him as his spirit departed this world. But she gritted her teeth. She had to get away. She had to find Æthelfrith.

Shouts from the battleground meant that they must have seen her. But the calls turned into roaring screams and the clash of metal. Glancing over, she saw that the remnants of Theobald's thegns were rushing at Maelumai and their dead lord. She didn't know whether they had seen her flight and deliberately tried to help her, or if they were fulfilling their loyal oaths to their leader and dying with him, but the effect was the same. They took any attention away from her and back to the battleground. She did not turn to see what happened but silently thanked Theobald's brave companions.

I will avenge you and your lord.

As she reached the forested slopes above their camp in the earthen-work defences, she coaxed the neck of her pony and dismounted to lead it along deer paths to the north-east. She would follow Theobald's dying wish and go to Æthelfrith. And she had last seen him at Degsa's Stone.

*

Edwin could not believe the foolishness of the giant who stood gloating over the body before them.

'Why did you not stop when I ordered you too?' he yelled.

Maelumai looked puzzled. 'I was told to kill him.'

'Who by?'

Maelumai's answer was drowned by a roar as the remaining group of Bernician thegns who had crouched together behind their shields during the combat, suddenly rushed forward, howling for revenge. Irish soldiers jumped to meet their charge but they could not fully stop the impetus. The thegns pushed their heavy shields forward, knocking Maelumai away from Theobald's body so that they could form a ring around him, where they stood, snarling defiance.

Edwin found himself caught up in the melee, almost bowled over by Irish soldiers forming up around their leader. He stumbled to one side and watched at close quarters as Maelumai unsuccessfully tried to grab the sword that he had stuck into the ground after the combat. It was within Edwin's reach so he yanked it from the earth and watched a mixture of blood and mud trickle down its blade. This was his chance to join a real battle and he held a champion's sword. It was heavier than any weapon he had ever wielded and raising it above his shoulders took considerable effort. He stepped forward to swing it towards an enemy helmet, feeling the grace of the well-balanced weapon as it cut through the air. The feeling of ecstasy as he made his first battle blow was short lived. A firm blade met his own before it reached its target, and he felt a painful jarring throughout his body as he was thrust back off balance.

'Give me that. You'll get yourself killed.' It was Maelumai who plucked the sword from Edwin's grasp and crashed it with a grunt onto the shield before him, which splintered and shook under the blow.

Edwin was shocked that he had not fared better. He stood trembling, unable to rejoin the fray but taking in the foul smell and the raucous din of men as they fought and died. Perhaps he would not make a great warrior after all. He stumbled away, feeling vomit in his throat, but not daring to be sick.

'Are you alright, m'lord?' It was Forthhere, who had run forward to protect his king. 'I don't think they need your help now. It will soon be all over.'

Edwin flinched as a thegn staggered screaming from the ring of fighting, clutching at a spear in his stomach whilst an Irish warrior hacked at his exposed back.

'Let's leave them to it, shall we? We need to go as soon as this is finished,' Forthhere said, leading him away.

'Go where?' Edwin felt transfixed by the fighting as he watched men die before his eyes whilst others gloated over their writhing bodies. Battle practice had never been quite like this.

Forthhere tugged at his sleeve. 'Come and talk with our council of war.' He pulled him towards Lillan, Herin and Rhun, who were in deep conversation at the side of the battleground.

'We agreed with King Áedán that we would join our two forces together as soon as our ambushes were complete so that we can face Æthelfrith's main army as one,' he heard Herin say.

'And where exactly is Áedán?' Lillan asked.

Herin looked frustrated. 'As I told you, he came down from the western isles by ships to the coast of Strad Clud. King Rhydderch did not openly join him in rebellion against Æthelfrith but he did give him free passage through his lands. Áedán should be near the border with Bernicia by now with his Irish allies.'

'How many men do they have?' asked Forthhere.

'Including the Gaels, Áedán was expecting to muster more than two hundred warriors,' Herin replied. 'Together, we will have more than enough to deal with Æthelfrith, even if he does evade Áedán's ambush.'

Edwin was still recovering from his first fleeting experience of the brutality of the battlefield, and he shuddered at the thought of what the news of Theobald's death would do to Æthelfrith's legendary ferocity. But he realised there was no going back.

'We have to kill the devil whilst we have the chance, don't we Brother Rhun?' Edwin was pleased to see Rhun vigorously nodding his agreement. 'I should comfort my sister. She will be shocked by all this.' He looked around the field, where the last of the fighting seemed to be over. 'Where is Acha?'

'I saw her ride from the battlefield, lord. She said she was going home,' Rhun replied.

'Good, she will be safer in Deira.' Edwin said. 'We can find her a suitable husband when we have dealt with Æthelfrith.'

*

Æthelfrith watched as ten of his mounted warriors crashed into the shield wall that blocked their path back towards Degsa's Stone. As the defenders staggered back under the impact of men and mounts, others came to their aid from further along the wall, which was what Æthelfrith expected and hoped. He gave orders to unleash the second charge at the section of the wall that had been weakened by the movement of men to help defend against the first assault. He grimaced as he saw warriors swoop onto the first wave of his companions, drag them from their horses and brutally slaughter them with axes and spears before they could find their feet on the ground. But the second wave were not quite so outnumbered and, although they did not break the line, they were keeping their seats on their mounts, slashing down at the enemy, who backed away to avoid the blows.

It was Æthelfrith's chance. He spurred his war-stallion forward, closely followed by his most experienced thegns. He had seen the hole that he wanted to pass through but, as he charged, men from behind the wall stepped in swiftly to plug the gap. Too late. He wheeled away from the bristling spears that threatened the exposed flanks of his horse, desperately seeking another weak point. The men of his first cohort were all down, a few still fighting on foot, some lifeless on the ground, others writhing from their wounds.

It was the wounded that drew his attention. Two horses thrashed together on their backs in the mud, and Æthelfrith saw the wall open as men pulled back from their flying hooves

'To me!' he shouted to his ten men and charged straight for the injured horses. His mount reared up at the sight of the animals that kicked and whinnied on the ground, but Æthelfrith dug in his heels and his stallion jumped then stumbled over the wounded animals as if he were clearing a ditch. He was through.

As he galloped away he heard the whistle of arrows overhead and the thump of spears dropping close by but soon they were falling short. He turned to see who followed. No one was close behind. His fists tightened on the reins. He hated to leave his loyal companions to their fate. They were all the friends he had in the world, except for his brother and maybe his wife.

Slowing his horse, he brought it round to face the enemy. He wanted them to see that he had escaped so that they would follow him. He had his own trap to spring further along the valley. Kneeling up on his saddle, he yelled curses towards the blue and white banner that fluttered above Áedán's army.

'I spit on your god of the cross. He died, just like you all will. I will kill you all.'

At that moment, the wall of soldiers parted, and horsemen dashed through, not his men but enemy warriors coming hard towards him. He may have stayed too long. It was a long way to Degsa's Stone and a group of riders could usually run down a single horseman over that distance. He counted ten or more, not odds that favoured him. Putting his head low to his mount's mane, he urged it into a gallop over the soft ground.

Shouts from behind made him glance back. Several of his own horsemen had broken though the wall and were in pursuit of his pursuers. The odds were getting better but still not good enough for him to turn and fight. He glanced up to the sky that was brightening after the storm, patches of blue showing through the scudding clouds. The weather would not hide him. It would be an interesting ride.

*

Acha looked furtively past the brushwood at the edge of the forest. She saw the valley stretching green and empty below her. To keep herself hidden, she had guided her pony along narrow trails through the wooded hillside, pushing her way through thickets and brambles that tore at her clothes and scratched at her face. Could she now risk riding out in the open? It would be faster than in the tracks she was following though the trees, and she was sure she could make Degsa's Stone before nightfall. Æthelfrith would surely have posted some scouts to watch over his army and they would come to her rescue. She gingerly pushed her way through the undergrowth and onto soft grass still wet from the rain. She allowed her pony a quick drink from the stream that gurgled down the dale before she clambered thankfully onto its back for the final stage of the journey.

The sun had begun to dip towards the horizon behind her when she first glimpsed the Stone, standing like a solitary sign at the meeting point of two valleys. The area seemed deserted and eerily quiet. The wind had dropped and no longer stirred the branches of the trees, and even the birds had stopped their singing. There was no sign of Æthelfrith, nor his warriors. She dismounted and walked the final few paces to Degsa's Stone. Theobald had chosen this spot as the main base for the army. Why, oh why had he gone to meet Edwin with so few men, when they had such a large warband waiting here? If only he had taken more warriors, he would still be with her, smiling down on her from his horse as he always did.

'Lord Æthelfrith!' she yelled as loud as she could. 'Its Acha. Where are you? I've news.'

Her voice echoed around the slopes of the valley but there was no reply. She repeated her call several times before slumping to the floor, her back resting against the dark rock, closing her eyes to block out the solitude that seemed to surround her. She felt the solidness of the rock against her skin. It had probably been there for generations, unmoving, untouched by the turbulence around it. She wished the stone could take her back just one day, to the moment when she had set out in the rain with Theobald to arrange their marriage. How stupid they had been! They didn't have to ask Edwin's permission to be together. They could have lived happily for the rest of their days without marrying. Now—

'Lady Acha, is that you?'

She opened her eyes, blinking in the glare of the sun, and scrambled to her feet. A group of armed men stood looking curiously at her. She sighed with relief as she recognised their leader.

'Thank the gods. I've found you, Leax. Where is your lord?' She addressed her question to her father's thegn whom she knew was now one of Æthelfrith's most trusted captains.

'Are you hurt, my lady?' Leax asked, stepping closer, inspecting her face.

'Hurt?' Acha dabbed at her forehead, noticing the blood for the first time. 'No, its just a scratch. Take me to your king. I need to speak urgently with him.'

'He has not yet returned, m'lady. He rode north this morning to hunt down the raiders.' He pointed over his shoulder to the vale behind him.

Acha groaned. 'Then you must fetch him back. Theobald and his men have been—' She stopped herself from blurting out the awful news. 'They've been ambushed by a warband.'

Æthelfrith was sweating profusely even though the sun was sinking towards the tree line. The drubbing of hooves behind was much louder now, and he knew the sound came from his enemy's horses. His men had fallen further behind; maybe their mounts had been wounded in the fight to get through the wall or just tired after a hard day's ride. He patted the neck of his own stallion, knowing that it was blowing hard and had little left to give. A thud beside him and a glimpse of a spear quivering in the ground told him the enemy were close, very close. They had the range and would soon improve their direction. It was time to turn and fight. He wheeled his horse up a slope before a bend in the valley; he wanted to gain the advantage of height over the enemy riders. Drawing his sword as a signal to his own horsemen that it was the moment to fight for their lives, he steadied himself for the charge, calculating where to strike first.

To his surprise, the chasing horsemen reined in, pointing not at him but further along the valley. They had seen something and it caused them to pause and talk urgently amongst themselves. Although he strained up in his saddle, a hillock obscured his view from whatever it was. The distraction was Æthelfrith's cue to charge, yelling loudly, hoping that his own warriors would reach his pursuers at the same time as he would. He noticed that the leading horseman looked up at him and glanced once more along the valley before barking a command. Amazingly, they pulled on their reigns to turn their mounts and were soon galloping back the way they had come, swerving wide to avoid his men who were struggling up behind them. Æthelfrith jeered loudly at the fleeing enemy but he did not give chase. Finally, he could see what had caused them to run and he laughed loudly with relief. A cohort of his army was force-marching swiftly towards him. It was just what he needed. Enough men to save him but too few to deter Áedán's army further down the valley from giving chase.

*

For a heartbeat, Acha thought that Theobald had returned. Seeing the familiar jutting jaw, boyish grin and tousled blonde hair, she almost flew to greet him. But when he swung long legs to the ground and looked towards her with a puzzled expression, she blinked, knowing that it was Æthelfrith. Her mouth went dry. How was she to tell him?

'Acha, what's happened?'

'A warband surprised us, lord. Theobald sent me to warn you.'

'And Theobald is still holding them back, is that it? I should take men to relieve him?'

'No, lord. He is dead.' Acha could hardly believe she had said the word, and the look of disbelief on Æthelfrith's face almost made her doubt it herself.

'Dead? He cannot be dead.'

'I'm sorry, he died bravely, with all his men.'

There, she'd said it.

I wish I'd died with him. My life has lost all its meaning and joy.

'With his dying breath, he told me to come to you, to warn you, so I have.'

'He's... You've... ' His unblinking eyes did not move from her face, and she held his gaze, unsure of what to do or say. He covered his mouth with his hands and slowly walked towards the giant stone that stood close to where she had been waiting for his return. He gripped the dark rock as though he intended to strangle it and threw back his head with a deep roar.

'No! You should have taken me, not him.'

Æthelfrith began to beat the stone with his fists, slowly at first but rising to a frenzy of hitting and shouting. When his voice sounded hoarse and he could rail no more, he laid his head on the cold stone, snuffling and breathing heavily.

Acha could not watch and turned away to hide her own tears. Abruptly, Æthelfrith became calm and spoke to her again, wiping at his eyes.

'How many ambushed you?'

She had been estimating this for some time, knowing he would ask. 'A hundred or more, I think,' she said, trying to compose herself as he had done.

'Do we know where they are now?' He turned to his thegn for this information.

'We think half a day's march to the south-west,' Leax said.

'And Áedán's army, where is that now?'

'Close by, lord. They will be here shortly, before sunset.'

Æthelfrith's eyes narrowed. 'My brother told me to pull back to the Stone and that is what we've done. We'll spring the surprise he arranged for them.'

Nineteen

Æthelfrith sat, head in hands, on the rotten remains of a fallen tree, trying to compose his thoughts for the coming fight. He was aware that the warriors around him were quietly making their final preparations, honing already-sharp blades and tightening leather helmets, patiently waiting for his final battle orders. Yet his head was too full of the past to clearly consider the present. He was trying desperately hard not to think about Theobald; the time to relive his life would come later, in the mead hall when they would take turns to tell his story. Now, he had a battle to win. But hard as he tried, he could not help but hear his brother's voice.

What exactly is your plan for this battle?

Theobald always asked him that before every skirmish, no matter how small.

Always know how you are going to win, he would say.

Today Æthelfrith's answer was simple: his plan was to surprise the enemy when they rode into the valley. At sunset, his men would fall on them from their hideaways in the steep wooded hillside.

The disapproving voice was not convinced: *Their scouts*

will find you and warn them. They will halt on the hill above the valley. What will you do then? Attack them up a rise?

That was a good point. Unless he could ensure that the enemy army descended into the valley, he could not spring his surprise assault. If Áedán halted his troops overnight on the ridge, the warband that had ambushed Theobald might join him. That could give the enemy superior numbers. When he was younger he might have been content to let the gods decide such matters. He thought he could win wherever and whenever he engaged the enemy because Thunor and Tiw were with him. After several close-run encounters, his brother had convinced him otherwise. Theobald did not believe that the gods decided who would have victory. Nor that brave individuals won battles, despite how they bragged of such feats in the mead hall. Theobald said that what happened before a sword was drawn counted for more than the events on the battlefield itself. Æthelfrith had laughed at him at first. But when they won encounter after encounter and had beaten back an enemy that had taken their very own stronghold not so long ago, he had begun to realise he was right. The intensive practice drills and the defensive earthworks they built across their territory made his army hard to beat. Their thorough gathering of intelligence and careful manoeuvring before any battle meant that they could defeat forces that were invariably more numerous than their own. As their leader, Æthelfrith always took the glory with his flamboyant fighting, but he came to recognise that it was Theobald who was really behind their victories. What was he to do, now that he was—? No, he could not bring himself to even think about that.

His brother's voice was badgering him again: *You're up against Áedán the Wily. He will have some tricks of his own. What do you know about his plan?*

He had assumed that his plan was to invade Bernicia and drive out his kin for good. That's what the British had been striving to do ever since his grandfather Ida had landed his warships on the coast near Bebbanburg. So why had they raided farmsteads? And what role was Edwin playing in all this? Was is just a coincidence he was nearby when the warband struck, or was it all part of an elaborate plot? If only Theobald was still alive, he could tell him. An image of his brother flashed into his mind, walking up the courtyard of Bebbanburg, a smile on his face and Acha on his arm. She would have made him a good wife, no doubt, but why had he used his last words to tell her to come to him? She said she had to warn him, but of what? It wouldn't have been Áedán's ambush, because she couldn't have known about that. It must be something else. It would be painful to question her closely about Theobald's last moments, but he had no choice.

Leax raised his eyebrows when the king asked him to fetch Acha, but he ran to do his bidding nonetheless. When she arrived, Æthelfrith could not help notice her red eyes and drawn face, a very different girl to the one he had watched strolling happily through his fortress.

'Tell me how you were trapped?' he asked curtly, knowing that the time remaining to deploy his forces was running out. 'Why didn't Theobald retreat back here as he'd planned?'

Acha's brow furrowed. 'He couldn't. They attacked from the rear whilst we were talking to Edwin and his thegns.'

'Were they British?'

'I don't think so. They spoke in a strange tongue and wore checked garments that I did not recognise.'

'Gaels! Must be a warband from Ireland.'

'They kept chanting their leader's name. Maelumai, I think it was,' Acha continued.

'And did Theobald say exactly what you were to warn me of?'

'No, he started to say something about Herin, but he didn't finish.'

'Herin? Was he there?'

'I've never met him, lord, so I wouldn't recognise him. I didn't see Ælfric, just Edwin and his thegns. But there was someone else who came with the attackers but was not dressed like them. He was the only one who wore a helmet.'

'With a boar's crest?'

'It did have a crest that could have been a boar but it was too far away for me to be certain. He hung back from the main fighting.'

Before Acha could say another word, Æthelfrith brushed past her and called to Leax. Suddenly, he knew why Theobald had told her to warn him. He felt like hugging Acha. Trust Theobald to think of sending her with his last breath. But it was not the moment for thanks. He had to change his battle plan.

*

Acha felt confused when Æthelfrith pushed past her and started giving orders to Leax and other thegns, who gathered quickly around him. Perhaps she should have said how Edwin had tried to save Theobald; she didn't want her brother blamed for his death, but there was no time to explain. The warband was on the move. Men swung their shields onto their backs and crept quietly along the hillside, touching the charms around their necks, mouthing silent appeals to the gods. She stood alone in the forest and watched as Æthelfrith prepared his men for war. She heard him tell Leax to keep his warriors hidden in the trees until Áedán's army had advanced to the Stone.

'It is important that you wait until you can attack from the rear,' she heard him say. 'Don't forget to use the archers first, but not on us!'

Soon a group of about thirty warriors had gathered around Æthelfrith, and she watched, engrossed, as they quickly redeployed out of the dense forest and into a clearer patch of woodland higher up the valley. There, they erected makeshift shelters and seemed to be setting up camp for the night. To her, it was a strange strategy until Leax explained that Æthelfrith was setting a snare to lure the enemy down towards the narrow, steep-sided gully around the Stone. And by the way Æthelfrith was making himself visible around the camp, she realised that he was using himself as the bait.

Leax told her to return to where she had been stationed with the small band of thegn-sons, who were too young to fight but old enough to act as servants to the army. As she trudged back up the hillside away from the battle zone, she found herself gnawing at her fingernails, willing Æthelfrith to survive. She wanted him to live because – she hesitated to admit it, even to herself – he seemed like the only person left to her in the whole world right now.

*

Æthelfrith watched with satisfaction as the enemy scout galloped hastily back to the crest of the hill. He could have run his sword through him when he surprised him in the woods, but he had feigned injury so that he would survive to tell Áedán that his prey, the King of Bernicia, was not far away. Now that he knew of Herin's treachery, he could answer his brother's questions: he knew his enemy's plan. It was simply to ambush and kill him so that Herin could rule in his place, no doubt under Áedán's authority. They did not want to fight his army and still did not know that it was nearby. They would find out soon enough. First, he had to make them believe that they could achieve their plan.

'We need to move out,' he shouted loudly in case other spies were within hearing. 'Leave the shelters and the cooking gear, just grab your weapons.'

Out of the corner of his eye he saw foot soldiers appear on the hilltop.

Closer than I thought, much closer. We really do have to hurry.

He stumbled from the clearing and turned to race down the side of the valley followed by his warriors. Ahead, he could just make out Degsa's Stone, the killing zone he intended for Áedán's army. It seemed to beckon to him from the shadowy gully but it was still far off and suddenly he was not sure they would make it. Shouts from behind told him that the warband was in hot pursuit. Soon he heard their high-pitched keening and he glanced around. They were lightly armed and much quicker than he had expected. Soon, they would be within a spear's throw of his men. Should he risk losses or turn sooner than he had planned? The fleet-footed enemy outnumbered them and they could be overwhelmed before they made it to the safety of his hidden army around the Stone. At that moment, he felt his long legs tripping on the rocky surface and he slithered in the mud. It was a sign.

'Turn to face them,' he gasped, sliding to a halt, drawing his short stabbing seax to face the first onslaught. 'For Theobald!' he yelled, and his thegns echoed his cry as they jostled into position to stand shoulder to shoulder with their king.

They hit them like hailstones drumming on a hard roof, countless men throwing themselves against the wall of their stout shields. They surprised Æthelfrith with their tactics for they did not stay to slug it out toe-to-toe as opponents normally did. Rather they darted in, making quick thrusts with light spears and small shields before they fell back to leave another line to throw themselves forward, always probing for the weak points. The speed of their attacks was most effective at the two ends of the wall, where they ran behind the defensive line to stab at the exposed backs of the hard-pressed thegns. Æthelfrith's warriors were well drilled and knew how to deal with that tactic, curving their wall into a semicircle to make it harder to penetrate. But they had never before met such fast and furious probing. Æthelfrith heard the desperate cries of his wing men and saw one stagger from the line to be hacked down by a swarm of attackers.

'Tighten the line!' he shouted, urging his men into a ring as the only way to stop the enemy from getting behind them. He knocked his heavy shield into the face of a screaming attacker and cursed as the thrust of his blade fell short of the man's body. His short sword was the weapon of choice when men stood shield against shield, close enough together to smell the stinking breath and hear the grunts from the other side as they tried to maim each other with quick jabs and prods. But for this fight he needed a longer weapon so that he could counter their darting attacks with a scything swing or the stab of a long spear.

Worse, the tight ring they had been forced to adopt made it almost impossible to retreat towards the Stone, where his reserves waited. They were stuck where they were, surrounded by fleet-footed fighters who buzzed around them like swarming bees. His patience snapped as he smashed his shield into an attacker and he chased him from the wall, stabbing at his exposed chest when the man stumbled, feeling his blade slice between ribs as he fell. Roaring his defiance, he grabbed a spear from the ground so he could reach more of the enemy who now stood taunting him, daring him forward. Time slowed and he felt the red mist flow through his body.

No brave sorties.

The voice in his head stopped him just as he was about to leap forward. The enemy were standing off him and now he could see why. It was not because they feared him, but because a new wave of heavily armed warriors were arriving and archers were readying their bows. This was not the moment for him to be caught exposed in front of the shield wall. His thegns were urging him to retreat and he heeded them for once and withdrew to the protection of the ring. He waved his spear towards the forest behind, hoping that Leax would realise their predicament and launch his attack even though they had not reached the Stone. But as a shower of arrows rained down on them, followed closely by a wave of yelling warriors thrusting spears between their shields, there was no sign of reinforcements.

*

Acha waited anxiously amongst the thegn-sons in the makeshift camp high above the valley floor. They were unable to see much through the thick branches, so no one spoke as they strained to interpret the shouts of triumph and pain that drifted up from below. She found it impossible to even guess what was happening and grew increasingly exasperated.

'Why don't you climb a tree to get a better view and tell us what is happening?' she suggested to one lad who seemed to be in charge. He shrugged, unsure if he should obey the princess he'd been told to look after. A slim thegn-son looked at Acha with wide, admiring eyes.

'I'll do it,' he said, and before anyone could stop him, he was expertly shinning up the tallest tree. As he reached the highest branches, they bent and swayed under his weight but he scrambled on until he reached a point where he could peer down into the valley.

'The king and his band are surrounded. There's troops dashing all around them. There's more coming along the valley, archers too,' he shouted. 'He's got a whole army against him.'

Acha's mouth went dry as she pictured Theobald in exactly the same predicament.

'Where's Leax and the rest of our army?' she shouted up to him.

The youth moved branches to clear his line of vision towards the Stone.

'Can't see them nowhere,' he called.

Why aren't they doing something?

Acha's mind flashed back to the moment when Theobald and his small band were caught between the fire of archers and the assault of heavily armed troops smashing into their frail wall. She could not let that happen again.

Before anyone could stop her she ran to her pony that was tethered nearby, jumped onto its back and kicked it hard.

'Hey! Where do you think you're going? We're meant to guard you,' she heard the thegn-son say, but he was too late to stop her. She had to find Leax.

Urging her pony along a rocky trail between the trees that descended on either side of the crest, she rode quickly to the point that she calculated lay above Degsa's Stone.

'Leax!' she called as loudly as she could; but her voice vanished, unreturned, into the thick forest. Cursing to herself, she slid from the saddle and stumbled down through the trees, still calling for Leax and his men. As she struggled through brittle branches, a strong hand caught her arm.

'Quiet m'lady. You'll give our position away.' A burley thegn appeared from behind a tree, and the forest seemed to spring to life as she made out one warrior after another crouching in the undergrowth.

'Where's Leax? I have a message from the king,' she blurted, breathing hard, knowing how costly every lost moment could be.

The thegn whistled twice like a bird and she heard the call repeated in the distance.

'Be quick,' she urged, straining to make out figures in the shafts of sunlight that shone through the leaves.

Someone standing by a stout trunk waved and the thegn pointed in his direction.

'Follow me. Quietly,' he said.

She knew that silence was not what was needed but she scurried along behind the thegn as softly as she could. When she recognised Leax outlined in a pool of light between the branches, she sighed with relief and nearly tripped over deadwood in her haste to reach him.

'The king is in grave danger. You must attack the enemy now,' she blurted as soon as she was within earshot. At that moment, a breeze blew distant sounds of battle to their ears and she could see Leax's eyes widen in disbelief.

'Where is the king? Our orders were to wait until he had retreated to the Stone.'

'I know, but the enemy caught him and surrounded him so he cannot retreat. They used the same tactics to kill Theobald. First the fast soldiers, next the archers and finally the heavy troops. You must attack now before it's too late.' She was gabbling, realising that she had to convince Leax but not knowing quite how to make him trust a woman in military matters.

'Æthelfrith himself ordered it,' she added seeing the doubt still on his face.

'The king—'

'Yes, we were close by and he shouted, and I had a horse and the thegn-sons didn't, so I came with the order. Attack now. To save your king.'

It was the best she could do.

*

Æthelfrith heard the arrows whistling skyward towards them.

'Shields up!' he ordered.

At that moment, foot soldiers attacked in unison. As they struck his men, he realised this was a different type of assault. These warriors wore thick leather armour and carried long shields. They did not turn and run but stayed to stab and jab whilst yelling in a tongue he did not fully understand. As he braced his shield to check the charge of a bulky warrior, Æthelfrith heard his howling change to a scream of pain and he pitched forward, clutching at an arrow in the back of his neck. His head slammed against the boss of Æthelfrith's battered shield, almost forcing him off balance. Stepping back, he knocked into one of his own thegns who was staggering with an arrow shaft in his cheek. His men looked bewildered: they didn't know whether to use their defences against the deadly hail of arrows from above or the assault of fresh soldiers to the front. Áedán didn't seem to care that he was killing some of his own men. He had plenty enough of them, it seemed. They were lining up four of five deep around Æthelfrith's small band, waiting their turn to batter at their defences. Æthelfrith cursed as another thegn fell, and he sprang forward, shouting for the ring of shields to tighten once more.

He had never before fought in a circle as enclosed as this and the longer it went on, the more he realised that there was no escape. It was impossible to make a sally into the enemy and nowhere to run and regroup. Why wasn't Leax coming? He began to wish his orders to wait at the Stone had not been so specific. If only he could get a message to him. The point of a spear appeared through the linden wood of his shield. He needed to concentrate on his fighting and think less about the tactics. He used to leave that to Theobald and let the red rage in his head take care of the rest. That was something that would have to change if—

The men behind him began roaring in unison. It was the battlecry that invoked the most famous of their ancestors: 'Ida!

Ida!' He could only admire their spirit and he threw himself forward, plunging his seax towards a shoulder that had strayed within range, slicing into soft muscle before he met hard bone. The enemy captains barked orders, unintelligible to him but which seemed to lift the pressure on their defensive ring as the ranks of warriors surrounding it began to melt away. The light was fading, so maybe they were calling a pause before one final assault before nightfall. The warriors at his back continued to chant and shout defiance and he risked a glance over his shoulder. What he saw almost brought tears to his eyes.

An army – his army – was advancing swiftly along the valley floor. They had finally sprung Theobald's surprise.

Twenty

Once more, Acha stood in the forest wondering what to do. Leax had used urgent whistles and hand signals to order his men to move rapidly out of the woods. They didn't wait to take up any particular formation but scampered as fast as their heavy clothing and weapons would allow towards the battle that soon became visible to them in the distance. Acha had been told to return to the thegn-sons on top of the wooded slopes but what was unfolding before her was too interesting to miss. Looking down at her tattered, blood-stained clothes, she realised that no one would recognise her as any sort of princess, so she tucked up her tunic and ran after the troops.

The quickest men were the archers with their light equipment and they soon outstripped the main force. Theobald had been passionate about his bowmen. He had once explained to her that it took a lifetime to train a warrior who did nothing but fight, drink and eat at the king's cost.

'Bowmen, on the other hand, can be farmers' sons who train by shooting at rabbits during the harvest and who eat from their family table, not ours,' he'd said to her.

As a result, this army had a large cohort of Theobald's archers and they were about to wreak their revenge for his death. Some in the rear lines of the enemy saw them coming but their warning shouts to turn were too late. The first volley hit the Irish troops with deadly effect. As the shafts tore into their exposed backs, men crumpled, screaming, and the next line turned to try and ward off another torrent of missiles. Acha could see that the rear of the enemy was made up largely of the light soldiers whose small shields did little to protect them from the hail of arrows. Maddened by this stinging attack, they did what they were trained to do. They ran, yelling wildly, towards their tormentors. Acha gritted her teeth in anticipation, having watched Theobald train his bowmen what to do in this very situation in the fields near Bebbanburg. They loosened off their final shots and turned to the shelter of the warriors who were approaching rapidly behind them. Gaps opened up in the defensive wall for the archers to scurry through before the toughened shields crunched together to meet the charge.

As the formations clashed, Acha heard Æthelfrith's men begin to chant the name of their illustrious forefather, Ida, before an even louder cry of 'Theobald!' echoed around the valley. The well-equipped thegns who had been resting, pent up in the forest, tore eagerly into Áedán's weary warriors who had done nothing but march and fight all day. Once they had slashed and smashed their way through the first rank, they ran to attack the next who were still confused as to which way to turn. Acha saw the ground littered with injured men, some imploring their god to take them swiftly to his heaven, others just moaning with pain. Although she shuddered at the sight of such carnage, she was enjoying the panic that was now besetting the enemy that had been attacked in the rear – just as Theobald had planned. She hoped Æthelfrith was alive to appreciate it too.

*

After the traumas of the day, energy and elation was pouring into Æthelfrith in equal measure. He could see a way out. His small band was still shackled by a ring of warriors, but he could sense the doubt in their nervous glances to see what was happening elsewhere. And doubt bred fear and disorder. This was the moment to break out of their encirclement, but which way?

Don't become separated. Keep your forces together. He could hear Theobald's voice on the practice field as he drilled his captains in how to lead. He should fight towards his own, advancing army. But he was facing the wrong way.

'Close ranks around me!' he ordered and withdrew his shield from the wall. He hardly dare look down as he stumbled over bodies to the other side of the circle. Too many familiar faces lay there, their bodies broken and battered, some unmoving, others trembling and cursing their pain. No one asked for his help and he gave none. There was a battle to be won. They would understand that.

He looked over the heads of his thegns to get a sight of the battle outside their circle. His troops were rampaging forward, scything down Irish soldiers like farmers cutting corn. He caught sight of a hunched figure on a tall stallion whose chainmail glinted in the setting sun as he urged his retreating troops to form a shield wall to stop the rout.

It was the unmistakeable figure of Áedán.

They must be desperate for an ancient like him to be in the action.

But Áedán's urgent orders were having the desired effect. His mixed force from Dál Riata and Ireland were no longer running away but were forming a human barricade across the valley to stop the advance of Æthelfrith's men, who would soon be forced into a slugging match, a battle of attrition in which there would be no certain winners, only countless casualties.

The Bernician archers had retired, unable to fire when friend and foe were at such close quarters. And Æthelfrith was still trapped on the wrong side of the battle.

He made a gap for himself in the front line of his own beleaguered band.

'Advance together!' he called, urging them to break through the enemy ring and head towards the bigger battle that raged beyond them. Moving such a tight formation whilst still fighting was difficult. Gaps in their defences would appear as they struggled forward but he had to take the risk. There was a second problem: push as they might, the enemy did not budge. Rather, they shoved back even harder, so they were in danger of losing ground. They were up against relatively fresh Dál Riatan warriors, Æthelfrith realised, and they knew about fighting in a shield wall. He had to do something.

As they heaved again, Æthelfrith felt his foot catch on the limb of a fallen body. Cursing, he glanced down and saw something of his brother in the thegn's face that lay senseless beneath him. Maybe it was the glazed blue eyes or the blonde moustache smattered with blood. Whatever it was, the red rage took over his senses. He let out a blood-curdling howl and used the full power of his mighty frame to lunge forward, crashing his shield into a warrior on his left and stabbing his short sword into a helmet to his right. The enemy sagged before his onslaught as if some supernatural being had charged into their midst. He countered a spear thrust with his blade and swatted away the slash of a sword as bodies fell away before him and the enemy lines opened up. His thegns urgently hacked and parried behind him, forming into a wedge shape with Æthelfrith as the deadly tip that sliced through the ranks surrounding them.

Once they had broken through, they could move at speed, almost running whilst still clinging to their formation.

Æthelfrith did not stop until he reached his target: the rear of the shield wall that stood against his army.

'Spread wider,' he yelled as they smashed into the backs of Áedán's men. Having been turned once, the enemy had to turn again and face the mighty king of Bernicia in all his fury. He struck at the tip of the embattled lines so that Leax's troops could use the gap that opened up to get behind the enemy formation.

From that instant, the battle changed. From a slugging match of two equal sides, it suddenly became a slaughter. When Áedán's left flank broke and scattered, the disorder infected the rest of the line like a virulent plague. The Irish troops had suffered badly in the first assault and were the first to turn. The Dál Riatan troops fought on but once their king could see the outcome and reigned his horse around to ride hard to the north, his men soon followed him and ran in confusion from the conflict.

Æthelfrith shook his fist at the retreating army. Dusk was falling fast and the evening star was already twinkling above the horizon. Theobald was watching, nodding his approval.

*

Acha watched transfixed as the battle unfolded before her in the dying light of the day. Æthelfrith's soldiers had finally burst through the line of enemy troops and poured after them like a river breaching its banks to flood the surrounding fields. Suddenly she could see him, towering above those around him, bellowing orders and chasing down a group of fleeing warriors. Æthelfrith had survived. He was her last hope, the only person who could avenge the terrible deed that had been done earlier. She closed her eyes and began sobbing with relief now that the enemy was in full flight.

As the din of battle receded, she became aware of noises closer to her: low moaning and sharp cries, muttered prayers and vulgar curses – the sounds of men suffering. She scanned the grassy slopes, suddenly shocked by the sight of so many shattered bodies, some motionless and silent, others thrashing and twitching, some heaped up one on the other, others doubled over in pain. One in particular caught her eye because he was watching her and began to crawl agonisingly slowly in her direction, an arm outstretched, beckoning to her. He wore no helmet and his fresh face and unkempt hair told her that he was young, probably no older than she was. She wanted to turn and run from the horrors around her but something in the youth's desperate look made her hesitate. Surely she should do something for him? His checked clothing told her he was probably an enemy warrior and he might harm her if she allowed him near. She fingered the knife she had taken earlier from Theobald as he lay dying, knowing that she would have wanted someone, anyone, to have cared for him in a similar situation.

'Wait and I'll be back,' she shouted, scurrying towards the edge of the woods, immediately realising what a ridiculous thing she had just said: he was hardly in a state to run away. Searching around in the undergrowth, she found some moss to dig up with her knife and even nettles to cut. Hilda and other healers of her village had taught her something of their craft, so she knew that the first treatment for flesh wounds was to stem the bleeding before the patient's strength ebbed away with their blood. Folding up the bottom of her tunic to make a carrier for her finds, she little thought about how much of her slender legs she was exposing to view. The young man was looking expectantly in her direction, crouched on one knee as she ran back.

'I thought you were an angel,' he gasped. 'But angels don't show a man such fine flesh.'

Acha blushed and let go of her tunic so that it unfurled, dropping her pickings to the ground.

'Just lie still and don't try anything or you will be dead.' She waved her knife at him and grabbed the sword away from his side.

He rolled over obediently and she immediately saw the gash in his thigh beneath red-stained trousers. It did not take her long to staunch the flow of blood with moss and bind it with cloth that she tore from his tunic.

'May the holy Columba bless you. My name is Conaing mac Áedán and you will be well rewarded for saving me.' It was the first time that she had heard either name but it would not be the last.

*

Æthelfrith rested wearily on his sword and waved Leax over to him. His men were chasing down the remnants of Áedán's army but he did not want to overextend his forces in the twilight.

'Regroup our warriors, Leax. We don't want to be caught off guard by the other warband that must be close by. Oh, and well done for rescuing me from my little predicament,' he said.

Leax chuckled. 'Just following your orders, lord. Although I did not expect them from a woman.'

'A woman? How so?'

Leax looked puzzled. 'Why, the Lady Acha, who told us of your plight and your instruction to attack.'

'Acha? I—.' He stopped himself. 'Where is she now?'

'I asked her to return to the thegn-sons for safekeeping, lord. They should have descended to the battlefield by now to help our wounded.'

'Then I must find her and thank her.'

It did not take Aethelfrith long, although he could scarcely believe his eyes when he did see her. She was bent over a wounded warrior binding his wounds, her hands covered in blood, her face grubby, her tunic dirty and torn.

'Hardly the work of a princess,' he called as he strode towards her. 'We train the thegn-sons to do that.'

She looked up and half-smiled. 'I wish I could do more, m'lord king. Too many men have died for one day.'

'Not enough of Áedán's men for my liking. They must pay the price for what he has done,' he said.

Acha tossed back her hair and wiped grime from her forehead. 'There is at least one of the enemy you should save.' She pointed towards Conaing, who crouched close to where she worked. 'He is Áedán's son.'

Aethelfrith stared at the young man, who grinned and tried to stand until Acha put a restraining hand on his shoulder. 'I told you not to move or you will bleed.'

The man grimaced and sat down again. 'You said he was a king and it is good manners to stand… '

'Which son are you, lad?' Æthelfrith quickly knelt beside him, looking him up and down for weapons, noting the red-stained cloth around his leg.

'Conaing, half-brother of your wife – if I'm right in thinking you are King Æthelfrith?'

'I am. You know where Queen Bebba is?'

Conaing grinned. 'Oh, I can tell you where she is alright, your boy too, but I'm thinking my life might be worth less if I did.'

'You'll be dead if you don't,' Æthelfrith snarled, reaching for his knife.

'Then we'd both be none the wiser,' Conaing chuckled.

Acha was surprised at his confidence, perhaps over-confidence considering his predicament.

'I think you owe something of your life to me. You would have bled to death if I hadn't tended to your wounds.'

'To be sure I'm in your debt and in return I offer you my protection in the land of the Dál Riata, should you ever need it.' Conaing spat on the palm of his hand. 'I so swear in the name of the Holy Father.' He stretched out his arm towards Acha.

Æthelfrith pushed Conaing's hand down impatiently. 'If you are the king's son, you'll be secure enough. I will hold you hostage against the safety of my own family. Now, tell me what you know of Bebba and my son, Eanfrith.'

'Your boy was held in Dunadd when I left.'

'And his mother?' asked Æthelfrith.

'She was the one holding him,' Conaing said, laughing.

*

Edwin felt an involuntary tremor run through his body and he clenched his hands to stop them shaking.

'Defeated? Áedán's army has been beaten?'

It was Rhun who had woken him, just as he had finally fallen asleep amongst the trees where they had pitched camp for the night.

'Yes, lord. Our scouts are sure that Æthelfrith prevailed last night. He will come after us with a much larger army than we can muster. Maelumai and the Gaels are preparing to leave. We have no choice but to go with them.'

'Go where?'

'They are heading west to return to Ireland. We should go with them to the coast for protection. I will return to Gwynedd. You could come with me.'

'To Gwynedd? You mean go into... to exile?' Edwin hated that word. It sounded worse than death to him. He had heard stories of warriors forced to leave their kin through some misdeed to live a miserable life in damp caverns or forest groves, friendless and unprotected, to die of hunger or eaten by wolves. That was not a life for him. He was still a king.

Lillan arrived with Forthhere, dragging their horses and packs, alarm in their faces.

'We must go, lord. Æthelfrith is camped so close that his scouts must find us soon. He will blame us for his brother's death and he will not be in a forgiving mood.'

'What of my sister, Acha?'

'We have no news of her,' Lillan replied.

'She told me she loved Theobald and wanted to marry him. She'll be very unhappy now too,' Edwin said, gazing out at the early morning sky.

'The good Lord works in wondrous ways. She will find contentment through her grief, as will we,' Rhun said, following Edwin to his horse.

'Does your god always run before the devil like this?' Edwin asked.

Rhun put a comforting hand on Edwin's shoulder. 'We will pray for our Lord's protection. His kingdom will come and Satan will be defeated. But we need to survive long enough to see it.'

Twenty-One

Æthelfrith saw the first glimmer of daybreak and scrambled to his feet.

'Up, up. Let's move,' he shouted, watching to make sure the sentries echoed his orders throughout the camp of weary warriors. He had only managed a few moments of fitful dozing during the short night, his mind full of bitter regret. If only he had heeded Theobald's warnings, if only he had not divided his forces, if only, if only... He could think of countless ways he could have changed what had happened. Maybe the gods were punishing him, but for what? Taking the kingship when it could have gone to Herin on his father's death? He looked up at the sky that had cleared of cloud and glimmered with stars, the torches of the gods. A flash caught his eye, a brief trail of light illuminating the greyness to the west.

A sign. Theobald was surely with the gods now, urging him to take revenge.

'We go after the villains who killed my brother,' he called to Leax, who was awaiting orders. His first thought had been to pursue Áedán back to Dunadd to finish off the Dál Riatans for good and to retrieve Bebba and his son now that he knew where they were. But Áedán had been badly mauled and would not pose a threat for what remained of his life, which surely would not be long. He held one of his sons as hostage for the return of his own, thanks to Acha. He would send a messenger to arrange the exchange and a tribute from their farms. Otherwise he would leave them to lick their wounds.

As his army stirred into life and prepared to march out, Æthelfrith strode to the rear of the column that was forming up, casting his eyes around the small band of thegn-sons and servants who were busily packing away the remnants of pork, apples and bread left over from the evening meal. He found Acha tending her pony by a tree.

'Can you find the place where Theobald died so nobly?' He tried to be matter of fact, honouring his brother by speaking of his glory, not weeping over him like a woman.

'Yes, lord.' Acha looked cleaner than when he had last seen her on the battlefield, but he could tell from her eyes that, like him, she had not slept much.

'You may find it difficult to see his—' he began.

'I have seen him, lord, and still have his blood on my tunic,' she said proudly, brushing at a dark stain above her waist where she had briefly cradled Theobald's head.

'Yes, of course. We have the scent of his killers nearby and I will hunt them down like the vermin they are. If I divert to find Theobald, we could lose them. Could you find him and take him back to Bebbanburg? I will give you an escort and you can take the prisoner too. He will only slow us down. I can only spare the one horse that you will need to carry Theobald but at least you will not have to walk,' he said, indicating her pony that cropped casually at the grass. 'Take good care of Theobald and don't listen too much to that jester, Conaing. He has enough words for ten men and not many of them make sense. And see my men hold him close. We will need him as barter for my wife and son.'

Acha straightened her back, honoured that he trusted her with an important undertaking.

'I will. You think my brother is with the prey you are chasing?'

Æthelfrith shrugged. 'My scouts have picked up trails and seen warriors retreating westward, but we don't know exactly who they are until we catch up with them.'

'Be merciful to Edwin, lord. He's still only a boy and easily led by those around him. And he did try to save Theobald.'

'So you've said. Unfortunately he didn't succeed. Otherwise I could ask my brother for his opinion on what to do about yours,' he said and turned to go.

*

Seated astride her pony, Acha held her head high, not daring to look down at her tattered and stained clothing as Æthelfrith's column of warriors waved their farewell and disappeared over the horizon. She was certain they would be making coarse comments about her bedraggled appearance once they were out of her hearing, but her thoughts were focussed on her own mission. As Conaing was not up to walking, she had given him the horse, a guard on either side, one holding a leash to his body, the other leading his mount. He looked refreshed and relaxed despite the deep cut that Acha knew must still be causing him some pain. His easy-going manner made her want to trust him, but she could not risk failing in the task given to her by the king she had come to respect. Besides, once they started along the same trail that she had taken only a few days before, she needed distraction. She could not help but remember the fine figure of Theobald riding by her side, beaming down at her from his saddle, always cheerful even in the rain that had soaked them that day. Luckily, Conaing's chatter was a rich source of diversion from such thoughts. She began by asking him about his home and sat back to listen as he spun his tales.

He told her of Fergus the Great, son of Erc, the first king to lead his people away from the mainland of Ireland to settle on the western isles of the country they called Alba, thus founding the dynasty of the Dál Riata. Fergus and his descendants, Domangart, Congal and Gabran, had carved out a kingdom in the western highlands before Bruide, the mighty King of the Picts, stopped their expansion to the east. Acha grew a little weary of hearing of the battles of his illustrious ancestors and remembered another name he had mentioned.

'So who was this Father Columba you swear by?' she asked.

'I was just coming to that,' he said. 'The one true faith was preached by the holy man, Patrick, a priest from Roman times who came amongst the Scotti.'

'Wait, wait,' Acha interrupted. 'When were these Roman times and who are the Scotti?'

'Do you know nothing? It's time your kin wrote things down like our priests. The Scotti was the name given to the Gaels of Ireland by the Romans. And if you don't know who the Romans were, God help you. They left stone piles all around here. Have you not seen the Wall?'

'Oh, you mean the giants. I grew up next to their ruins,' Acha said.

Conaing nodded. 'I have heard them called giants, although I'm told that many were in fact shorter than us. Anyway, Columba was a monk, like Patrick, only born much later, and he sailed from the north of Ireland to get a bit of peace and quiet and set up home on an island called Iona. Except he didn't get much peace because the Picts had beaten poor old King Gabran into submission and he died. So the people of Dál Riata were casting around for a new king who could beat the Picts. Which is when Columba had his vision.' Conaing paused at Acha's puzzled expression.

'What do you mean, a vision?' she asked.

Conaing scratched his head. 'It's like, well, something sent by God to tell you about something. Like when I lay dying on the field of battle and I had a vision of an angel come to take me to heaven. Only it turned out to be you sent to keep me on earth a while longer. For what, I have yet to find out.'

Acha did not want to think about the battle sights she'd seen in recent days. 'Tell me about Columba's vision.'

'He had a dream that he was to ordain a certain Áedán as King of the Dál Riata. And so it was that my father was crowned by a priest, which if you saw him today you would know was long, long ago because the skin has dried and tightened around his bones so that it doesn't fit him any more.'

Acha laughed and the thought crossed her mind that this young man might just help her to forget the love she had lost.

'Tell me about your sister, Bebba,' she asked, curious to know why Æthelfrith had been so taken with her. The woman she had met had been quite a misery, although she could see the glamour in her appearance.

'I'm thinking it would be easier to speak without all these ropes dragging on me.' Conaing fingered the leash around his body.

'You could walk without the leads but for the sake of your health, you must ride. And as you ride on our only horse, other than my pony, I must take precautions that you do not escape.'

'Escape? Why would I want to do that when I have in prospect a long ride beside a lady who has considerable charm and the healer's gift, not to mention good looks?'

Acha tried to ignore the burning in her cheeks. 'Good, then tell me about your sister.'

'Actually she is my half-sister. My father, King Áedán, first took a Briton as his wife and next a Pictish princess called Domelch, who is Bebba's mother. My mother was an Angle as you may tell from my name. Father didn't seem to have had much taste for Gaelic women. Maybe that's why he's called Áedán the Wily.'

He chuckled as he seemed to do after almost every sentence. 'Bebba is a one-off. I don't think I'll ever meet her like again. She has all the ambition and cunning of our father mixed with the wildness of her mother's kin. When we were children, I never knew what she was going to do next. One moment she was all kind and cuddly. She even kissed me once, you know, like a woman when I was just a lad, and all to get me to give her the little knife I had made. The next thing I knew she was throwing it at me in a fit because I said she was ugly. Can you believe that, my own sister trying to kill me?'

Acha felt tears in her eyes, remembering her own childhood tussles with Edwin. She had tried to push thoughts of her brother from her mind, knowing that he was probably in considerable danger, but she was helpless to do anything. Where had he gone after their fateful meeting? Hopefully straight back to Deira. Surely Æthelfrith knew he was too young to have plotted against him?

'How did Bebba come to marry a king who was the enemy of her father?' she asked.

'Now, that is an interesting story. You must have heard about it.'

She knew the version that Theobald had told her about how his brother had won her in a tournament. Yet Acha had always sensed there was more to it than that.

'Only that Æthelfrith had married her on an impulse,' she said.

'It wasn't an impulse to her. She will never be content as just the daughter of a king. She wants to be one.'

Acha choked. 'How can she—'

'Not really king, but married to one who let's her have her own way. Her first scheme was to try for an addle-brained, older king but she picked on Rhydderch in Strad Clud, who was smarter than she thought and saw her game. When she heard Mynyddog was looking for someone to tempt Æthelfrith to his side, she jumped at the chance.' Conaing paused to ease himself up from the saddle to scratch his bottom.

Acha frowned. 'But how could she control Æthelfrith? He is hardly weak.'

'Not in the physical sense, no, not at all. But she has a way of getting into a man's mind so that he will do her will.'

'Which is what exactly?'

'Now you are asking me about deep secrets that could get me into big trouble if they get out.'

'Are you suggesting I'm a gossip who does not know how to keep my tongue to myself? If you are, then I prefer to ride alone.' She urged her horse ahead of Conaing's mount.

'I would never dispute your honour, m'lady, but I'm not one to betray my own kin,' he called after her.

'Then keep your tales to yourself,' she muttered.

He kept his distance, and the silence hung between them like a heavy curtain as they wound their way down a stony trail to the valley floor. Finally he coughed and spoke in a soft voice. 'Maybe I can be discreet by telling you a similar story,' he offered.

'As you wish,' she said indicating that he could ride beside her once more.

He made his cheeky chuckle. 'I see you're a strong woman yourself. Father Columba told me this story from the ancient book he refers to all the time. It was about a great warrior called Samson who had such huge strength that his enemies could never overcome him. One day he pulled down the gates of their fortress with his bare hands, which made them realise they had to use cunning rather than brute force to beat him. So they sent out their spies and found out he had fallen in love with a woman called Delilah. They went to her and promised her great wealth if she could help them subdue him. She was obviously ambitious because she agreed and set about him with her womanly ways to find out the secret of his strength. It took a while but he finally told her. You'll never guess what is was.' He paused, combing his long hair in a deliberate fashion with his fingers.

Acha watched, puzzled when he next groomed the mane of his horse in an exaggerated way.

'He had magic hands,' she guessed.

'No, it was his hair. His strength was in his hair.'

Acha had heard more tales of warriors with great powers than she cared to remember but she had never heard of one who claimed strong hair.

'How could his strength grow out of his head?'

'Well it did because when she cut it off one night while he was asleep, he was as weak as a baby in the morning. She called in the enemy soldiers, who put out his eyes and made him work like a slave.'

By now, Acha had realised that this was some sort of riddle. She had to work out what Aethelfrith had that was equivalent to Samson's hair and how Bebba might cut that off. But before she could give much attention to the puzzle, her thoughts were distracted by the distant view of the earthen fortification where she had spent her last hours with Theobald.

*

To Acha's surprise, the tent where she had camped had survived the fighting. It was flattened but still secured by wooden pegs, and she felt a moment of joy when she discovered her bag of clothes safely nestling under the cow-skin covering. Glancing around to make sure no one was looking, she tugged her stained and torn tunic over her head, kissing the cloth where it was caked with Theobald's blood before she carefully stowed it in her bag and put on a fresh tunic. The touch of clean cloth on her skin helped prepare her for the difficult task ahead.

She knew the exact spot where Theobald had died. It was marked by the broken and battered bodies of his loyal thegns who, even in death, formed a protective wall of flesh and bones over their lord. She quickly organised the grim work of dragging away the corpses one by one to make them ready for the funeral pyres. As they identified the bodies, her warriors shouted their names, making sure they securely grasped what weapons they had, ready for their voyage to the next world. Where they found an enemy soldier intertwined with their own they tossed the corpse into a shallow pit, contemptuously breaking and bending their swords and spears to render them useless for their onward journey.

She saw Theobald's arm before his face, recognising the golden bracelet around his wrist that had been given to him by his father the day his brother had become king, a gesture of recompense for being the second son, he had once joked to her. His hand seemed to beckon to her and she felt a strong urge to kiss his ashen cheeks, even his lifeless lips. But once her warriors had carefully stretched his body onto a patch of grass, she knew they were watching her and that this was not the moment to grieve. His corpse was not for the pyre but was to be placed with his ancestors in the cemetery by the dunes back home, so she ordered one of her escort to construct a comfortable bed for him to lie on. The others took their axes to collect branches of hazel and oak from the forest to build up the pyres they would need to burn the bodies. They took Conaing with them so that at last she was alone with Theobald.

His eyes had closed and he seemed strangely at peace despite the angry red weald on his neck where the sword had spilled the life force over his leather jerkin and onto the grass. She greeted him meekly as she began the work of cleaning and tidying him, apologising for leaving him to die on his own, but she was only obeying his orders after all. When she told him of Aethelfrith's battle, she particularly emphasised the role that his archers had played in the victory. They had often joked about his obsession with the bow, as she reminded him now.

'You remember your riddle? No? I'll remind you. One day this lord was riding through the forest when he came upon a clearing where a young boy stood with a small bow. Around him were seven separate trees with arrows stuck in the very centre of each of the targets that had been painted onto the trunks. "Who has shot these arrows so accurately?" the lord asked.

"Why I did, my lord," the boy replied.

"You? From what distance?" the lord asked incredulously. "From one hundred paces," the boy replied. The lord of course did not believe him, but the boy was telling the truth. How had he done it?'

She paused, brushing the wetness from her eyes in the silence that followed, knowing that he would've remembered because she had often heard him tell the story.

'Yes, you're right. He had first shot the arrows into the trees and afterwards painted the targets around them.' Her laugh sounded hollow and turned into a cough as she breathed in the fumes from the burning of the dead that had started nearby.

'Yuk, your thegns smell even worse now than when they were alive. I am going to take you home so we will have more time together.' She glanced over her shoulder to make sure that no one was watching and kissed him gently on the lips.

Preparing the pyres was a miserable task even for the hardened warriors. She knew they had brothers and cousins amongst the dead. One of the youngest thegns amongst her retinue laid his own father carefully onto a bed of kindling before covering him in a blanket of logs. As was the custom, he had the honour of applying the torch to the firewood and he stood erect as the flames took hold and smoke billowed up to the sky to signify the voyage of the dead to the land of continuous feasting.

Acha thought of the Christian god as she watched, wondering if the dead did go to his heaven, where creatures called angels healed wounds and made wine from water. Conaing's story of Samson and Delilah had come from that god's book and she needed the answer to Conaing's riddle. For inspiration she turned towards Theobald, who lay next to her on his makeshift bed. She imagined him with his brother discussing their plans before they had set out for Degsa's Stone, arguing over their strategy as they often did. Aethelfrith had relied heavily on Theobald's counsel and advice. Her pondering was interrupted by a loud bang as one of the skulls exploded, and she watched, hands over ears, as shards of white bone flew into the air with the flames. The answer to the riddle came to her in that moment.

Once the pyres were burning well and smoke filled the skies above the valley, she gave the order for her band to gather up their possessions and make ready to move out. With the stench of burning flesh in her nostrils, she had to decide how to get Theobald home in one piece. Her guards suggested they take it in turns to carry him, one on each end of the wooden frame that he was lying on. But that would be too cumbersome and slow, she argued. The heavy rains had left the trails quite wet in places and she could not take the chance that a tired warrior might slip and drop their precious load. Conaing suggested they abandon the frame and sling him across Acha's mount but she could not bear the thought of such an undignified mode of travel for his last journey. Finally, she made the guards strengthen the wooden structure with stout branches, then strap one end to the rump of her pony so that it could bump along the ground behind her.

As they set off, she turned to watch Theobald's progress, wincing at every stone that shook the makeshift sled, fearing it might either break or he would slip from it. Yet she was happy that having abandoned him on the field of battle, she had returned to take him home. Once she was convinced he was secure enough, she turned her thoughts again to the riddle and she waved Conaing to bring his horse alongside her own.

'Theobald would be curious to know that Bebba's brother was accompanying him on his final journey. He was never fond of her,' she said.

'I'm with him on that. I wasn't fond of her either. Put me off women altogether for a while. Luckily I have saintly ladies like yourself to give me a more balanced view of the female side.'

'Why did you dislike her so much?'

'You promise you won't tell anyone?'

She nodded her agreement and he took a deep breath. 'She made me scared of boats. There I've said it. Haven't told anyone else except my ma and she's dead.'

Acha thought at first it was another of his jokes, but he wasn't laughing as he went on.

'Bebba woke one day and said she'd had a vision in the night. She insisted on telling my six brothers and me about an angel who had told her about how each one of us would die. We didn't believe her of course. She was always tormenting us with her tales. Anyway, it's normally the holy men who have the visions. I took no notice of what she saw for me until two of my elder brothers were killed exactly how she said they would be – in battle.'

Acha was all ears. 'What did she see for you?'

'She saw me drowning in a boat. It gave her great pleasure to tell me because she knew that the one thing I love more than anything in this world is fishing in my curragh and she could take that joy from me. It did the trick. I've been terrified of boats ever since. And amongst seafarers like the Dál Riata, that is very serious, I can tell you.' Conaing laughed his merry chuckle. 'There, now you know all about me and my kin. So why not come and live with us? It's a wonderful land and it seems pretty miserable around here.'

The invitation shocked Acha at first and she laughed to show she was not taking it too seriously. Yet she felt drawn to the idea. She didn't know why but she sensed that Dál Riata would have a special place in her life.

The journey to Bebbanburg was slow, which gave Acha time to brood on the riddle that Conaing had set for her. She was certain she was right, so during a rare moment of silence from Conaing she decided to test her answer.

'Am I right in thinking I am looking at Samson's hair?' she asked as she turned towards Theobald's body bumping along on the sled behind her.

Conaing blinked, the smile disappearing from his face. 'What do you mean?'

'I have the answer don't I? Bebba took away Æthelfrith's power by having Theobald killed. Theobald was equivalent to Samson's hair.'

'I really can't say. It's more than my life's worth.'

As he hadn't denied it, Acha took that as confirmation. Next, she had to find out who else was in on the plot. She just prayed it was not her little brother.

Twenty-Two

Edwin had never seen a curragh before. It looked similar to the boats of planked oak that berthed at Eoferwic, but, judging by the way it was carried between just two of Maelumai's men, it had to be much lighter. It was dark and they were quietly removing the branches and foliage under which the boats had been hidden and hurrying with them to the shore. He ran his hand over the hull of one that had been placed near him on the mud bank, feeling the taught animal skin that had been stretched over a wicker frame. No hard wood. No wonder it was light even though it was over ten paces in length.

'Are we really going to travel in such a flimsy vessel?' he whispered to Rhun, who stood next to him, bags in hand.

'We have no choice. Æthelfrith is close by and he will come for us at first light. We must be gone by then.'

Edwin watched as Lillan and Forthhere quickly loaded their possessions into the boat. He pointed to the bleak shoreline on the other side of the estuary.

'Is that where we are going, to the opposite bank?'

'No point in that, unless you want to stay in Deira, which I wouldn't advise,' said Rhun.

'Where then?'

Rhun pointed his brown sleeve into the darkness. 'We will sail west and then turn south, towards Manaw and Mon.'

'To the open sea in such a slight craft?' Edwin looked alarmed at the small fleet that was now bobbing in the water as the Gaels quickly launched their curraghs.

'These boats have been good enough to take my brethren to far parts of the world to preach the word of God. They took Columba to Iona and Brendan to many strange lands. So yes, we will be taking these craft into the open sea. Two layers of ox hide soaked in resin are as strong as oak if you avoid sharp rocks. God has changed the wind in our favour. It blows from the east, straight down the Firth. We should make Manaw by nightfall.'

Rhun proved right. They were blown so quickly down the estuary in their light boats that Æthelfrith's warriors appeared only as small dots on the distant beach when they arrived there in the early dawn. They had escaped, for the moment at least.

Once into the open sea, Maelumai held his course due west with the main fleet and headed for Ireland. Edwin had not spoken to him since their argument over the killing of Theobald. Nor did he acknowledge the departure of Herin, who had decided to stick with the Gaels

Good riddance to them. They failed me. Next time I will decide how we are to kill Æthelfrith.

Rhun ordered their steersman to head south and the curragh with its small complement sailed onwards, alone in the open waters. Edwin had insisted on taking his place at an oar alongside Lillan and Forthhere and the five other men who made up their crew. It took his mind off the rapid change in his fortunes from king to fugitive in just a few days. He had Ælfric to blame for that. He would not be following his intrigues again. Nor would he ally himself with an arrogant fortune-seeker like Herin, who was now fleeing to Ireland. He would have to find another way to destroy Æthelfrith. But how was he to do that? Rhun said he should ask his God for guidance. If he accepted him as the one true God, he would show him the way to regain what he had lost. As the skies darkened and still the only sight was endless, unbroken sea, Edwin felt ready to pray to the Christian God for the smaller favour of a safe landfall. No sooner had the thought crossed his mind than there was a shout from the bows and all heads turned to look at the dim outline of a shoreline.

'The Isle of Manaw. We'll sleep and eat there,' Rhun announced.

Once they had landed, Edwin judged that there was not much else to do other than sleep, eat and pray on the island. It was a desolate place inhabited by a few monks who seemed disgruntled by the intrusion into their solitary world. They hardly spoke as they offered them sparse portions of fish cooked quickly over a fire in the spitting rain, before they shuffled off to a huddle of tiny shacks of rough-hewn rocks protected by a mound of turf around the base. Edwin was famished and gulped down his food without a thought, but Rhun nudged him as he wiped his lips on his sleeve.

'Come and pray with me,' he said indicating the entrance to one of the small buildings.

'That's a church?' Edwin asked, astonished that such an insignificant stack of earth and stones could be a monument to a god.

'The locals call it a keeil, but yes it is a church. Anywhere that is dedicated to the word of Christ is a church, no matter how humble.' Rhun said.

Lillan and Forthere scrambled to their feet as their king stood up but Rhun waved them back.

'There is only space for one or two at a time,' he said.

As Edwin ducked into the dark space of the tiny chapel, he began to regret his decision to follow Rhun. There were no windows and the roof was too low for him to stand up fully. Rhun placed a candle on the stone slab at the end of the room and handed Edwin the burning taper.

'Light this and ask for divine guidance,' he said.

Edwin touched the flickering flame to the wick of the candle and blew out the taper. With his head bowed because of the low roof, he watched as wisps of smoke danced to the ceiling and the candle began to glow. His skin prickled as he stared at the halo of light around the flame and for a moment he forgot the agitation in his mind.

'Just as we have passed this light from one holder to another, so does our life move from one phase to another. Have faith in the one true God to change yours for the better,' Rhun said quietly.

Edwin was tempted by his advice to put his trust in this new god. What had he got to lose? Thunor and Tiw had done little for him. Maybe the Christ God would give him back his kingdom. Rhun put a hand on his shoulder as they returned slowly to the monk's shelter.

'Whatever your belief, we should baptise you when we arrive in Gwynedd. The king there believes fiercely in our God and he will protect you more securely as a Christian fugitive.'

Edwin was too tired to argue and, although the straw he was given as a bed was stale with other men's sweat, he fell asleep as soon as he lay on it.

He did not wake until he saw the monks shuffle out of the door for morning prayers. Soon after, Rhun called his crew back to the curragh and as the sun began to climb above the horizon, they were on their way around the island and into the grey waters to the south. The early banter in the boat gradually dried up when the wind swung round to blow a stinging rain against them. With little help from their sail, they had to strain hard at the oars to make progress. A long day of strenuous rowing ended with no sign of land.

'It is too deep to anchor this far from shore so we'll take turns to sleep and row, or else we'll be blown back to Alba,' Rhun announced as darkness fell.

Edwin insisted on continuing to row as he felt his mind too troubled for sleep. Lillan sat opposite pulling on a bow-side blade and when Edwin was sure Rhun was asleep, he asked for his advice in a quiet voice.

'What do you think of this Christ they say is a god?'

Lillan turned so Edwin could just make out his weary expression in the dark. 'We must seek a friendly mead hall to take us in and we may have to accept their customs as our own. For myself, I will always ask Woden and Thunor for their favour, but I am prepared to pray to Rhun's god if it brings me food and shelter.'

'That was Rhun's advice. Yet he insists there is only one god who will not look favourably on us if we also follow others.'

'We are wanderers now and will need the help of all the gods. Maybe you should try the new one if it suits our purpose for a while.'

To be a wanderer sounded better than an exile to Edwin although he realised that he had become both. From now on, he would have no rights, no authority, no home, nothing other than that which he begged from others. He remembered the words of his sister urging him to be strong if he wanted to become a king. If only she was with him now. In his mind, he saw her standing next to him, rain dripping from her hood, during their last, fateful meeting.

'I wonder what has become of my sister?' he mumbled.

Lillan looked away and did not reply for a while. Edwin sensed there were tears hiding in his eyes when he turned back.

'My main regret in not returning is that we cannot protect her. But she's a resourceful girl. She will look out for herself, you'll see,' Lillan said.

It was their turn to rest. Rhun had woken and was prodding the other half of the crew from their sleep to take over the oars. Edwin was too exhausted to mind the discomfort of lying in the damp bottom of the boat and was still asleep when the coast of Gwynedd came into view. When he did sit up, he was amazed at what he saw. Before sleeping, he had prayed to the Christ God to take him to a land of fertile fields and friendly people, and before him now stretched a green peninsula just as he had imagined. As they rowed closer, he realised that there were narrow straits that made it an island.

'The Isle of Mon, or Monez, as the Saxons call it,' Rhun called to him. 'My adopted home.'

Edwin studied the sandy bay that seemed to invite them to land.

Maybe my new God has answered me.

The steersman ignored the bay and guided the curragh through the narrow channel between the mainland and the island until they reached an inlet on the southern shore. As they rowed further inland, it became a winding river and Edwin was comforted by the familiar sight of workers in the fields and groups of thatched huts. Eventually he spotted a long hall surrounded by a group of smaller buildings set back from a jetty.

'Welcome to the royal vill of King Cadfan of Gwynedd,' Rhun said as a horn blast announced their arrival.

Edwin saw a group of warriors forming up near the jetty. 'They don't seem too welcoming.'

'From the look of our boat, they'll think we're Irish and there's a lot of history between the Gaels and the local folk here,' Rhun replied. 'They'll be pleased enough when they find out who you are. It's not often another king visits.'

Ex-king, Edwin thought.

'Wait in the curragh,' Rhun said as he scrambled ashore to talk to the captain of the guards, who had carefully watched their approach. After a hurried conversation, a messenger disappeared towards the buildings set back from the harbour.

Edwin shifted his sore bottom uncomfortably on the hard seat of the boat and dreamt of a long soak in a hot bath. After what seemed like an age, Rhun finally waved him ashore and he took his first unsteady steps onto the land of Gwynedd.

'King Cadfan has granted us an audience in his mead hall,' Rhun explained as they were led towards a collection of thatched huts that stood on a hillock above the banks of the river. Edwin brushed at his dirty clothes and tried to tidy his salt-caked hair.

Begging for a bed from a minor king. So this is what my life has become.

The hall was smaller than his own in Eoferwic but built in the same way with low thatched eaves supported by stout posts and planked walls. As he ducked through the doorway, he felt the familiar sting of smoke from a fire burning in the centre of the floor. The smell of meat roasting on a spit raised his spirits and, as his eyes became accustomed to the dinginess of the room, he was surprised to see two young girls curtsy before him. One offered him a warm, damp cloth to wipe his brow whilst a second gave him a cup of wine which could only have come from sunnier climes judging by its rich taste. He happily returned the welcoming smiles of the girls.

Being a wanderer may have its merits.

A singsong voice interrupted his musing. 'May the Lord God be praised for sending us such an honoured guest.'

Edwin could not at first see the speaker but, spinning around, he saw a stocky, dark-haired man with a bushy beard that almost covered the silver torc around his neck, approaching through a side door.

'Welcome to our humble kingdom Edwin, son of Ælle of Deira, although we might have wished for happier circumstances for your visit.'

Rhun stepped forward as Edwin tried to recover from his surprise. 'My lord, can I introduce you to King Cadfan ap Iago and his son Cadwallon?'

Edwin nodded and bowed his head. 'These are my thegns Lillan and Forthhere,' he said indicating the two who had hurried forward to stand alongside him.

Edwin's eye was caught by the appearance of the king's son: he was a thin, reedy youth, already taller than his father although he looked a similar age to Edwin. He wore a leather helmet but no body armour, preferring a tunic that clung unevenly to his skinny shoulders. He did not speak but fidgeted first with his clothes, then with a knife at his belt and finally with the strap of his helmet that he kept on despite the warmth of the hall. His eyes were unblinking as they darted from Edwin to his two thegns and back again.

'I hear you have had a long and arduous journey to our shores, so I'm sure you need rest, but first let us eat.' The king indicated benches at the long table. 'There is a newly killed lamb that looks ready to slice.'

Edwin found himself sitting opposite Cadwallon, who still glowered unsmiling in his direction. Desperate to eat, Edwin made a grab for the bread already on the table just as Rhun stood and cleared his throat.

'Let us pray,' he began.

Edwin quickly dropped the bread back into the wicker basket, and Cadwallon sniggered loudly.

'We thank you, Lord God, for delivering us safely to these shores and for the food we are about to eat,' Rhun continued.

'Bring vengeance on those that have done us wrong and deliver us from the evil ways of the disbelievers. Amen.'

At last, Edwin thought he could eat but, at that moment, the king addressed him and he felt obliged to resist the bread for a second time.

'I hope you can stay with us for a while, my lord Edwin. We would welcome your views on the sinister work of the devil in your kingdom.'

Edwin had to think back to his conversation with Rhun about Æthelfrith, the devil king, to follow his meaning.

'I believe that the devil should be destroyed so that the work of the one true God can continue,' he said, pleased with himself for remembering Rhun's phrases. Cadwallon guffawed and clapped in a deliberate, slow beat.

Cadfan's shaggy eyebrows shot up. 'Does this mean you are a follower of our God?'

'I am,' said Edwin firmly, aware that Lillan and Forthhere were looking curiously at him as he spoke. 'I am to be baptised by Brother Rhun.'

'Praise be to God,' said Cadfan. 'The faith is spreading in the north as well as the south.'

Edwin furrowed his brow. 'How so in the south?'

Brother Rhun leaned forward. 'You may remember, lord, that Æthelbert, the Saxon king of Kent, recently turned to Christ with many of his subjects.'

Edwin nodded at the vague memory he had of that news. 'Does that mean he will help us to defeat the devil king?'

Cadfan looked amused. 'Kent is a long way from Bernicia, but who knows? Our God works in wondrous ways. Even non-believers may come to your cause.' His bushy eyebrows shot up again. 'Which reminds me, Cearl, the Mercian king is due to pay us a visit soon. He is interested in marrying his daughter into our kin.' Cadfan nodded towards Cadwallon, who was grinning inanely. 'Maybe there are other possibilities to explore,' he said, looking knowingly first at Edwin and back to Rhun.

Cadwallon stopped grinning and glared again at Edwin.

*

When his scout returned, Æthelfrith found it hard to believe him.

'Ælfric has asked for my protection?' he asked, scratching his head.

'Yes lord,' the scout replied. 'He says that King Edwin and Lord Herin were plotting against him and went off to get support from the Gaels to overthrow both of you.'

'Does he know where they are now?'

'No, lord, but he is worried they will return to Eoferwic with a warband from Ireland. That's why he asks for your protection.'

So Edwin had deceived his sister. He was part of the plot. Æthelfrith had cursed his captains for letting the Gaels escape in their boats during the night, although, in truth, he knew it was his own misjudgement. He should have attacked them immediately and risked fighting in the dark even though the shoreline was thickly wooded. He had checked the beaches for boats of course, but he should have realised they had hidden their light craft in the forest. Theobald would have known. So close to his quarry yet he had let them slip away. Edwin and Herin might even have been with them. He had scoured the lands as far as his scouts could safely ride and the only news he had received so far was from Eoferwic. He would go there and hear Ælfric's story from his own lips. And if Edwin had truly fled, there was a vacant throne to be filled.

His men were tired after continuous marching hither and thither after an unseen enemy. But the promise of a rest at a

Deiran royal compound spurred them into one last effort and they made good time to Eoferwic. There, Æthelfrith found Ælfric where he had last seen him: sitting in the king's seat on the high table of the mead hall.

He took just Leax and a few trusted companions into the hall with him, leaving the rest of his men to set up camp amongst the ruins of the old citadel.

Ælfric rose immediately. 'My lord, King Æthelfrith. Welcome. What news of the rebellion?'

Rebellion. That's an interesting word to use. I thought I was fighting foreigners not rebels.

'We have routed Áedán's army, but who are these rebels you seek protection from?' Æthelfrith asked.

Ælfric raised both his arms in a gesture of thanks. 'The gods be praised! I warned Edwin that he would not defeat the great king Æthelfrith, but he would not listen. He wanted to become king in his own right at too early an age and your cousin Herin encouraged him. He seems to harbour some sort of grudge against you for becoming king instead of him when his father was killed. Together, they decided to flout your authority. I hope they both died in the battle?'

'No, they did not. I came here to find them and understand exactly what part this court played in all of this.'

Ælfric looked surprised. 'Why, we are loyal to you lord and always will be. We must find the traitors and have them killed, of course.'

'Why did you not send me any word of this rebellion when it was fermenting here?'

'You did not receive my message? But we sent someone days ago didn't we?' Ælfric turned to one of the warriors behind him, who nodded a curt confirmation.

'I had word that you sought protection but many days after we had won the war.' Æthelfrith strode quickly forward so that he could look more closely into Ælfric's eyes. 'At the price of my brother's life.'

Ælfric recoiled with shock in his eyes. 'Theobald killed? No, I am so sorry. He was such a wonderful brother to you. Having lost my own brother, I would not wish that on any man.'

He waved his arms, and some slave girls jumped up from the shadows at the edge of the hall.

'But we are forgetting our manners. Prepare a hut for the king. After such a gruelling time, you must take a soothing bath that these girls will prepare. After, we will have a great feast to celebrate your victory and honour your brother.'

Æthelfrith was about to protest but, when he glanced towards Leax to see his reaction, he saw how tired he looked. Maybe it was time for his men to rest and celebrate. And he knew that the one thing Ælfric was good at was organising festivities.

*

Æthelfrith proved right about that. At first he resisted the luxuries that the Deiran court offered him. The memory of his brother's death still nagged at him like a raw wound. Yet the slave girls eased some of his pain when they bathed the dirt of the long march from his skin and massaged the knots of anxiety from his muscles. When he made his way back towards the mead hall, he was surprised at the reception that awaited him. His army was too numerous to all fit into the hall, so men were already seated at benches and trestle tables set up outside. It reminded him of the festival in Din Eidyn where they had dined under the stars, courtesy of King Mynyddog. How fortunes had changed since that night. He had defeated every one of the kings that had paraded themselves so proudly at that feast, leaving them all dead or dying. He was overlord of all their domains just as he was here at Eoferwic. Yet he still felt empty inside. At the very moment when his power was at its greatest, his spirits were at their lowest. He needed his wife, his son and his brother at his side to enjoy this time. And they had all disappeared.

A sudden shout broke through his dejected thoughts. The nearest warriors had seen his approach and they were on their feet roaring a welcome for their leader.

'Æthelfrith! Æthelfrith!' they chanted and soon the entire army outside the hall were up, raising their goblets, shouting his praises and banging rhythmically on the tables. He acknowledged their greetings with an embarrassed smile, waving forward the serving women to recharge their glasses. As he ducked inside the door to the hall, the din became overwhelming, reverberating around the wooden walls like rolls of thunder that made the building tremble. By now, the chanting had become a roll call of the territories over which he held sway.

'Gododdin! Strad Clud! Rheged! Dál Riata!'

As he approached the top table, he noted that the king's chair had been left vacant for him and, as soon as he stood by it, a few changed the cry.

'Deira! Deira!'

Æthelfrith held up his hands to ask for quiet but this chant was soon taken up by the entire gathering so that it echoed inside and outside of the hall.

He knew that Ælfric was standing next to him, but he dare not look to see if he was frowning or smiling at this latest outburst. Waving a bench maid forward to fill his glass, he sat down and absorbed the glory that was being showered upon him. If only his brother and his son were here to share it with him.

What would Theobald do in this situation? Seize the moment, of course.

He turned to speak to Ælfric, but he could not make himself heard above the din. Standing once more, holding up his hands for quiet, the noise gradually subsided until he could speak.

'Warriors of Bernicia and Deira, when I stood before you after our victory at Catræth, I said that if we fought together, we could vanquish all our enemies. Well we did, and we have.'

A mighty roar arose around the hall and was repeated beyond the walls as his words were relayed to those outside. He waited for the noise to subside before continuing in a quieter voice.

'Yet there were those who did not believe in our unity. There were those inside the royal families of Bernicia and of Deira who betrayed their oaths to me and allied themselves with foreign enemies. What is to be done with these traitors?'

His warriors were on their feet again, roaring for vengeance and demonstrating their judgements by drawing imaginary knives across their throats.

'Thank you for your advice,' he said turning particularly to address the warriors from Deira, some of whom sat alongside Ælfric at the top table. 'According to the testimony of Lord Ælfric, your own King Edwin was a leader amongst those that betrayed us. According to our ancient custom, he has therefore forfeited his right to be king, has he not?' They all nodded their agreement, including Ælfric.

'So who is to be king in his place?'

For a heartbeat, the hall went quiet and Æthelfrith thought he had gone too far. Ælfric had a black expression as his eyes darted around the hall, seeming to dare anyone to speak. It was Leax who broke the silence.

'Æthelfrith!' he yelled and his call was taken up by the Deiran warriors, swiftly followed by the Bernician troops.

'Æthelfrith, King of Deira! Æthelfrith, King of Deira!' became the new rhythmic chant. Ælfric did not join in.

Finally, Æthelfrith managed to quieten the hall down again. 'Thank you for your advice. I will ask the council of Deira for their decision tomorrow.'

He knew the council members were all in the hall and they would not go against the will of the warriors.

Theodore would be proud of me.

Æthelfrith did not intend to drink heavily that night. He knew the dangers of being drunk in a mead hall that was not his own. Yet the euphoria of the occasion went to his head as much as the wine that filled and refilled his cup. Once the roast pork and cabbage had been served, the noise in the hall changed from shouting to chewing and slurping so that Æthelfrith could at last speak with Ælfric.

'It seems the mood is to make me king in Edwin's place. But I will still need a loyal lord to keep things in order when I am absent. You can continue in much the same role as now if you have a mind to do it.'

Ælfric's eyes narrowed. 'That is generous of you and I think it is in both our interests. I will serve you well.' He paused, licking around his lips to wipe off the pork fat. 'Especially if you grant me one request that will help remove further threats to your kingship.'

'Threats? You mean Edwin returning?'

'No, no one is going to side with a boy of thirteen against the most renowned warrior king for generations. No, I mean the threat of his sister, Acha.'

'Acha? What threat can she pose?' Æthelfrith's head had begun to spin from the heady mixture of praise and dark wine.

'King Ælle is still thought of highly in this land. Whoever marries his daughter has a claim to kingship. And their sons will rival yours.'

He remembered Theobald making exactly these arguments as a reason why Æthelfrith himself should marry Acha. He also remembered Ælfric's obsession with marrying her.

'Would not that apply to you if you were to marry the girl?'

Ælfric chuckled and patted his ample belly. 'Look at me. I am not a warrior to challenge a leader like you. I have sons enough by my dead wife and slave girls who satisfy my needs. I would not be troubling the bed of a thin, young thing like her. She would be safe in my hands.'

So why is he so keen to marry her?

His thoughts began to spiral around in his head and made no sense. Maybe Ælfric's motives were as he claimed.

'If I support you in this, will you propose Edwin's exile and my kingship to the council tomorrow?' Æthelfrith took another swig of wine, trying to ignore the screaming in his head that he knew came from Theobald.

Ælfric's wide smile was his first of the evening. 'Of course.'

Twenty-Three

When she finally arrived at the fortress that was now called Bebbanburg, Acha's mind was filled with Theobald. Everything in the area reminded her of him, from the mudflats where they had ridden at low tide in search of sea food in the coves, to the grassy slope within the palisade walls where they had strolled in the evenings. She didn't know how she was going to bear it.

'Do you have your own boat at all?' Conaing asked, looking with interest at the small harbour that nestled under the rocky outcrop.

'I thought you had a fear of boats since your sister—'

'I do,' Conaing said quickly. 'But I was hoping you might help me overcome it. If it took one woman to put the curse on me, I was thinking it might take another to lift it. And this bay looks a wonderful spot for fishing.'

So Acha found a diversion for her grief by helping Conaing overcome his fear. Whenever the sea was calm, he would pluck up the courage, with her encouragement, to row her in a small boat to explore the islands or fish in the shallow waters off Bebbanburg. The captain of the fortress had frowned when she had first made her wishes known.

'On my oath, I will not harm the lady nor seek to escape. We will be back if the good lord permits it,' Conaing said to the captain, who reluctantly agreed, providing they took a guard with them; and he pointedly told them that a fast war boat would be at the ready in the harbour. Acha was mostly content to drift through the day, soothed by the gentle rocking of the waves, listening with one ear to Conaing's tales of the Gaelic people and dreaming of what it would be like if Theobald were there to take the oars. But more and more, her mind turned to the woman who had given her name to the fortress. She had to find out how she had arranged the ambush. She was also desperate to hear news of her brother Edwin and her kin in Deira.

She wasn't the only one to be thinking of home.

'You know your rock reminds me of Dunadd,' Conaing said pointing back at the fortress. 'It sits on a similar dark lump of stone close to the sea but its walls are made of boulders, not wood. The way in is the same though. A cleft in the rock with a strong gate at the top, and beyond that, workshops for smelting and working metals, just as you have. Our wine is better than yours, though. We buy it from the Franks.' For once, he didn't chuckle, but looked around at the guard, who had nodded off to sleep in the bow. He leaned close to Acha and whispered.

'Why don't you come there with me when I am released? You could find a new life. There's nothing here for you now is there?'

Acha blinked in surprise. 'And what exactly would I do in Dunadd?'

'Why, marry me of course,' Conaing said, as if it were obvious. 'You've captured me in more ways than you think.'

For a moment, the idea sounded attractive to Acha. She could escape from her memories of Bebbanburg and her worries in Deira. Conaing would certainly make her life interesting.

'I am honoured by your offer,' she heard herself saying. 'But I must find my young brother, Edwin. I promised my mother to look after him.'

'Let me help you look for him. He's probably in hiding with the Gaels.'

'I also need to find out why Theobald died. He and I were… well sort of betrothed and I can't just leave him un-avenged. I want to know exactly who plotted to have him killed.'

'And you'll marry me if I tell you?'

Acha blinked and looked away, her mind racing. She did need to know and one day she might be ready to pay that price. But not yet.

'Well I certainly can't marry you if you don't tell me. You would have secrets from me. I couldn't trust you.'

Conaing sat in silence, watching the waves that gently bobbed their boat up and down.

'Let me think about it. I'll have to ask for God's guidance.' For once he did not laugh.

The wind had begun to shift and, by the time they had returned to the harbour, a stiff easterly breeze was blowing. As they pulled into the shelter of the wharf, Acha noticed that a new vessel had sailed to their shore. A young thegn waited beside it with the fort captain, who pointed in Acha's direction as she stepped onto the harbour wall. As he walked briskly towards her, Acha recognised him as one of Æthelfrith's companions and her heartbeat quickened at the thought of what news he might bring.

'I come from King Æthelfrith, m'lady. You are to come to Eoferwic with all speed.'

'In your ship?' she asked indicating his sleek craft.

'Yes, m'lady. On the next tide.'

Acha turned to Conaing, who was busy shipping the oars and tidying their rowboat. 'Oh good, you will enjoy that won't you?' she said laughing.

The thegn looked surprised. 'I am sorry m'lady but King Æthelfrith did not mention any other passengers.'

'Then I cannot come, for he ordered me to carefully guard this prisoner,' she said pointing to Conaing, who looked bemused as he climbed up the harbour steps.

It took a moment for the thegn to decide, but he must have seen the determined look in Acha's eyes.

'Very well, but we need to sail with all speed.'

*

Acha could hardly wait for the ship to dock at the quayside in Eoferwic. She did not wait for the planking to be run out to the wharf but jumped nimbly across the gap to the shore before the stern line was attached. Her instincts told her that Edwin had somehow returned home and now awaited her. Why else would Æthelfrith tell her to come with all haste? She left Conaing with the guards as she ran along the path towards the royal village. When she caught sight of her hut still standing as she had left it, she almost cried. When she burst through the door expecting to see Edwin sitting on his usual bench, she did cry.

He was not there. There was no sign of the clothes or weaponry that he normally scattered around the floor. Maybe he was quartered in the great hall now with the other thegns. Yes, that was it; he would be there.

Two of the guards from the boat caught up with her as she walked briskly from the hut. 'We have instructions to take you to the hall,' one of them panted.

'Good, that's where I'm going,' she announced, quickening her pace. Taking a deep breath whilst the guard opened the door to announce her, she tidied her hair and brushed dust from her tunic. Good, it seemed as though they were expecting her. Blinking in the smoky interior, she instantly recognised the tall frame of Æthelfrith sitting at the high table. But next to him was not her brother, but her uncle.

Ælfric! How could he still be here? Surely he was part of the plot.

Æthelfrith clearly did not think so because he was chatting with him like an old friend. Her heart pounded and she nearly panicked and ran out.

Stay calm. There must be a simple explanation.

She tried to smile as Æthelfrith rose. 'Welcome home, my dear. I was just explaining to the Witan what an important part you played in the battle with Áedán's forces.'

Facing her alongside Æthelfrith and Ælfric were the elders of the king's council, all studying her intently as she held her breath, feeling increasingly uneasy. She must have stumbled into a meeting of the full council. 'I am sure you would like to rest after your journey but I thought I would give you important news as soon as you arrived.' Æthelfrith coughed and looked down.

'There is evidence that your brother Edwin played a significant role in the rebellion against our authority and he has fled beyond the reach of our forces. This council has therefore pronounced him an exile.'

Acha was about to blurt out that he'd made a mistake and that her brother must have been misled by the man sitting next to him, but Æthelfrith spoke again.

'The council have also honoured me with the title of king here as Edwin can no longer play that role. And, as king, it is now my duty to secure your future as the marriage we had foreseen for you is no longer possible.' He paused and wiped his brow. 'To prevent further intrigue against the royal kin, this council has agreed that you will marry Ælfric.'

She recoiled as if she had been slapped hard in the face. They could not be serious, yet she could see by Æthelfrith's stern look and Ælfric's smirk that they were. She felt her knees buckle and looked around for help. The elders and the guards all returned her startled look with impassive expressions. She would get no help from them. A red rage filled her mind so that she spat out her reply without caution.

'Never, not to him!'

Æthelfrith looked taken aback. 'Careful what you… '

Acha ran forward to the high table. 'This man you would have me marry helped kill the man that I should have married.'

She glared into Ælfric's face as he struggled to stand up.

'You want me to take his hand in marriage? I will. Like this!' She whipped Theobald's small knife from the folds of her tunic and stabbed it into the back of Ælfric's hand as he pushed himself up from the table. He yelled and went white as blood spurted onto the cuff of his jerkin. Pinned to the wooden surface, he collapsed back towards his chair as guards ran forward to support him and grapple with Acha.

She didn't know why she had acted as she had. As they bundled her out of the hall and into her hut, she realised she had just made her problems worse. But it had been worth it to hear Ælfric scream. And it had bought her some time. She needed to talk to Æthelfrith.

'Tell the king I have very important information for his ears only,' she yelled through the door, knowing guards would be stationed there.

It did not take long before the door swung open and the tall frame of Æthelfrith stood before her.

'What do you mean by such bad behaviour?' he asked.

'I mean that Ælfric is guilty and my brother is innocent of the rebellion against you,' she said, her voice trembling with either rage or fear, she wasn't sure which.

'How could you know that?'

'Ask Conaing mac Áedán. He will tell you.'

'Conaing? Where is he?'

'He came with me. Bring him to us and he will tell you.'

At least she hoped he would. He had yet to tell her all that he knew, but if he still wanted to marry her, she now had an unexpected lever to encourage him to talk.

*

Æthelfrith found Conaing squatting outside a tent with some of his warriors, throwing dice.

'You. Follow me,' he said turning on his heel.

'Where would I be following you to, lord?' Conaing asked, jumping up.

'To your grave, if you don't tell the truth.'

Æthelfrith was seething. She might be the daughter of a king, but how dare a mere girl flout his authority by assaulting the person he had picked for her to marry. He should have her whipped before sending her to Ælfric's bed. He did not expect much from Conaing. What could a youth from Dál Riata know of the intrigues of the court of Deira? If it weren't for the fact that Theobald had held Acha in such high esteem, he would not be taking the trouble of asking him.

He threw open the door of Acha's hut without knocking, expecting her to be weeping in a corner. Instead, she stood defiant, facing him squarely as he marched in, both fists clenched at her side.

'This better be good,' he said as he ushered Conaing forward.

'Conaing, I need you to tell us who was involved in the plot to overthrow the king and his brother Theobald.' Her eyes narrowed, pleading. 'If you don't, I am to be married tomorrow.'

Conaing looked shaken. 'Who to?'

'That's none of your business. Just tell us what you know,' Æthelfrith snapped.

There was a long silence as Conaing looked at Acha, frowning. Æthelfrith had a sense that communications passed between them, although they spoke no words. Conaing deliberately cleared his throat.

'You're asking a lot and I would not do this for anyone else. I just hope it helps you out of whatever corner you're in.' He turned towards Æthelfrith. 'I will tell you what I know but some of this involves my sister, your wife. It will not be pleasant for you, so I need your word that you will not harm her or me for reporting the truth.'

Æthelfrith swallowed hard. Theobald had always warned him about Bebba. Could she have betrayed him? He needed to find out.

'You have my word.'

'It's a long story but… ' Conaing began.

'Keep it short. I can always ask questions,' Æthelfrith said.

'Well for me, it all started when Mynyddog sent word to my father, King Áedán, asking him for his help against the newcomers, as he called you Angles in Bernicia and Deira. Áedán couldn't spare any soldiers as he was too busy defending himself against the Picts, but he did give Mynyddog this advice. Divide and conquer. Keep the two kingdoms at each other's throats so we can defeat them one at a time. I'm not sure how the ruse to marry you to Bebba came about but that was to distract you whilst they finished off Deira. Bebba was only too happy to marry a young king, and in return she sent information back about your whereabouts and how many warriors you had, that sort of thing.'

Æthelfrith felt his mouth go dry. In his heart, he had known for some time that Bebba had made a fool of him, that Theobald had been right. He wanted to ask questions but he could not find the words to speak.

'But you ruined that plan by kicking the sh... ' Conaing paused, smiling at Acha. 'Begging your pardon, I was forgetting I was before a lady. I mean by defeating the Gododdin and their friends at Catræth. That victory made Áedán realise he could ignore you at his peril, so when he received an approach from Deira through your cousin Herin and Ælfric... '

'You are sure it was those two?' Æthelfrith asked, scrutinising his face for signs of deceit.

'I met your man Herin myself when he came to Dunadd. The first time he came was with Bebba, helping her to pick up her clothes, they said, but it was clear she wanted to involve him in the intrigue and he was only too happy to go along with it. They couldn't believe their luck when you left Herin in Eoferwic so he and Ælfric could scheme away together. Herin came to see us more than once with messages from Ælfric. Áedán finally made peace with the Picts and was mighty disturbed to find you were overlord over all his other neighbours. So when Herin reported on one of his visits that Ælfric would support him from the south, Áedán sent word to our brethren, the Gaels, to come over the water to help.'

'You keep saying Ælfric as though he acted alone. Surely Edwin as the future king was involved too?' Æthelfric asked.

'In all the talks I was involved in, his name hardly came up. Herin just said that he was too young to be interested and Ælfric made all the decisions. Don't forget, this all kicked off some time ago, so Edwin was younger then.'

Æthelfrith stroked his chin. He glanced at Acha. She had stopped trembling. Maybe she had put Conaing up to this to save her brother and herself. He sensed they had formed some sort of bond on their travels together

'It was certainly Ælfric who came up with the ambush idea,' Conaing continued. 'I remember the night well. It was cold so we all sat round the fire enjoying our wine when Herin said that Ælfric was always thinking of ways to avoid fighting battles and his latest idea was to somehow kill you and put Herin in charge of Bernicia and Ælfric in Deira. Áedán agreed as long as they accepted him as their overlord. Herin laughed at that. He was always a little on the arrogant side. But they agreed to it in the end.'

Æthelfrith nodded. That sounded like the Herin he knew. How could he have been so blind to it all?

'What role was Bebba playing in this?' he asked.

'I was coming to that,' Conaing said, looking at Acha. 'This was her Delilah moment.'

Æthelfrith felt irritated when he saw Acha half smile to show that she knew what Conaing meant, whilst he didn't know what he was talking about.

Conaing chuckled. 'Sorry I had forgotten you don't read our holy book. It has this story in it about a woman called Delilah who made a super–strong warrior weak by cutting off his hair. Well, Bebba said we would not defeat you unless we cut off your hair.'

'What nonsense is this?' snapped Æthelfrith.

'Not literally your hair. Bebba meant Theobald. She said he was the one behind your strategies. She said we had to kill you both, if we were to take over.'

Æthelfrith almost blushed. Was it so obvious that Theobald did his thinking for him?

A sharp tap at the door interrupted them and Æthelfrith opened it in a daze, taking a gulp of fresh air to clear his head. A guard was standing outside with a white-haired woman.

'My lord, you said you wanted a report on Lord Ælfric's health as soon as we knew it. Hilda is here to give it,' he said.

Æthelfrith exhaled wearily. 'Then speak, Hilda the healer.'

Hilda peered through the entrance and stepped cautiously forward. 'I see the owner of this knife is with you.' She held the weapon towards Acha, its blade cleaned of the blood that must have stained it.

'It was Theobald's. I took it from him when he was killed,' Acha said, quickly taking it.

Æthelfrith recognised the knife as the one that his brother always carried in his belt. He had almost forgotten that Acha had been with him when he died.

Hilda's eyes were wide and watchful. 'So it came to pass, did it? Was it that brutish Gael who killed him? I could tell he was sent by the elves.'

'You know him?' Acha asked, looking surprised.

'No, but I smelled him when he came here.'

Æthelfrith had been about to ask after Ælfric but this was more important news. 'Are you saying the Gael who killed my brother came here?'

The woman nodded. 'I was gathering bark for a remedy against the spotted fever. I found the quickbeam, apple and elder but I still needed willow, so I wandered further up the river to a small stream where I spied a strange boat stitched together with sticks and skin.'

'That'll be a curragh. Nothing strange about that,' Conaing interjected.

'I suppose not if you're a Gael all done up in chequered cloth like he was. I got his scent from fifty paces and thought he was a bear. Bigger than a bear when I saw him. As tall as you, lord king,' Hilda said looking up at Æthelfrith. 'If not taller. Wider too. I could tell he wasn't up to any good so I didn't go too near in case the guard saw me. '

'That would be Maelumai, the Irish champion. I was just getting to that part,' Conaing piped up.

Æthelfrith held up a hand to quieten him. 'Who else was there?'

'Someone with a sweeter smell who now has a bloodied

hand. And your cousin and a Christ man who hid his face in a brown hood,' Hilda said.

'You mean Ælfric, Herin and a monk,' Æthelfrith said. 'Did you hear what they said?'

'I watched and listened with my ear cupped but the wind only blew fragments my way. Names. Yours, lord king, and your brother's. And the Lady Acha.'

'Was Edwin there?' Æthelfrith glanced at Acha.

'He was briefly. He ran past the bush I was hiding behind carrying a giant rock and nearly threw it on Ælfric's foot. Thank the gods, he didn't stay long because his two thegns stood close by me, waiting for him and I feared they would uncover me at any moment.'

'Did you hear what he said?' It was Acha who stepped closer to Hilda, her eyes searching her face.

'I believe he was the one who spoke your name, m'lady.'

Æthelfrith looked at Conaing and Acha. There was more to this than he had realised. He needed to think, but he remembered the healer had come with news of Ælfric's health.

'How is Ælfric's wound?' he asked her.

'It will heal, m'lord. If you want it to,' Hilda replied with a wry smile.

*

Acha's mind was in turmoil when Æthelfrith turned to leave. Surely he was now convinced of Ælfric's guilt and Edwin's innocence. It was hard to tell from his set jaw and stern expression. What if the words of a foreigner and a healer were not enough for him?

'Wait, I have a further question,' she called to Hilda, who had begun to follow the king out of the door. Hilda turned and Acha waited until Æthelfrith was out of earshot.

'What did you mean when you said Ælfric's wound would heal *if we want it to*?'

'Exactly what I said m'lady. Once the skin has an open door, like that hole in his hand, evil spirits can creep through and poison the body. I can apply a poultice to either close the door or leave it open a while longer to see if any spirits come visiting.'

'Or maybe the poultice can make sure they do?' Acha whispered.

Twenty-Four

Edwin desperately hoped that the wheel of fortune would begin to spin in his favour. It had spun him to the depths of despair when he was forced to flee and become an exile, wandering through lands so foreign that he thought he must be on the edge of the world where goblins and dragons dwelled. Yet the wheel had taken an encouraging turn and he had landed in a hospitable place where Christ-men held sway over the people. Once he had accepted their god, they treated him like the prince he was, not an exile. Brother Rhun had swiftly taught him the rudiments of their faith and taken him to the river where he had splashed water at him and declared him a Christ-man too. He'd told him not to make sacrifices to his new God but pray on his knees with his head bent low instead. So every day he visited the strange building they called a church and asked for the power to drive out the devil king who had murdered his father and the return of the kingship that was rightly his. There was little sign that the Father, as he had learned to call him, was listening until the day the King of Mercia arrived in Gwynedd.

It was clearly an important moment for King Cadfan, who lined up his family and companions, including Edwin, to watch the sleek boat arrive. As the crew tightened ropes to the wharf so that the visiting king and his entourage could disembark, Edwin scrutinised the Mercian royal family. King Cearl stood out clearly in his gleaming chainmail and golden belt, although his plump body indicated that he had not stood in a shield wall for some time. But it was the young girl who followed him ashore that caught Edwin's eye. Her thick, honey-coloured hair immediately made him think of his sister and, when she stood before him whilst introductions were made, one glance from her soft blue eyes made him feel warm, just as he did when Acha had smiled on him. He wasn't the only one drawn to her. He noticed that Cadwallon was staring intently at her, fiddling with the strap of the helmet that never seemed to leave his head. As she walked up the incline towards the village, Edwin quickened his pace to draw level with her.

She flicked a strand of hair from her eyes. 'You're Edwin, yes? Although my name is Cwenburg, most people call me Cwen, which makes me sound like a queen even though I'm not, although father says I might marry an ætheling who will become a king, so then I would be. A queen I mean. I'd be Queen Cwen,' she said without seeming to pause for breath. 'Will you be a king one day?'

Edwin stumbled on a rock, his attention absorbed by the elfin figure beside him. 'Yes, I'm sort of a king now,' he replied, straightening up.

'Are you looking for a wife too?' she asked.

He felt his cheeks redden. 'I'm… no, maybe… '

She glanced over her shoulder towards Cadwallon, who was glowering behind them.

'He is, but he gives me the creeps. He should marry my sister. Her breasts are big enough to peep out of her dress. That would give him something to stare at.' She pulled the neck of her tunic forward and peered down. 'Mine are growing fast and they're a good size for my age, so mother says, but my sister just laughs and waggles her great udders in my face to show how small mine are.'

Edwin could not speak. Was she real or a fairy come to entrance him? Her eyes sparkled in the sunlight, softly studying him. He felt his heart beating like a drum in his chest as he struggled to find words. She hopped onto one foot as they walked along the baked mud path and sprang forward like a fawn. Landing awkwardly, she overbalanced and grabbed at Edwin's arm to keep her balance.

'Sorry. I'm not allowed to walk on cracks today.'

'Why not?'

He watched transfixed as she lifted the bottom of her long tunic, pointing to a deep crack in the pathway.

'I might disturb Loki if I walk on that.'

'What's a god doing down there?'

'My sister says it's so he can look up our skirts. Mother says it's so he can protect me. She says he will find me someone important to marry one day. Are you important?'

Edwin puffed out his chest. 'Yes. Yes I am. I am the son of Ælle, son of Yffe, King of Deira. He was powerful and ruled over many lands.'

She was studying him carefully. 'So why are you here?'

He could not take his eyes from her. Why was he so fascinated by this slip of a girl who talked too much? Maybe he should tease her, like he did Acha.

'Actually I am looking for a wife. Perhaps I should marry your sister if you are promised here.'

'Perhaps you should. If you want a life of misery.' She took a skip to avoid another crack in the path.

'I thought you said everyone wanted to marry her. Isn't she beautiful?'

She stopped her legs astride the crack, wobbling to keep her balance. 'Yes, that's why she would make your life a misery. Men with beautiful wives are always looking over their shoulder to see who is taking them to a different bed.'

He chuckled, emboldened. 'And I would not have that problem with you?'

'No, although they say I look like my mother and she is the most beautiful woman you'll ever see.' Edwin glanced around, looking for the queen. 'No, she's not here, Cwenburg said. She said it was not auspicious for her to travel. She's a soothsayer as well as a queen. She's teaching me her skills.'

'What have you learned?'

'How to look at someone's face and see not just their nose, eyes and mouth but their thoughts also.'

Edwin was mesmerised once again by her wide-eyed gaze. 'So what am I thinking now?'

'You are wondering if the buds on my chest will grow into big breasts like my sister's.'

She laughed and he did too, knowing just how right she was.

*

The next day, Edwin realised that the King of Gwynedd was sparing no expense to entertain his guests from Mercia. He had organised a rowing competition to take place across the narrow straits between the Island of Mon and the mainland. Edwin admired the boatmen's skills as he watched two curraghs of four oarsmen and a steersman race to the other side and back again. The distance was not far, a thousand paces of so, but there was a wicked stream running with jagged rocks to navigate. The steersmen seemed expert at impeding the opposition as the boats raced side by side, clashing oars and ramming each other as they weaved across the channel, around a marker and back to finish by the spectators. Cwenburg stood next to Edwin, jumping and clapping at the spectacle. She pulled at his sleeve, pointing towards one of the craft lined up for the next race. Cadwallon was in the steersman's seat, his face distorted as he screamed orders to his muscly oarsmen as the race began. He proved a skilled cox, cutting in front of the opposition, forcing them wide around a sandbank so they lost ground. His boat finished comfortably ahead and, as he leapt ashore to the wild acclaim of the onlookers, he looked towards Cwenburg and grinned. It was the first time Edwin had seen him remotely happy.

After more races, two boats remained undefeated: Cadwallon's crew and another who looked equally powerful and determined. To Edwin's annoyance, Cwenburg yelled encouragement for the king's son in a shrill voice as the boats sped through the swell, their bows level, their oars overlapping as Cadwallon tried to nudge his opponents towards a rocky outcrop. His tactics did not seem to be working until they hit the current in the centre of the straits. He must have known that the tide had strengthened because he veered sharply away from the other crew, seeming to take an unnecessary loop. The opposition realised the power of the current too late and were swept onto sharp rocks that tore through their craft's leathery skin. Cwenburg squealed loudly as the oarsmen floundered in the fast-flowing water and Edwin expected the men to drown. To his amazement, they used arms and legs to propel themselves to the shore unharmed, as Cadwallon urged his men home to claim victory.

In the absence of his queen, King Cearl asked his daughter to present the prize to the winners. When Cadwallon stepped forward to accept the trophy of a small silver blade from Cwenburg, he clasped her hand, pulled her firmly towards him and kissed her hard on the lips. He held the trophy aloft to the cheers of the crowd, grinning triumphantly towards Edwin.

You haven't won the main prize yet, thought Edwin.

That evening, the mead hall was full for the feast, the climax of the entertainment. When Edwin followed his host into the hall, he was pleased to be shown a seat of high status next to the Mercian king. Table-women elbowed their way between braying warriors who pinched and fondled them as they charged the tables with sizzling lamb and jugs of mead. Edwin felt at ease: it was just like home. He was not surprised to see that the women guests were seated at a separate table away from the boisterous menfolk. A sharp tap on the table brought the hall to silence as Brother Rhun rose to say prayers. Edwin wondered what the Mercians made of this Christian ritual; when he glanced towards Cwenburg, she did not seem to be taking it too seriously. She had already begun to munch her bread and stuck out her tongue at him when he caught her eye.

'I'm told you have adopted this strange god who speaks of peace.'

Edwin turned to the flabby figure of King Cearl, who had spoken to him as soon as prayers had finished.

'Yes, but he also speaks of driving out the devil in the form of wicked kings who usurp the rights of others.'

'Ah, you know of such one?' asked Cearl, swigging at his wine cup.

Edwin saw the cunning in his eye and wondered if he should speak warily.

No, there is no time for caution.

'Brother Rhun believes that the king who has forced me away from my kin is one such devil. He says that the Christ god will help me win back what I have lost.'

Cearl chuckled. 'You'd be better off with a large army.'

Edwin glanced towards Cwenburg before he replied. 'If I marry your daughter, would you support me? Your grandchildren would inherit the northern kingdoms after me.'

Cearl choked into his cup. 'Have a care, young man. You sew your seed on ground you have not yet prepared.'

Edwin glanced at Cadfan, who was eyeing them warily. 'The land here is fertile enough. This king has an appetite for my purpose.'

'Does he now? But there is another who you will need before you can succeed,' Cearl said, lowering his voice.

'The Saxon kings to the south?'

'No, my overlord, Rædwold, the Angle king to the east, is the only one who can command enough warriors to defeat your devil.'

'You will speak to him on my behalf?'

'I might, if you marry my daughter.' Cearl held up his hand as Edwin smiled towards Cwenburg. 'I don't mean that one. She is promised here. I have another at home who will be to your taste, I'm sure.'

Edwin grabbed Cearl's hand. 'I don't want her sister. I want Cwenburg.'

King Cearl stared hard at Edwin before excusing himself and staggering outside, a call of nature Edwin supposed. But he did not return even when the crackling pork was served. Edwin ordered more wine and munched thoughtfully at his food. He cast his eyes around the hall to where Lillan and Forthhere sat on a nearby table. Maybe he should have consulted with them before being so bold. The Mercian king had looked startled at his request, and he may have spoiled his chances. Why had the girl made him so imprudent? He recalled his sister's words when she had explained her affection for Theobald in the fateful moments before the battle. Could he be feeling something similar? He looked for Cwenburg on the women's table and watched as she laughed with her neighbours. Her giggling face took him back to his childhood once more when he had teased and played with Acha. He had been happy then and he could be once more with Cwenburg, he was sure of it. He would not give her up easily. That thought took his attention towards Cadwallon, who had been seated on the other side of his father, Cadfan. Both had left their seats.

A British warrior tapped his shoulder. 'The king asks to see you in private, m'lord,' he said, indicating the side door.

Edwin jumped up, wondering if it could be a trap and he should take Lillan and Forthhere with him, but there was no time to hesitate. He followed the warrior to an adjoining hut that he knew to be the king's dwelling. Both kings, Cearl and Cadfan, were waiting for him.

'Ah Edwin, come sit in my humble abode for a moment. Difficult to hear yourself speak in there.' Cadfan nodded towards the hall where the noise level had steadily risen as the wine flowed. 'Time is not on our side so I will be direct. Cearl tells me you have asked to marry his daughter, Cwenburg. I have to say I was not amused. It is not our custom to accept a king's hospitality and protection, and ask for the woman who has been promised to his son.'

Edwin hung his head.

Where are you, God? I thought you were answering my prayers.

'My son will be even more upset at the news. Probably challenge you to a duel,' Cadfan continued.

Edwin lifted his head. He would not be afraid to fight for Cwenburg.

Cearl stepped forward. 'Yet, there are advantages in the match. You may not be aware of the situation in Mercia, but I am without a direct heir since the death of my son and there are factions who would take advantage. If my daughter were to marry an ætheling from another court, it would serve my purpose.'

'I'm not just an ætheling. I should be king,' Edwin blurted out.

'Your pedigree is well known to us and you would be most welcome in our land.'

'So do I need to fight Cadwallon to marry Cwenburg or not?' Edwin asked.

Cadfan chuckled. 'We are too short of æthelings to have them bludgeon each other. No, you will not fight Cadwallon. You must become his blood brother to prevent enmity between you.'

Blood brother to that weird oaf! That means I can do him no harm. Well, at least I will have one less enemy to worry about.

'He will agree to this?' asked Edwin.

'He will,' Cadfan said.

'You and your thegns will give your oath to me,' said Cearl. 'And you will marry Cwenburg.'

Twenty-Five

Acha sat on a rock that had fallen from the crumbling walls of the old citadel and threw a pebble angrily into the bushes that had taken root amongst the ruins. It seemed a lifetime ago that she had run to this very spot to watch the thegn-sons practice their warrior skills, eager to admire their muscles gleaming in the dying light of the day. That was the time when her father had announced that the northern kings were gathering an army and that she must marry Æthelfrith to unite the Angle kingdoms against them. She smiled to herself when she remembered how she had believed all the tales about Æthelfrith the Ferocious so that she had railed against her father's choice. He was not at all like those stories, yet he was infuriating her right now. Although he had put off her wedding to Ælfric, he still insisted on talking to him before he would pronounce on her fate. Ælfric's hand wound had refused to heal, festering into a weeping puss, and he had a fever so that he no longer spoke any sense. The uncertainty was almost worse than the nightmare of her uncle recovering and persuading the king of his innocence once again. She had to wait to hear her fate with only a few guards to keep her company.

Tired of weaving with the women, she had thought it might be distracting to watch the battle training in the ruins once more. There were many more warriors now than the handful of thegns that used to entertain her. Æthelfrith's army had grown so much that she did not know all their faces, let alone their names. Where were Lillan and Forthhere? Hopefully, protecting her brother, but for all she knew they could be buried in some foreign field. She turned her back on the fighting. It no longer gave her any pleasure to see men struggle against each other even if it was not for real. The clash of swords still reminded her of the blow from the wicked blade that had sliced into Theobald's neck. Why did men always have to fight? She buried her face in her hands and began to cry.

'Lady Acha, are you alright?'

She heard a familiar voice and quickly wiped at her face with a sleeve, brushing the dust from her tunic. Leax was striding towards her, waving away the two guards who stood close by.

'The king sent me. I bring news,' he said, stopping at a respectful distance.

At last, Æthelfrith has come to his senses and realised the truth.

'Your Uncle Ælfric has died,' Leax said.

Dead! How dare he die before confessing. Or perhaps he did?

She cleared her throat and tried to feign sorrow.

'How so?'

'From a fever.' Leax shifted uncomfortably and looked down. 'His kin are holding you responsible and claiming wergild.'

Acha felt faint. Wergild was compensation for a crime and the price for killing the brother of a king would be well beyond her means. If she didn't pay, the family could claim her life instead.

Æthelfrith looked down at the festering hand of Ælfric's portly body.

'It did not seem like a mortal wound,' he said to Hilda, who crouched by the bed.

She dabbed at the yellow puss with a cloth. 'He died from a fever in his head. It could have come from anywhere.'

'But most likely from the stab to his hand?'

'Who knows? Men die of many things.' Hilda straightened her back with a grimace and looked the king in the eye. 'His brother died after a blow to his head, but it was not that which killed him.'

Æthelfrith narrowed his eyes. 'What are you saying, old woman? What has Ælle's death got to do with this?'

'King Ælle did not die from a simple fall, we both know that. Nor has Ælfric died simply from a flesh wound to his hand. No, other forces are at work.'

Æthelfrith glanced over his shoulder to see if anyone was listening. He knew she was hinting at something that he would not want others to hear.

'What sort of forces?'

'Could be the work of men who might gain from their death. Or it could be the elves punishing them for misdeeds.' She looked down at Ælfric and snorted. 'This one had plenty of those.'

He turned on his heel. 'Find Lord Leax and bring him to my quarters,' he called to one of the slaves who crouched by the eaves.

He need not have bothered. Leax was already outside his hut, questioning a scout who had recently arrived, judging by his mud-splattered appearance.

'We have news of Edwin, lord,' Leax explained. 'It seems he fled to the south-west and has taken shelter in Gwynedd.'

'Gwynedd? How did he get that far?'

'Probably in one of the boats the Gaels had hidden in the forest.'

'Anyone with him?'

'The trader who gave us the news says he was alone except for a couple of thegns.'

Æthelfrith saw the concern in Leax's eyes. 'Your son, Lillan?'

'One was described as tall and thin, so yes, probably Lillan. And Forthhere. They are both oath-bound to Edwin.'

'Lets talk inside,' said Æthelfrith as Leax dismissed the scout and followed his king through the door. Æthelfrith sat wearily in the throne-like chair in the centre of the hut that had once belonged to King Ælle, trying to absorb the torrent of information that he felt was drowning him: stories of Ælfric's plots and now news of Edwin with a British king, no doubt fermenting more trouble.

'How do we winkle him out of Gwynedd?' he asked.

'Do we need to? He can't do us much harm from there. Perhaps we should resolve our problems here first. The men are growing restless,' Leax said.

Æthelfrith knew he was alluding to the issue of how to govern Deira now that Ælfric was dead and what to do with the king's daughter who had stabbed him. He trusted Leax in matters of war but had never taken him into his confidence on these more delicate matters. He stroked his moustache thoughtfully.

'There is something we could do that would please them, lord, although I fear you may find me bold to suggest it,' Leax continued.

'Try me,' said the king.

*

Acha lay on her bed, feigning sleep, her mind alert. She could hear the roars and shouts from Eoferwic's mead hall. It was time for Conaing to come. He had surprised her with his deep concern for her safety when he had heard about the claim of wergild against her. He had also heard rumours of disquiet amongst the Deiran warriors who had become disillusioned with the heirs of King Ælle and were looking to other families for a successor. He had strongly advised her to escape with him and seek refuge in Dál Riata and find her brother. With no word from Æthelfrith and the council, she had still hesitated. But when word came that Edwin had been seen in faraway Gwynedd and pronounced to be an exile, stripped of any inheritance, she had reluctantly agreed to Conaing's plan. He would come for her during the mead hall feast. She didn't know how he would deal with the guard permanently outside her hut, but he had assured her he would come when the warriors had drunk their fill so that they could sneak away during the night.

A sharp tap at the door told her he had arrived, so she shot up, clutching a small bag, ready to run.

It was not Conaing whose outline appeared in the doorframe. It was a much taller figure who swayed as he approached.

'M'lord Æthelfrith. What are you doing here?'

I've come to marry you,' he said with a slur.

Acha's mind raced. Was he playing a cruel joke on her? What had happened to Conaing?

'What do you mean, marry you?'

Æthelfrith giggled as he stumbled over a stool but managed to catch it and sit down unsteadily.

'Ælle told me. Theobald told me. Now Leax has too. I should marry you. You are the one.'

'Which one?' Acha asked, straining to understand his speech.

'The peash… peace-weaver,' he managed to say.

Acha's mind flashed back to the moment her father had used those very words to inform her she was to marry the man who now sat slumped before her. So that was it. Once more, her fate was to be decided by the political wishes of land-grabbing warlords. And just as she was on the verge of escaping to the far north with someone driven by romance, rather than power. She glanced through the door hoping Conaing would not choose this moment to arrive.

'Sorry I didn't believe you about Ælfric. I was stupid. Can't think straight since… ' He put his hands over his eyes. Æthelfrith's enormous frame crumpled and he began to sob. Acha felt a mixture of sympathy and panic.

Is he crying? Should I call someone for help?

He snuffled and glanced at her through red eyes, but he could not control himself and almost fell off the stool. Acha's instincts took over. She quickly put her arm around him, steadying him and making comforting noises as if he were a baby. He grabbed her around the waist and put his heavy head on her chest, weeping and weeping until she thought he would never stop. She ran her fingers through his hair.

He's crying for Theobald. How familiar his hair feels. Just like his brother's.

He tightened his grip around her, desperately trying not to fall from the stool. 'Will you ever forgive me?'

Yes, I can forgive you. But I'm not sure I will ever love you like…

'And marry me, just like Theobald said?'

She could not support his weight any longer and tried to protect his head as his body crumpled to the floor

I have a difficult choice to make.

*

Æthelfrith woke in a strange room. He almost called for a guard but memories from the night before came flooding back. He sat, hands to his head, remembering first his conversation with Leax, who had convinced him that the solution to his problems was right before his eyes. Except he shouldn't have got so drunk before he came to tell her. Now he was in her room. He had vague recollections of talking to her, but what had he said? He had intended to say that he had grown very fond of her, that he admired her courage and determination, that he wanted her as a wife. But he could not remember what, if anything, he had told her. A slave-maid advanced from the eaves of the hut.

'Where is your mistress?' he called.

'She bade me look after you and went to sleep elsewhere, lord.'

Æthelfrith scrambled to his feet, brushing at his crumpled clothing and trying to untangle his hair.

'Bring me water. Lots of cold water,' he muttered.

Once he had bathed his face and rubbed at his eyes, he called the guard who stood outside the door.

'Where did the Lady Acha go?' he asked.

The guard looked at him curiously. 'She went to find Hilda, m'lord. She said you had fallen ill.'

'And did she return?'

'Hilda came and said that the Lady Acha would rest with her as you were not to be disturbed here, m'lord.'

Æthelfrith barged past the guard, casting his eyes around the small village, breathing in the fresh morning air, trying to clear his head.

So I did see her. But did I tell her that I wanted to love her so that we could be as happy as she and Theobald had been?

He did not know where Hilda's dwelling was so he made first for the hall. Sleeping warriors still lay on the benches around the walls whilst slaves cleaned the mess of the feast from the floor. The stench of vomit and stale ale almost made him wretch. It had been a really good night. He called to the women crouched around the embers of the fire, stirring the pots of breakfast stew.

'Where's Hilda?'

'She sleeps over there, m'lord,' one of the women said pointing to a table.

Æthelfrith felt like kicking her awake but he bade the woman do it for him. Hilda peered at him through narrow eyes when she finally managed to drag herself out from under the table and present herself.

'Where is Acha? I'm told you were with her last night.'

'Yes lord, I was. And with you. I gave you a potion to help your sombre mood. Are you improved?'

'Much better, thank you. So where is Acha?'

'I gave her my bed in the women's hut, but she said she had to see to some travel arrangements first.'

'What travel arrangements?'

'Why, she said she had been ordered to return to Bebbanburg for her own safety. With Conaing.' Hilda raised her eyebrows as if thinking that Æthelfrith would know all about it.

'Find Conaing mac Áedán and bring him to me at once,' Æthelfrith said to the guard who had come into the hall with him.

'I think I saw him come in here after I had returned.' Hilda was looking around the benches of the hall. 'Yes, there he is,' she said pointing to a prostrate figure snoring by the wall.

'Find me Lady Acha instead,' Æthelfrith shouted after the guard. 'No wait. I will find her myself.'

*

Acha felt a tug at her sleeve. She was dreaming of rowing into a small cove with Theobald. Or was it Conaing? Their images blurred as she tried to drag open her eyes.

'The king wants to see you,' the old woman said.

Good. I just hope he hasn't completely forgotten what happened last night.

When she was led outside she was surprised to see him standing alone, fiddling agitatedly with his sword belt.

'Good morning, lord. I hope you have recovered.'

'Yes, yes. Hilda gave me something. I hope I was not too… too disturbed?'

'You were distraught, missing your brother I think.'

'I was, yes but I… well I also wanted to say something to you.'

'You did, lord,' Acha said trying to stay calm and not blurt out that, based on what he had said, she had taken one of the most difficult decisions of her life.

'Did I… ?' Æthelfrith hesitated, seeming to realise that he was standing in front of a hut full of women, some of whom had begun to peer at him through the door. 'Can you walk with me a while?'

Great. He's forgotten what he said. Pity. He did look so like his brother.

Acha smiled through gritted teeth. 'Of course. Shall we go to the ruins?'

They always had a special meaning for her and she still hoped this might be a special moment. They walked in silence until they passed the waste pits that marked the edge of the village. As they made their way through the fallen stones of the citadel, Æthelfrith cleared his throat.

'Did I make a complete fool of myself last night?'

'No, not at all. Quite the opposite. I began to understand you for the first time. But you were very drunk.' She took his arm and chuckled. 'I had to hold you like this to stop you falling. And you cried, which was good.'

'Is it ever good to see a man cry?' His shoulders drooped and he avoided her gaze.

'Oh yes, especially when it is over someone you love. It shows you can.'

'Can what?'

Acha sighed inwardly. Perhaps this was going to be more difficult than she thought.

'It shows you can love someone. Which was good as you had just said you were going to marry me, although I knew you were crying about your brother, not me.'

He looked relieved. 'Did you reply? About marrying me I mean. I know I can order it, but I would rather you agreed.'

'I didn't reply because I was hoping to know first if I was anything other than just a peace-weaver to you.'

His face reddened. 'I didn't tell you?'

I know you felt something, which is why I am here now.

'No you didn't, but you can now.'

He took a deep breath. 'I know Theobald had deep affection, some would call it love, for you.' Acha tried to look him in the eye but he glanced down as he continued. 'He and I were very close and thought the same way about most things, so it's only natural I should share his feelings for you.' He looked relieved and pleased with himself.

Acha smile. *That's probably as good as I am going to get. At least I'm not just a peace-weaver.*

Epilogue

One Year Later

Acha cradled the perfect baby on her knees and looked into the blue eyes that stared up at her. Æthelfrith was not yet home. Time to admire their baby. He had wanted to call him Theobald but Acha had said she could not bear to be constantly calling out that name, so they had compromised and named him Oswald. The ending of the name honoured his dead brother and the beginning would represent a new lineage for their future sons. There were plenty of names to choose from: Oswin, Oswy, Oslac and more. They both knew of the tragedies that could befall a small group of siblings so they planned to have a large family. Besides, she was enjoying the process of making babies more than she had expected. Her husband was always particularly attentive when he returned from his travels and the thought that he might soon be home made her skin tingle with anticipation. She had raised the subject of girls' names but, when Æthelfrith had suggested Ebba, she had quietly dropped the subject. It reminded her too much of his former queen who had disappeared with his first son. It was bad enough having Bebbanburg, her home, named after her.

She only wished she knew more of what had happened to her brother, Edwin. There were rumours that he had been seen in Mercia but she had heard nothing from him. She still believed he had been tricked into playing the role he had in Theobald's death, but he probably still felt too guilty about it to send her a message. Although he had been pronounced an exile, she had persuaded Æthelfrith not to pursue him too hard. They could live in peace, even if there was only silence between them.

At last, she heard the lookout's cry and the clanging of the bell. That would be her husband returning. She wrapped baby Oswald in a woollen shawl and carried him proudly towards the gate of the fortress to see his father return.

*

Æthelfrith urged his horse into one last effort. The first sighting of his fortress as he came over the hills always spurred him on and now he had the added incentive of being reunited with his new son. He hadn't felt like this the first time he had become a father. When Bebba had given birth, she had handed Eanfrith over to maids so that he hardly ever saw him and, once his mother had taken him into the mountains of Pictland, he had suppressed all affection for both mother and son. Instead he directed his fatherly feelings towards Oswald. He could already see what a great warrior he would become by his strong-looking arms and the firm grip of his fingers.

The boy was lucky to have Acha for a mother. She had changed abruptly from a girl to a woman the moment he was born and he loved the way she cared for his son. Theobald would be proud of her and pleased that he had taken her as his wife. He often thought how lucky he was that his brother had insisted she should come with them to Bebbanburg, away from her odious uncle. Despite his earlier misgivings, he had grown to appreciate her to the point where he could not imagine being without her. Was that what some people called love? He wasn't sure but it was good enough for him. And they would soon have a family large enough to secure his line for generations to come. The days of his hot-blooded youth were over. He no longer risked himself in wild skirmishes as he had done. Life with his family was too precious for that. Now he was a wise and serious king who ruled because he had the largest army of all the northern kingdoms. He paraded his warriors around his territories to demonstrate his power, knowing that no one would challenge him in pitched battle, unless... No he didn't want to put himself in a bad humour by thinking of that just as he arrived home. He would send scouts to check and see if Edwin really had married into the Mercian royal family before he worried too much. For now, he just wanted to enjoy his beautiful wife and son.

*

Edwin gazed at Cwenburg's swollen tummy and wondered at the miracle that was creating a child inside her. His new God truly worked in wonderful ways, as Rhun often reminded him. He closed his hands in prayer, kneeling before her curled body on the bed. He prayed that she would survive the birthing so that he could continue to enjoy this wonderful creature who had somehow fallen into his arms. He also asked God for a son. The birth of a grandson to King Cearl would reinforce his position within the Mercian ruling elite. Cwenburg's mother had already divined his name as Osfrith. She had seen a vision of a line of kings whose names all began with *Os,* and the ending of his name, *Frith*, signified peace. So she had declared that Osfrith would become a mighty but peaceful leader. Edwin had not argued. His new God preached peace and forgiveness and for the moment that was a convenient cloak for the real ambition that he always turned to at the end of his prayers. He prayed for revenge against another *frith* who had stolen his kingdom and his sister. He would not rest until he had destroyed him and won back what was rightfully his.

Historical Notes

When I read historical fiction, I like to know what is based on reliable evidence from the past and what is derived purely from the author's imagination. Unless I am familiar with a particular period, I often find it difficult to draw the line between fact and fiction. If you share this need, or if you are just interested in knowing more about the setting of this novel, I hope you will find these notes of use. As it is a relatively unknown period, they are more detailed than perhaps is usual.

Society in Britain, AD 600

From its origins in the fifth century to its demise in the eleventh, Anglo-Saxon Britain evolved from simple tribal groups into one of the most sophisticated societies in Europe. It began in the 'Dark Ages', so called because written records all but disappeared when the Roman army withdrew from Britannia around AD 400 and plunged the country into chaos. Society disintegrated into a multitude of rival tribal groups made up from the British population of mixed Celtic origin, and Angles and Saxons and other immigrants from northern Europe.

Two hundred years later in AD 600, when this book begins, these factions had consolidated into a number of territories led by both British and Anglo-Saxon kings. A social hierarchy had developed with a warrior elite at the top and slaves at the bottom whilst literacy was reborn as Christianity spread. But the more sophisticated society, with the towns, trading centres, laws, literature, mints and stone-built churches that came to typify the Anglo-Saxon world by the time of the Viking invasions, remained many years into the future.

British and Anglo-Saxon societies were probably quite similar by this time. Economically, they were very dependent on agriculture with few options for employment outside farming, unless you were born into the warrior elite. The vast majority of the population lived in scattered, self-sufficient communities. There was minimal coinage, so trading relied heavily on barter. It was a world without towns: trading ports or 'wics' had just begun to develop, for example at London (Lundenwic), Ipswich (Gyppeswic) and York (Eoferwic), but there were no settlements of any size. Royal families had begun to construct centres for use by themselves and their warriors based around large halls, but these housed relatively small numbers of people. They built almost exclusively in wood; stone working on any scale was not reintroduced into Britain until the building of churches and ecclesiastical centres later in the seventh century. The remains of Roman stone-built towns and villas were left to decay as memorials to a past generation, referred to as 'the work of giants' in Anglo-Saxon poems such as *The Ruin*.

This does not mean that the people of Britain in the sixth and seventh centuries led primitive lives. Archaeological finds have revealed artefacts of elaborate household articles, stylish clothing and finely made tools and weapons, many with intricate ornamentation that has astonished even the experts. The excavation of the boat burial at Sutton Hoo was one of several finds that overturned the notion that this was simply a 'brutish' period of history. The iconic Sutton Hoo helmet found amongst the treasure illustrates not just the warrior class of the buried chieftain but also the sophistication of a society capable of producing the intricate decorative motifs and gold embossing found on the headpiece.

Timber-built halls were at the centre of Anglo-Saxon life and used extensively for eating, celebrating and meetings. Satellite huts around them were for everyday living and working and often had pits beneath the flooring for storage and ventilation (referred to as sunken-featured buildings by archaeologists). Anglo-Saxon buildings consisted of one, single-storey room, so privacy was hard to come by. Cloth partitions may have been used, and by the late sixth century some huts did have small chambers at one end, possibly acting as an entrance porch to give residents some separation from the outside world. Their villages were not intended as defensive military bases as they had no fortifications or even fences. That all changed later in the ninth century with the development of walled towns or 'burghs' initiated by King Alfred and his successors in response to the Viking invasions.

As kingdoms developed, their leaders began to demonstrate their status through larger buildings on elite, royal sites. Imposing halls with tall, timbered interiors richly decorated with tapestries became the status symbols of powerful kings. A ruler such as Ælle of Deira may have built a number of such royal compounds, including the one at Eoferwic, in order to travel around his territory to ensure loyalty and collect tributes.

Both Anglo-Saxon and British communities adopted a code of values typical of a **'heroic'** society that stressed physical and moral courage. Much depended on the bond between a lord or chieftain and his military retainers who formed a close-knit group of **'thegns'**, often based on family ties. Loyalty was much prized, the blood feud the unhappy consequence of betrayal. To be outside of this 'kin' was to be an exile, a greatly feared and distrusted fate (as experienced by Edwin). As the 'ring-giver', the lord rewarded his followers with gifts such as precious metals and land and provided a feasting hall that brought the rural community together for social interchange, entertainment and news. In return, he demanded not just loyalty but a 'render' of agricultural produce from his farming followers.

In the halls, heroic tales would be narrated, poetry recited, and riddles posed, sometimes by travelling performers and poets (Anglo-Saxon 'scops' or British 'bards'). The stories were recounted orally and passed on by word of mouth so only a few have survived. These include the epic *Beowulf*, which reflected the values of its Anglo-Saxon listeners even though it tells of heroic deeds in Sweden and Denmark. Others, such as the *Wanderer* and the *Wife's Lament*, are cautionary tales that warn the audience of the consequences of living outside of their tightly organised society.

Riddles in the form of extended metaphors that conceal everyday objects were also popular. These, more than the epic poetry, reflect the life of ordinary people, rather than the elite warrior group, as they are more concerned with crops and household objects than battles and weaponry. Nearly a hundred such riddles have been preserved in the *Exeter Book*, which stands as a testament to the earthy humour of the period. (See Chapter 1 and elsewhere for examples.)

The love of riddles flows through into the language of the literature, which often used expressive, condensed metaphors (or 'kennings') to describe ordinary objects: for example, the sea became the 'whale's path' or 'ship's road' in *Beowulf*. The name 'peace-weaver' was applied to a woman who married into a rival group in an attempt to establish peace between feuding families. The Anglo-Saxon warrior culture demanded revenge for the death of a chief from loyal followers, so feuds were a common feature of society and it often took a woman to stop them.

Although the farming communities produced surpluses for exchange, **trading** was difficult during this time. With no established trading centres, it was dependent on itinerant merchants (such as Guthlaf, the Frisian trader). Without coinage, exchange relied on barter often using balance scales and weights. However, there is evidence of long-distance trading relationships: Britain was known for its export of slaves (see Bede's story of Gregory in the slave market in the Prologue); and imported goods from continental Europe, Egypt and India were present in the Sutton Hoo burial site.

The commonest **clothing** for early Anglo Saxon women was a tube-shaped dress (or 'peplos'), worn over an undergarment and fastened at each shoulder by a long, oblong-shaped brooch. Cloaks and capes secured with a single brooch were also common. Long strings of amber beads were the favoured jewellery. At the end of the sixth century, fashions began to change, (as Acha discovers in Chapter 3). The introduction of Christianity into Kent brought continental tastes with it. The tubular peplos gave way to the tunic, previously worn as an undergarment. These were often brightly coloured in a woven woollen cloth, with silk trimmings to the hems and sleeves for the more wealthy. The festoons of amber beads largely gave way to smaller necklaces, with decorative items in silver, gold, amethyst and shell. The shape of brooches changed from square to circular as annular and disc brooches became more common. Some of these were quite elaborate, built up of metal discs decorated with garnets and lined with gold foil.

Men also dressed in colourful clothes and were particularly fond of belts with large, highly decorative buckles. Small cloaks or capes, some made of fur, were commonly used as a versatile garment that could also be used as a blanket at night. The basic dress seemed to have been a short, girdled tunic over loosely woven trousers. Leggings of stronger material such as leather afforded further protection if needed. Long hair, beards and moustaches were probably the norm. Protective clothing for the warriors would have been predominantly made of leather and heavy material, including the helmets. Metal protection was expensive, so only the richest leaders could afford the chainmail or metal headgear as displayed in the famous Sutton Hoo finds.

Many aspects of Anglo-Saxon and British cultures had begun to merge by this time as the races mingled, but one key differentiator remained: **language**. During the Roman occupation, many Britons spoke Latin but also a common British language labelled by scholars as 'Brittonic'. By the end of the sixth century, Brittonic had become the common language of the indigenous British population, although it then developed into various dialects including Welsh and Cornish. In contrast, the immigrant Angles and Saxons spoke a Germanic language that developed into Anglo-Saxon or Old English. As the Anglo-Saxon influence spread, so did their language.

The political landscape

The story opens at the end of the sixth century in the Kingdom of **Deira**. Archaeological evidence suggests that immigrant groups of Angles from modern-day Denmark, allied with Anglian mercenaries already in Britain, gradually established this kingdom to occupy much of modern-day Yorkshire between the Humber Estuary and the River Tees. Later, a small group of Anglian warriors established a foothold in the neighbouring territory to the north of Hadrian's Wall, in **Bernicia**, approximating to Northumberland today.

These territories, later to become known as Northumbria, were surrounded by a number of British kingdoms. In a region covering southern Scotland and the northernmost parts of England were the realms of 'Hen Ogled' or the 'Old North': **Gododdin** centred on Din Eidyn (Edinburgh) in an area roughly conforming to Lothian; **Strad Clud** based in Strathclyde around Alt Clut (Dumbarton Castle); **Rheged** in what is now Cumbria; and **Elmet** around modern-day Leeds. Further north were the kingdoms of the **Dál Riata** in the western highlands, and the **Picts** to the east, whilst to the south was **Gwynedd** in northern Wales. (See map page 301.)

Over the rest of England, the Anglo-Saxons had become the dominant ruling class, establishing kingdoms in Mercia, East Anglia, Kent, Sussex, Essex and Wessex. Further west, British kings were in control in Cornwall (Dumnonia) and southern Wales (Powys and Dyfed).

Historical sources and the return of Christianity

Written records begin again at this time largely because Christianity re-emerges to become the predominant religion. The Roman Empire had adopted Christianity as its official faith from the time of the Emperor Constantine in the fourth century, but when Britannia broke away from the Empire in the fifth century, the influence of the religion dwindled. The Anglo-Saxon immigrants were pagans, following Woden, Thunor and Tiw, who mirrored their warrior culture, and Frigg, goddess of love.

However, the Christian faith was preserved amongst communities of Celtic monks in the West Country and Ireland. By the sixth century, they had reconverted many of the British kingdoms that survived in western England, Wales and Scotland. In AD 597, Pope Gregory (of the 'Angles or angels' fame – see Prologue) sent a mission under Augustine to the Anglo-Saxon court of Æthelbert of Kent, who was duly converted along with his followers. During the next century, all of the Anglo-Saxon kingdoms adopted Christianity as their main faith. At the beginning of this story, the Angles of Deira and Bernicia still worshiped their old gods.

Both British and Anglo-Saxon monks instigated a tradition of historical writing, so written records began to reappear in the British Isles. British clerics compiled 'annals', many of which are summarised in the *Chronicle of Ireland* including writings at the monastery of Iona from the seventh century. A Welsh monk, **Nennius**, wrote the *History of the Britons* in the ninth century.

The most celebrated historian of the time is **Bede**, an English monk from Northumbria who compiled the *Ecclesiastical History of the English People* in the early eight century and set the standard for such works. Later in the ninth century, the *Anglo-Saxon Chronicle* was commissioned and gives some details of this era.

Some early British poetry has also been preserved from this time including *The Gododdin* by **Aneirin**, which eulogises many famous contemporary warriors (some of whom appear in the chapters on the Battle of Catræth, including the poet himself).

Later medieval historians also recorded some of the events from these times, including the twelfth-century clerics **Reginald of Durham** and **Geoffrey of Monmouth**. They are less reliable witnesses as they were writing centuries later but they may have had access to earlier histories that have now disappeared.

This means that after a gap of around two hundred years, we finally know a little more about the individuals who made history at this time. Real people begin to populate a landscape hitherto shrouded in the mythical mists surrounding characters such as King Arthur.

Wherever possible, I have adopted individuals who are referenced in the historical records as the characters for this book, so most of the people in this story were actually alive around fourteen hundred years ago. (See the 'Key Characters' at the beginning of the book that lists those who did, or did not, exist).

How did the Anglo-Saxons take over England?

So exactly how did immigrant Anglo-Saxon warlords come to rule England and impose their culture, laws and language on the more numerous British population?

That is the big question from these times. Unfortunately, the availability of written history does not mean we have accurate records of the period. Archaeological and DNA evidence is often at odds with contemporary chroniclers, so it is difficult to understand how events unfolded. The traditional portrayal is that, after centuries of constant warfare between the rival races, the indigenous population was wiped out, only surviving in the 'Celtic fringes' of Scotland, Wales and western England.

The reality was much more subtle. Although the Anglo-Saxon culture did eventually prevail in England, there was no widespread killing or removal of the native population. Ruling elites based on immigrant families gradually acquired power over a population that still retained many roots in the old Romano-British population. Intermarriage and further immigration over a long period meant that the population reflected many ethnic influences, especially in the non-ruling classes of society. There were alliances as well as conflict between Anglo-Saxon and British rulers, as this story illustrates, and the lineages of Anglo-Saxon royalty included British names. The neat division of kingdoms into 'British', 'Angle' or 'Saxon' only reflects the family origin of the rulers and not necessarily that of the ruled.

Early mediaeval historians were often recording oral stories that had been doing the rounds of feasting halls decades earlier with many opportunities for elaboration and mistakes. Religion also played a key role in putting bias into history. A keen rivalry developed between the Celtic monastic institutions and the ecclesiastical hierarchy stemming from Rome. This religious divide reflected the ethnic origins of the ruling classes, as the Anglo-Saxon kings were converted mainly by the Roman Church, whereas the British rulers came under the sway of Celtic monks. This led the ecclesiastical chroniclers to exaggerate racial divisions in society and to distort the significance of events. The English historian Bede, whose loyalty lay with Rome, had little time for British Christians. He even praised the massacre of British monks by the pagan King Æthelfrith (see *Ecclesiastical History*, II, 2). This distinction between Christian clerics was emphasised in the hairstyles of the monks: the Romanised tonsure was to shave a circle at the top of the head, leaving a halo effect; Celtic monks were shorn over the head from ear to ear, leaving the back long.

Warfare and the two battles

The book is set at a crucial time, around AD 600, when the British kings of the 'Old North' could only defeat the Anglian kings by combining their forces against them, and they made several attempts to do so. Anglo-Saxon and British kings retained a number of warriors within their households as permanent standing armies that did the majority of the fighting. In later Anglo-Saxon times, ordinary farmers and other freemen were obliged to do military service in the so-called 'fyrd' (and I have suggested the beginning of this with Theobald's farmer-archers). But at this time, it seems that battles were slugged out between sides of professional warriors who did little else but fight, train, eat, drink and tell tales of their fighting. But such troops were expensive to keep, and the agricultural and trading surpluses to pay for them hard to come by. Their numbers were therefore low: early written sources document armies of less than one hundred. Sometimes these would combine to create a larger force of a few hundred, such as the one that drove Æthelfrith's predecessors into the sea. The Gododdin army was a relatively large unit of three hundred mounted fighters drawn from several British kingdoms, and it was probably defeated by a combined force of Deiran and Bernician warriors. Movement was often quicker by boat, so even in the pre-Viking age, the size of armies was often measured by the number of boats, with around thirty-five men to a boat.

The fighting itself was man to man and brutal. Warriors would form up close to the opposing force before attempting to maim and kill them with swords and spears. Protection was limited to wooden shields and thick leather coats and helmets, unless you were rich enough to afford chainmail or, even rarer, a metal helmet.

We are not sure exactly where the two key battles in this book took place. **Catræth** is widely assumed to be Catterick in North Yorkshire, which was the site of a small Roman fort, Cataractonium, strategically placed near Deere Street, forty miles north from York. But why did a British warband bypass its most immediate enemy in Bernicia, whose stronghold, Bebbanburg, lay eighty miles to the north-east, and thus expose itself so far from its base in Edinburgh? This issue has led some to suggest that the battle probably took place further north. My plot gives the British a reason to have the confidence to go so far afield: they believed Æthelfrith would remain neutral because of his pact with them. He became known in British literature as Æthelfrith the 'Twister' or the 'Artful', implying that he may have used cunning strategies such as this.

The site of the **Battle of Degsastan** is even more uncertain. Despite Bede's assertion that Degsa's Stone was well known, it has never been found. I have followed the commonly accepted siting in Dawstone in Liddesdale on the Scottish Borders. The Irish annals record that Áedán of Dál Riata set fire to homesteads on his way to the battle, which is surprising behaviour considering he was probably in the territory of his ally, the Strad Clud. I have used this to suggest Aidan was luring Æthelfrith into a trap. The *Anglo-Saxon Chronicle* records that 'Herin, son of Hussa led the host hither', which I have taken to mean that Herin had indeed defected to the enemy and showed them the way around the Bernician defences. We know from Bede that not only was Theobald killed but all his army was destroyed in the battle too. I have taken this to imply that Degsastan was more of a campaign than just a one-off encounter.

The people and the places

So what do the historical records tell us of the ruling elite and the places where they lived in northern Britain at the end of the sixth century?

In Yorkshire, the kings of Deira traced their lineage back through many generations to Woden, but the first one of whom we have any certain knowledge is **Ælle**, son of Yffi, who ruled from c. AD 570. Bede documents that he was still king at the time of Augustine's mission to Kent in AD 597, so his reign by Anglo-Saxon standards was very long, probably thirty years. He successfully enlarged his area of control at the expense of the neighbouring British territories including the old Roman capital at York (Eoferwic).

Although the *Anglo-Saxon Chronicle* records his death earlier in 588, I have used Bede's dating as the more reliable. How Ælle died is not clear: the twelfth century monk-historian Reginald of Durham states he was killed by Æthelfrith, although Bede and others are silent on what would have been a significant matter. I have therefore used this ambiguity to assume Æthelfrith's role in his death was largely hushed up.

Ælle's daughter, Acha, was born around AD 585, and his son Edwin circa AD 588. There is no other named sibling in the records, but Bede (*Ecclesiastical History*, IV, 23) records that Edwin had a nephew, so an elder brother who died at an early age may have existed, as I have suggested. We have no information about their mother.

Acha is recorded as Edwin's sister by Bede and by Reginald of Durham. She married Æthelfrith early in the seventh century. Marriages of convenience in which women would be offered as 'peace-weavers' between rival families were standard practice in this period. However, the fact that she had six sons by someone who had possibly killed her father and exiled her brother, provides some evidence that their relationship was more than just political expediency. It was the Anglo-Saxon custom to signify a common lineage by the first letter of their names. Æthelfrith had six sons, as listed in the *History of the Britons* and the *Anglo-Saxon Chronicles*, whose names all begin with 'O'. The first of these was Oswald, born around AD 604, and we know his mother was Acha (He was later to become king and sainted, but more of him in Book Two of the series.) So it is reasonable to assume she was also the mother of the other 'O' named sons. There is an odd-one out: a seventh son named Eanfrith, who is likely to have been the offspring of Bebba, Æthelfrith's other known wife. (More on Bebba and her son below.)

Acha would certainly have felt torn in her allegiances when Æthelfrith exiled her brother, took over her father's throne and became her husband. We do not know the nature of the relationship between Acha and Æthelfrith's brother, Theobald.

Edwin is extensively documented by Bede (particularly as he was one of the first Christian Anglo-Saxon rulers – again, more of that in Book Two). As told in this book, he was probably no more than twelve or thirteen when his father King Ælle died, so he was too young to rule. Several sources document that an interim king took over for a few years after Ælle's death and before Æthelfrith combined Deira and Bernicia into the one kingdom of Northumbria. The *Anglo-Saxon Chronicle* records that it was a certain Æthelfric who succeeded Ælle, but nothing is known for sure of his lineage. Bede mentions that Ælle did have a brother Ælfric and I have assumed that he and Æthelfric are the same person (partly to simplify the proliferation of names beginning with Æ) and that Ælfric effectively ruled Deira during Edwin's minority.

Bede relates how Edwin was forced into exile and 'wandered secretly as a fugitive for many years through many places and kingdoms' (*Ecclesiastical History* II, 12). He is reported (e.g. by Reginald of Durham) to have been received first by King **Cadfan**, the Christian king of Gwynedd. There he met Cadfan's son, **Cadwallon**, who was to become a most dangerous foe later in his life. Edwin came under the protection of King **Cearl** of Mercia when he married his daughter, **Cwenburg**, by whom he had two sons, Osfrith and Eadfrith. British sources record that he received baptism from **Rhun**, brother of Owain, and son of Urien of Rheged.

Bede also tells of two Deiran thegns, **Lilla** and **Forthhere who served Edwin** (I will not explain the context here as it would give away the fate that awaits them in Book Two). I have slightly amended Bede's spelling of 'Lilla' to 'Lillan' to avoid confusion with feminine derivatives of the name for the modern reader.

Anglo-Saxon kings spent a considerable part of their lives moving around their territory so they probably had a number of royal centres. **Eoferwic**, modern-day York, probably become part of Deira during Ælle's reign. The Romans who founded it as a strategic military centre in AD 71 knew it as Eboracum.

At its centre was a massive fortress, including the principia – the administrative headquarters. Either side of a courtyard were other buildings including a large aisled hall or basilica which stood where York Minster is today. To the Anglo-Saxons of AD 600, who built only modest structures in wood, these massive buildings must indeed have seemed to be the 'work of giants'. Excavations beneath York Minster have shown that the great Roman hall was probably still standing right up until the ninth century and many of the surrounding walls remain today. Modern tour guides of the area still have many tales of Roman ghosts from the past to tell.

Bernicia was established north of the River Tees probably by a small band of disaffected warriors from Deira led by Ida, Æthelfrith's grandfather, around AD 550. The paucity of Anglo-Saxon archaeological finds from this time suggests they imposed their will on the indigenous population, removing the native ruling class of the old British kingdom of Brynaich, but not their subjects. They established themselves on the coast around modern-day Bamburgh, named Din Guari by the British and Bebbanburg by the Angles.

After Ida a succession of his sons (including Æthelfric, Æthelfrith's father) succeeded in making inroads into the former British kingdom. But they suffered setbacks when a renowned British leader, **Urien of Rheged**, began a long campaign against the expansion of Deira and Bernicia. This culminated around AD 585 when he mustered a combined British force including warriors from Gododdin, and Strad Clud led by **Rhydderch**, to force the Bernicians led by **Hussa** (Herin's father) back towards the coast and onto the island of Lindisfarne (Ynys Medcaut). However, the British leaders fell out amongst themselves and Urien was killed by Morcant from 'jealousy, because his military skill and generalship surpassed that of all the other kings' (*History of the Britons*, 63). It was left to Hussa's young nephew, **Æthelfrith**, to take advantage of the in-fighting amongst his enemies when he became king in AD 593 and win back the territory his predecessor had lost.

After these attacks, Æthelfrith probably would have wanted to re-fortify his main fortress, renamed as **Bebbanburg**, on the north-east coast of Northumberland. A plateau of volcanic rock measuring 300m by 70m close to the beach forms a natural defensive site. Protected by the sea on one side, the landward defences were supplemented from the earliest times. *The Anglo-Saxon Chronicle* records that a hedge and later a wall first enclosed the site. This would have been a timber palisade as the Anglo-Saxons did not build in stone at this time. The volcanic base made digging post-holes difficult so it is probable that a box rampart would have been constructed. This consists of two parallel walls infilled with rubble and soil, (as described in Chapter 4). Archaeological excavations at the northern end of the citadel have revealed a stony clay deposit that may be the remains of the infill of a box rampart from this period.

The fortress was named Bebbanburg after Queen **Bebba,** Æthelfrith's wife, as testified by both Bede (*Ecclesiastical History,* III, 6&16) and Nennius (*History of the Britons*, 63). Bebba is an intriguing character. Her name has British origins and apparently did mean 'beautiful traitress'. It was not uncommon for Anglo-Saxon kings to take British wives, but Æthelfrith must have been quite taken by her as, according to Nennius, he did actually give his royal fortress to her as well as name it after her. We do not know for sure what happened to Bebba but her son, **Eanfrith**, gives us a clue. He later appears in the Pictish king-lists as the father of a king of the Picts, which strongly suggests that he was exiled in Pictland. I have therefore assumed that Bebba facilitated his flight to this land as she was herself of Pictish descent. We do not know that her father was Áedán, but one of his wives, Dolmech, was a Pict.

Æthelfrith developed a reputation as both fierce and cunning. Bede described his attacks on his neighbours as ferocious, and to the British he was known as Æthelfrith 'Flesaurs' – the Artful. Militarily he was very successful. Bede states that he 'ravaged the Britons more extensively than any other English ruler' (*Ecclesiastical History*, I, 34). Under his leadership, the boundaries of Bernicia advanced significantly inland from the coast, at the expense of British territory. His forces were involved in the overwhelming defeat of the British kings at the Battle of Catræth (Catterick). He became the first king to rule both Deira and Bernicia to form Northumbria from around AD 600, facilitated by his marriage to Acha.

Bede reports in some detail on his crucial victory over the Dál Riata in AD 603:

'Áedán, king of the Irish living in Britain, aroused by his successes, marched against him with an immensely strong army; but he was defeated and fled with few survivors. Indeed, almost all his army was cut to pieces in a very famous place called Degsastan, that is the stone of Degsa.'

He goes on to report Theobald's death in that battle. 'In this fight, Theobald, Æthelfrith's brother was killed together with all his army.' (*Ecclesiastical History*, I, 34) Irish sources confirm that Æthelfrith's brother was slain and name his killer as **Maelumai mac Baeton**, a king's champion from Ulster.

We do not know if Theobald influenced Æthelfrith's military strategy as I have suggested, but we do know that after his death, the king was undone by a mistake that someone more cautious and systematic may have avoided (as related in Book Two).

British literary sources tell us something of the kings who ruled in northern Britain at this time. **Mynyddog** is known to us through Aneirin's poem as the ruler of the Gododdin based at his citadel in Din Eidyn. There, Aneirin tells us, he entertained three hundred warriors from different parts of the Old North for 'a short year' with feasting, mead and 'sportive mirth'. Such lavish hospitality earned him the title of Mynyddog the Wealthy (Mwynfawr).

Owain is referenced in the same poem and in other sources as the son of Urien, the renowned king of Rheged, killed in the siege of Lindisfarne.

Rhydderch of the Alt Clud is a well-documented king of the Old North, ruling from AD 580–614. He was also present at the earlier siege of Lindisfarne during Urien's campaign against Bernicia.

Ceredig is believed to have been the last British ruler of the ancient kingdom of Elmet in southern Yorkshire.

Collectively, they were known as the kings of '**Hen Ogledd**' or **Old North**. The origins of the modern Highland Games in Scotland may lie in a form of war games that helped select the strongest and bravest soldiers during the early history of the area.

Aneirin. A number of Brittonic poets are known to have existed at this time from references in the literature. According to the Welsh Triads, Aneirin was the 'prince of bards', probably based at the court of the Gododdin around Edinburgh. He is best known for *Y Gododdin*, an elegy to warriors of the Old North that has survived in the *Book of Aneirin*. This refers to his mother as Dwywei. His father is less certain but may have been a chieftain from the northern Pennines, Nunod, nicknamed the Stout.

Y Gododdin is a wonderful tale of how three hundred British warriors feasted and prepared in Din Eidyn (Edinburgh) for a year.

> *The men went to Gododdin with laughter and sprightliness,*
> *Bitter were they in battle, displaying their blades;*

A short year they remained in peace.
... Fresh mead was their feast, and also their poison.
Three hundred were contending with weapons;
And after sportive mirth, stillness ensued.
(Aneirin – Y Gododdin VI and VIII)

After the festivities, they rode to Catræth (Catterick) where they were comprehensively defeated by the Anglian army. Aneirin's purpose was to praise the men who died rather than describe in any detail what happened. I have therefore included some of the warriors he describes: **Gorthyn** the Great, **Tydfych** the Tall and **Cynon** (one of the very few survivors), but I have invented the detail of the battle. Their leader was **Owain**, the son of Urien of Rheged, described by Aneirin as 'quicker to a field of blood than to a wedding, quicker to the ravens' feast than to a burial.'

Conaing is documented as one of the seven sons of King Áedán of Dál Riata but little is known about him except for a record of his death (which will be told in Book Two). His name is of Germanic origin, suggesting that his mother, one of Áedán's queens, was an Anglo-Saxon.

David Stokes

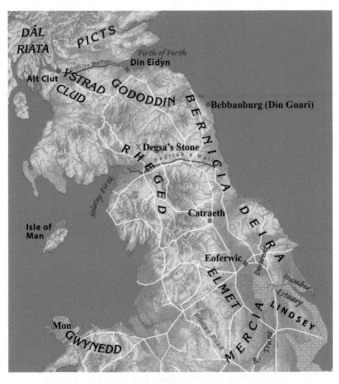

NORTHERN BRITAIN around AD 600
(Adapted from Wikimedia Commons)

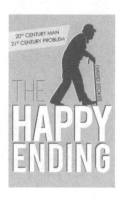

Also by the Author

This is a feel-good, heart-warming novel, full of fun and whimsy that also touches on a serious theme. Readers will be rooting for Harry, a 97 year-old widower from the very first page as they will find it easy to empathise with this down-to-earth, amusing character.

Not content to wither away in a nursing home, he strikes out to find a purpose in life while his fellow oldies doze in front of the TV. He is joined by a colourful cast of characters in a well-crafted plot where the action rarely stalls. Underlining the feel-good adventure, however, is a serious message about modern slavery, a real-life 21st century problem.

The Happy Ending can be purchased at
https://www.troubador.co.uk/bookshop/

For more information about the author and the Anglo Saxon period, including free downloads, go to:

davidstokesauthor.com